ALLERDALE

CONFIRMED BACHELORS BOOK 1

JENNY HAMBLY

Copyright © 2021 by Jenny Hambly
All rights reserved.
No part of this book may be reproduced in any form or by any electronic or mechanical means, including information storage and retrieval systems, without written permission from the author, except for the use of brief quotations in a book review.

The moral right of Jenny Hambly has been asserted.

www.jennyhambly.com

This book is a work of fiction. Names, characters, places and events, other than those clearly in the public domain, are either the product of the author's imagination, or are used fictitiously. Any resemblance to actual people, living or dead, are purely coincidental.

DEDICATION

To Ruth,
For all the laughter and encouragement!

CHAPTER 1

The Castle Tavern in Holborn was filled with gentlemen of the Fancy. Anyone with an interest in pugilism was welcome. Today, a thrilling if bloody encounter between Ned Painter and Tom Oliver, more widely known as The Chelsea Gardener, had ensured that the establishment was packed. Miles Gilham, Earl of Allerdale, son to the Marquess of Brigham, squeezed shut eyes that were stinging from the thick cigar smoke that hung in the air. Less than a year ago, he would have felt invigorated by the undoubted excellence of the hard-fought contest he had witnessed, yet he found himself strangely underwhelmed by the whole encounter. It seemed that seeing two well-matched athletes pounding each other to a pulp no longer had the power to excite him.

He opened his dark eyes and scanned the room for his friend Lord Carteret, who had braved the crowd of men standing three deep at the bar in order to furnish them with a drink. It was not yet eleven o'clock, but Miles suddenly wished for nothing more than to go back to his lodgings and make an early night of it. Over the past several months he had become used to retiring at a modest hour and rising with the sun, eager to face whatever challenges the day threw at him. He had thought that returning to Town would be as comfortable as putting on a well-worn glove, yet tonight, at least, he felt as though it was like putting on one that was too tight. He did not doubt, however, that it would soon stretch until it resembled a second skin.

It was not his friend but another gentleman who suddenly came towards him out of the smoke.

"Allerdale, where have you been hiding, you rogue? It used to be that you were forever haunting Town, but it is now past the middle of May and this is the first time I have set eyes upon you since I don't know when."

"I believe the last time I had the pleasure of your company, Sandford, was last July."

"That long?" Lord Sandford said. "Where does the time go? I might have suspected you had been hiding your latest barque of frailty away from prying eyes and been tempted to wrest from you the whereabouts of the rare beauty that could keep you away from Town for so long if it were not for your appearance."

Miles' lips twisted into a rather world-weary smile. "Temper your imagination, Sandford. I have been hiding no one away."

"You have no need to tell me that; your altered appearance tells me as much. Your skin is so brown I can see you have been spending very little time indoors and your hair has been cut in a severe style hardly likely to attract the ladies. I swear, it is shorn as close as a sheep."

Lord Sandford's words did not concern Miles; he knew he exaggerated. Even with his locks trimmed to such a degree that waves or curls no longer threatened them, he still boasted a healthy head of hair. He had become increasingly irritated with the effort it took to tame it over the past year, his not inconsiderable energy having been thrown into far more practical endeavours than how to ensure his appearance was everything that a man about town could wish it to be.

"How very appropriate a comparison," Miles said with a wry smile. "It is sheep that I have largely been concerned with for the last two months, but before your mock me, Sandford, I would point out that your dark locks have been brightened by a white streak that reminds me forcibly of a magpie since I last saw you."

The Marquess of Sandford grinned. "I cannot deny it. But I rather think that it adds a certain distinction to my appearance that, I am afraid to say, your close-cut crop does not confer upon you."

Miles looked into the rather pale, dissipated face of his acquaintance and said, "I am sure you are right, Sandford, but I can at least boast that I am in the best of health, whereas you look as if you need a repairing lease although the season has some way to run."

Lord Sandford's green eyes narrowed a little. "There was a time, Allerdale, when you did not judge your activities by the season. Every month was the season for play. Did you back the winner today? You usually have the devil's own luck. I must say, it was the best fight I have seen for some time."

"Yes, although it was brutal," Miles agreed. "I am amazed it went eight rounds. I thought The Gardener was gone after two, which I must admit caused me some dismay, as I had indeed put my money on him."

Lord Sandford pulled a face. "Mine was on Painter, lost a monkey on him." His eyes brightened with the gleam of the ever-hopeful gambler. "Never mind, the night is still young. Come with me to Watier's, why don't you?"

"Not this evening, Sandford. We would be there half the night, and my mother is expecting me in the morning."

Lord Sandford gave a scornful laugh. "All this talk of interesting yourself in sheep and keeping an appointment with your mother has me worried, Allerdale. Do not say you are turning into a paragon of virtue? You are the last man I would expect to turn into a dead bore."

Miles shrugged. "I doubt I will ever be a paragon of virtue, but I have spent the last nine months applying myself to more serious pursuits so perhaps I am a bore. I must admit that now I have a more intimate knowledge of just how much hard work and effort goes into producing the income that funds my lifestyle, I find I am a little less eager to squander it."

"And yet you are here, old fellow, and have placed a bet only today," Lord Sandford pointed out.

"Yes," he admitted, "but only a very modest one, I assure you."

A relieved smile dawned as he saw his friend Viscount Carteret approaching; Miles had promised his father he would behave in a more circumspect manner this year, and he never broke a promise if it was within his power to keep it. It would be far easier to fulfil his vow, however, if he were not cornered at every turn by some old acquaintance trying to drag him back into his old habits.

"Carteret! Perhaps you can be persuaded to accompany me to Watier's? Allerdale is being a dead bore and will not come."

Lord Carteret sent a swift glance in his friend's direction. His cynical grey eyes and firm chin were somewhat at odds with his haphazardly arranged, slightly overlong brown hair, which had a tendency to flop over his forehead. The former attributes suggested that he was astute and determined, and the latter that he possessed an easy-going carelessness.

"Not tonight, Sandford," he said softly, offering the marquess a lazy smile. "My luck is not in, and I do not believe in chasing my losses, especially not at Watier's; the play runs so deep there."

"Hen-hearted, the pair of you!" Lord Sandford declared, before striding off.

Miles tossed off the glass of daffy that his friend offered him and winced. "I do not think I will ever truly acquire the taste for gin!"

"I am quite in agreement, Allerdale, devilish stuff! As we have now partaken of the obligatory glass and listened to every aspect of the fight being discussed in tedious detail, might I suggest we repair to your lodgings where we can enjoy a quiet conversation without any reference to a flush hit, a doubler, or a cross-buttock?"

Miles lifted a dark eyebrow. "You are such an outstanding practitioner of the art yourself, Carteret, that I own I am surprised not to have heard you hold forth a little more on the bout. Didn't lose too heavily, did you?"

The viscount laughed. "When did I ever wager more than I could afford to lose, Allerdale? Sandford would have been justified in calling me a dead bore; I have always been one of your more sensible friends. Not that you have ever taken any of my advice! I am very pleased that you withstood his invitation, however, he is a dashed loose-screw and is running through the not inconsiderable fortune he inherited at a rate of knots!"

Miles smiled. "I believe that epithet has more than once been levelled at myself."

"Not by me," Lord Carteret said gently, guiding him from the establishment and raising his hand to attract the attention of a passing hackney. He instructed the driver to deliver them to Duke Street and followed his friend into the vehicle.

"You may have been a trifle profligate last year, but you never went beyond the line of what was acceptable for a gentleman. You have always been a staunch friend, and you have never to my knowledge, trifled with the hearts or reputations of ladies of quality. Unlike Sandford."

Miles frowned. "I fear your knowledge is not quite up to date, Carteret."

"Really? Then I am delighted that you invited me back to your rooms, Allerdale."

"I did not. You invited yourself!"

"An irrelevant detail. Now tell me, whose heart did you trifle with?"

"I trifled with no one's heart, but I certainly endangered a lady's reputation. I did intend to marry her, however, only she would have none of me! Didn't like my damnable temper."

"Yes," Lord Carteret said, meditatively, "it is usually that which leads you into trouble. Now come, tell me all."

"Very well, but only because I know you will keep mum about the whole affair. I lost heavily at cards to Devonan, and my father refused to pay my debt unless I married."

His friend blinked. "Lost to Devonan? You? Impossible!"

"My father said the same thing. When he could be brought to believe I had not been foxed, he was of the opinion that my drink had been laced with something to impair my judgement."

"The cad! Although I am glad you did not, I am surprised you did not call Devonan out."

"I had no proof. Besides my father won back everything I had lost and more. Instead, I abducted a guest staying in our house and headed for Gretna Green. When she refused my offer, I held the threat of keeping her overnight in Carlisle over her head and thus ruining her. Very pretty behaviour, wasn't it? Now tell me I am not a loose-screw!"

"It was certainly very rash," Lord Carteret said calmly. "Why did you not apply to me for a loan?"

"A man does not borrow money from his friends! At least, not such a large sum as I had lost. Heaven knows when I would have been able to pay you back."

"As if I would have cared, Allerdale. But you have proved my point. A loose-screw would have shown no such principles."

"Talk to Lady Georgianna Voss about my principles and she will laugh in your face!" He groaned. "I did not mean to mention her name, but it is too late now, I suppose. You will undoubtedly make the connection if she is in Town, although she is now Lady Somerton."

His friend chuckled. "I have indeed had the pleasure of making her acquaintance. She is elegant, beautiful, and quite formidable in her way. She does not suffer fools and is very forthright. I like her the better for it. But I am intrigued; you are neither married to her nor has any breath of scandal reached my ears. What occurred to make your foolhardy plan go awry?"

"She hit me over the head with a poker and made good her escape."

"How very intrepid of her," Lord Carteret murmured, a smile lurking in his eyes.

"I caught up with her but had by then come to my senses."

"I imagine you might have. What did you do next?"

"I took her home only to find her father and Somerton had arrived. The former was hellbent on making her marry me, and the latter, ready to murder me."

They had by now reached Duke Street. Lord Carteret followed his friend into the building and cast a surprised glance about Miles' sitting room. It was usually in disarray, with riding crops, invitations, gloves, and a myriad of other random articles littering the desk and furniture. This evening, however, he found it unusually tidy. A neat stack of correspondence graced one corner of the desk, and no articles of clothing or any of the accoutrements necessary to a keen whip and accomplished rider were draped carelessly over the two chairs or couch that were set about the fireplace. But then, his friend had only been in Town a matter of days, so perhaps that explained it.

When they were both comfortably settled in front of the fire nursing generous glasses of brandy, Lord Carteret took up the thread of their conversation. "And yet you are neither married nor murdered. How did you avoid either of these terrible fates? I, for one, would not wish to cross Lord Somerton."

"Impressive, isn't he?" Miles agreed. A fond, reminiscent smile softened his countenance. "It was all thanks to Georgianna. She was so calm and matter-of-fact about the whole episode that she took the wind out of everyone's sails." He laughed. "She coolly pointed out that she was home before nightfall and so her reputation was in no danger unless anyone in the room breathed a word about it. And when my father asked her how it was that we had arrived at Brigham together in such an amicable fashion, she merely said that when I wasn't being tiresome, I was very good company."

An appreciative smile curved Lord Carteret's lips. "She was in the right of it, Allerdale. The same thought has crossed my mind on more than one occasion. But I find it hard to believe that you were let off the hook quite so easily. What price have you to pay for your idiocy?"

"Damn you, Carteret. If we had not been firm friends since our first term at Eton, I would not let that pass."

"I doubt it not," Lord Carteret said. "But you can

hardly take umbrage at my calling you an idiot when I have been doing so almost from the moment that we met. Have you forgotten that it was I that fished you out of the pond when you lost your temper with one of the older boys who tried to bully me? I told you then that you were an idiot to square up to someone three years your elder."

"What ingratitude!" Miles protested. "How could I have done otherwise? You were as slender as a sapling, small for your age, and a prime target for any of the dolts who thought they could prise from you your pocket money, half your dinner, or persuade you to do their homework for them. I will say this for you, Carteret, your intellect was always far ahead of your years or your stature."

"Yet you would not listen to my counsel, even then," his friend said softly.

Miles threw up his hand in defeat. "I know. But how should I have known then that you have your own way of routing your enemy? I have never known such a fellow for biding his time and taking his revenge in a cold, calculated manner."

"It is a dish best served cold, I believe," Lord Carteret said. "Something I have been failing dismally to teach you for years. But we digress, you have still not informed me of the price you have to pay."

Miles was completely unconscious of the fact that his booted foot had begun to tap on the floor.

"I have spent the last nine months learning the business of running Murton, one of our estates in Yorkshire," he said curtly. "I have found the experience both illuminating and absorbing. But it is only half of the bargain. Although my father withdrew his insistence that I marry, my mother became quite carried away with the idea. When I returned to Brigham for Christmas, in a moment of weakness, I agreed that I would find a bride this season."

"Then your affection for your mother and your scruples have got the better of you, my friend," Lord Carteret said softly. "Your word has ever been your bond. For what it is worth you have my sympathy."

"You are still not reconciled to the prospect of marriage then, Carteret?"

"No," his friend said, his voice flat and his eyes hard.

Miles sighed. "It has been five years since Lord Haverham dashed your hopes of securing Diana Ramshorn—"

"They were not dashed by Haverham though, were they?" he interrupted, his voice silky. "They were dashed by Diana. She gave me every encouragement, furthermore, I told her I would call on her father and she did nothing to discourage me. She even allowed me to propose to her so she could have the pleasure of declining me. She tried to lay the blame at her parents' door, saying that they would not contemplate a viscount when an earl was in the offing."

"Perhaps it was true," Miles suggested.

Lord Carteret gave a hard crack of laughter. "You know as well as I that she was the apple of her father's eye. He would gainsay her nothing! My fortune was the equal of Haverham's and my address better, the only advantage he had over me was his rank."

"Then you had a lucky escape, my friend."

"I know it," he acknowledged. "I thought Diana's liveliness was all part of her natural vivacity, but she is a flighty piece. I do not resent Haverham at all, on the contrary, I feel rather sorry for him. I witnessed Diana in a clinch with Sandford on the terrace at a ball I attended only last week. She is clearly bored by her rather staid husband, but she is playing with fire. Haverham thinks so much of his consequence that I doubt it has crossed his mind that Diana is already playing such tricks, but if he gets wind of it, she will find herself whisked back to his pile in Staffordshire and kept there until she has provided him with an heir and a spare. She has thus far presented him only with a daughter."

"Were you not tempted to drop a word in his ear?"

Lord Carteret's upper lip curled into a sneer. "I do not take my revenge on women. Nor do I peddle gossip. You should know that."

"I do," Miles said gently. "You are always the gentlemen. Forgive me, I don't know where my wits have gone begging."

His friend's lips relaxed. "You are forgiven. The prospect of trawling the marriage mart for a suitable bride is enough to send anyone's wits begging. You are cutting it a little fine, however. You have only five weeks, six at most, of the season remaining and the most beautiful prospect has already been snapped up."

Miles groaned. "Do not tell me I have only the wallflowers left to me."

"It is not quite that bad, old fellow. There is one lady who is not quite in the usual style. She is a little older than some who have made their entrance into society this season, I judge her to be in her early twenties, and I would not call her beautiful—"

Miles dropped his head into his hands as if in

despair. "Say no more, I beg of you, or I will turn tail and return to Yorkshire!"

Lord Carteret laughed. "And leave your mother disappointed? I think not. But let me finish, Allerdale. It is not so desperate as you suppose. Miss Edgcott may not be considered beautiful in the traditional way, but she is not unattractive. She has spent some years abroad. Her father, Sir Henry Edgcott, was attached to the foreign office in some capacity or other. They were in Constantinople for some time but left when the city was unfortunate enough to suffer the plague. They made their way to Malta, but it followed them there, and Sir Henry fell victim to the contagion. Last season, Miss Edgcott was still in mourning for her father, and it is these circumstances that have kept her from making an appearance in society before now."

Miles did not look convinced. "In what way is she not in the usual style?"

"She has been used to moving in the first circles abroad. She is confident, intelligent, and unfashionably independent. Rumour has it that her father left her something in the region of fifty thousand pounds, and she does not appear to be very much interested in finding herself a husband."

"Has she had any offers?" Miles asked sceptically.

"At least three that I am aware of," Lord Carteret confirmed, "and only one from a fortune hunter. I believe there have even been some bets recorded in the book at White's as to whether she will succumb to the not inconsiderable attention she has attracted and finally yield to the lures of matrimony."

Miles raised a brow. "You think to tempt me with a challenge, Carteret, but I am not so gullible. It seems you approve of her and yet you evince no interest in her yourself."

"I like her well enough, but have we not agreed that I am not interested in the married state? There is the added awkwardness of her being a relation of Lord Haverham. She is a guest in his house, and she would have to be a very extraordinary woman indeed to make me wish to cross that threshold."

"But you think this less than extraordinary lady might suit me?"

Lord Carteret's lips twitched. "And why not? The only thing that I have known to tempt you out of your sullens when you are in a temper is your humour. Miss Edgcott can be very amusing and possesses an admirable sangfroid. I cannot help but think that these two qualities are desirable, if not essential in any woman you marry."

CHAPTER 2

Miss Eleanor Edgcott had not only been left a very generous sum of money by her father, but also a fine manor house by a loch in Scotland. She was very grateful that her cousin, Lord Haverham, had invited her to live with him during her year of mourning, however, for although the house was situated in an extremely picturesque spot, it was miles from anywhere, and the beauty of the country seemed only to be matched by the wet, cold climate. Three months there, in a house that was largely covered in holland covers, with a companion who had been hired by her family's solicitor and had proved as dull-witted as she was voluble, had been almost more than she could support.

Her companion, Miss Ryder, had accompanied her to Standon, Lord Haverham's estate in Staffordshire, and the problem of how to dispose of her had swiftly revealed itself to Eleanor. Although she had found her incessant chatter a constant irritation, Diana, Lady Haverham, had found Miss Ryder a most sympathetic listener and discovered she had a way with children. When her nursery maid was discovered to be carrying on with one of the footmen and been summarily dismissed, Miss Ryder had come into her own. She had stepped into the breach without a moment's hesitation. The child was approaching four years of age, and although it would have been beneath Miss Ryder's dignity to take over the position of nurse-maid, she had accepted the role under the title of governess.

Eleanor had been much more than a daughter to her father; she had also been his companion, social secretary, and hostess. She knew how to conduct herself in any company, was not easily shocked, and liked to be busy. She was thoroughly enjoying the variety of amusements London offered her and was seriously considering selling her estate in Scotland and purchasing a house in the metropolis.

Determined to employ her next companion herself, she had drawn up a list of the essential qualities this lady must possess, the most important of these being intelligence, humour, and discretion. She had advertised the position in the paper and now had only to interview her candidates.

She glanced at the clock and felt a little rush of anticipation as she realised it wanted only a few minutes until two o'clock. She had received fifteen letters of application for the post and had chosen the three that were the most coherent, legible, and also came with the benefit of a glowing character reference. She had kept quiet about her plans not wishing to give the impression to either her host or hostess that she was at all unhappy with her current situation, as well as being quite unwilling to brook any interference in the matter.

She did not expect to be disturbed; Lord Haverham was almost always at his club on a Wednesday afternoon, and Diana invariably liked to rest between two and four if they were not otherwise engaged.

Her eyes swivelled towards the door as it opened. Clinton, Lord Haverham's butler, stepped softly into the room and announced Miss Crevel. Eleanor rose swiftly to her feet.

"Good afternoon, Miss Crevel. Your timing is all that it should be."

Miss Crevel looked to be somewhere in her forties. She held herself well, possessed a quiet elegance, and had rather sharp grey eyes that suggested a keen intelligence. This impression was reinforced when she smiled and replied swiftly, "I should hope it is, ma'am. You could hardly wish for a companion who would always be keeping you waiting."

Eleanor's lips twitched at this humorous sally, but her smile quickly faded as she observed Miss Crevel's puzzled glance and realised that the comment had not been an example of the lady's wit but rather of a literal mind.

"Please, sit down," she said.

Miss Crevel sat and favoured Eleanor with a confident stare. Both her list of accomplishments and her reference had been particularly good so it was perhaps not surprising that she should not doubt herself.

"Tell me, Miss Crevel," Eleanor said, "how do you see your role as my companion?"

Miss Crevel looked surprised. "Surely it is for you,

Miss Edgcott, to tell me what you expect from a companion?"

"And so I may," Eleanor said, "after I have heard your own ideas on the subject."

"Very well. I should expect to always be with you when we receive visitors of the male variety and accompany you wherever you may wish to go. In short, Miss Edgcott, as you are still quite a young lady, I would see my role as that of protectress of your reputation. As well as this, I hope that I would be able to keep you tolerably well entertained when we are at home. I am very well read and am perfectly capable and willing to discuss any number of subjects."

Eleanor was reasonably sure that those subjects would be of a serious nature and an imp of mischief prompted her to say, "Well read? Excellent. I do so enjoy reading myself. What is your favourite novel?"

Miss Crevel's lips twisted in distaste. "I do not read novels, Miss Edgcott. Novel reading encourages idleness at best and immorality at worst. Reading should be an intellectually uplifting experience rather than one which panders to sensation and irrationality. I think a person's taste and character is more easily revealed by what they read than anything else."

"I see," Eleanor said reflectively. "I have never thought myself idle and yet I have read many novels. I must admit that although I found some of the stories to be so improbable as to be laughable, they did help a rainy afternoon pass more quickly. And others, you know, had the benefit of being witty, amusing, and true to life."

"If you engage me as your companion, ma'am, I am confident that I could introduce you to a wide selection of histories, sermons, and moral essays which would persuade you that your time reading novels has been truly wasted."

Eleanor rose and smiled. "I am sure you are right, Miss Crevel. I shall not keep you waiting long but will send a message to you by tomorrow at the latest, informing you of my decision."

As if possessing some sixth sense that alerted him to the imminent departure of guests, Clinton appeared at that moment and showed Miss Crevel out. Eleanor still stood in the middle of the room, a faint frown between her brows when he came again into the morning room.

"Miss Ripple arrived some five minutes ago, ma'am. I have put her in the book room. Would you like me to show her in?"

"Yes, of course," Eleanor said. "Thank you, Clinton."

A slender lady with a pretty shawl draped about her shoulders tripped into the room with a restless energy and a smile on her lips. Eleanor judged that Miss Ripple was a few years older than Miss Crevel.

"I am early, I know it," she said in a rush. "I am fully aware that guests who arrive early are just as annoying as those who arrive late!"

Eleanor jumped as Miss Ripple made the most extraordinary sound. Never before had she heard such a laugh; it began as a gentle whinny, before deepening as it gained momentum and ending on a hoarse, donkey-like bray.

"Not that I am a guest, but I am sure the principle is the same."

Although Miss Ripple appeared confident,

Eleanor was inclined to think that her hideous laugh might be put down to nerves.

"I am sure I have no objection at all to you being early," she said kindly. "Please sit down, Miss Ripple, and tell me how you see your role as my companion."

Miss Ripple did not seem at all thrown by this question. "Well, I have a great deal of experience in the role," she said confidingly. "Although thus far, I have served ladies far older than you, Miss Edgcott. I must admit, I think it would be refreshing to be a companion to a young lady such as yourself."

Eleanor saw the hopeful gleam in Miss Ripple's faded blue eyes and asked, "In what way would it be refreshing, ma'am?"

"Well, I imagine that you would like me to accompany you to a variety of entertainments."

"Would you enjoy such an arduous task even though it might keep you out very late?"

Miss Ripple clapped her hands together and said eagerly, "I would indeed, Miss Edgcott. I have been used to spending my evenings reading to my employer, which is something I do not mind at all for I do enjoy a good novel or poem as much as the next person, I am sure, but just think, if you were to take me about with you, I might meet the great man himself!"

Eleanor considered the various gentlemen she had met during the weeks she had been in Town. Most had been pleasant, a few impressive, but she would apply the term 'great' to none of them.

"The great man? Can it be that you have hopes of meeting the prince regent, Miss Ripple? If it is indeed your ambition, I must disappoint you, I fear. He is quite above my touch."

This time Eleanor could not quite suppress a wince as Miss Ripple abandoned herself to mirth. After a few moments, she made an effort to gather herself, dabbed at her leaking eyes with a handkerchief, and gasped, "You are funning, of course. I am sure the prince has much to recommend him, although I have heard that he is not what he once was and has become sadly fat, but that is neither here nor there, suffice it to say, I have no ambition to meet him. The person I refer to has such an exquisite sensibility, so perfect a command of the written word, and such a noble countenance that one cannot help but hope for at least a glimpse of him. I am sure anyone who has read Childe Harold could not fail to describe its author as great."

A vision of Miss Ripple accompanying her to a ball or musical evening and swooning at Lord Byron's feet came into Eleanor's mind. She brought the interview to a swift close, and once Miss Ripple had left, picked up the letter that lady had written and read it carefully. She could find no evidence of the breathless, rambling style the lady evinced in person in her missive. She sighed. All her hopes must be on Miss Gissop.

It seemed that this lady would not disappoint. She could have been no more than ten years Eleanor's senior, was pretty in an understated sort of way, and had bright, intelligent eyes. When Eleanor asked her to describe how she saw her role as companion, those eyes twinkled.

"How very clever of you to ask such a general question, Miss Edgcott, and one that is so seemingly innocuous."

"Seemingly?"

Miss Gissop's soft, deep laugh was gentle on the ears. "Indeed. You have given no clue as to your own preferences in a companion and so provided me with enough rope that I may either jump blindly through hoops in an effort to please you or tie myself up in knots!"

A glimmer of amusement brightened Eleanor's deep, brown eyes. "You make me sound like such a scheming female! I assure you I am no such thing!"

Miss Gissop smiled. "Then I shall answer your question as honestly and simply as I may. I would endeavour to be just what the word implies; a companion to you. I am old enough to be able to offer the respectability the position requires and perhaps offer you some advice if my opinion is sought, but not so old that I will be unable to enter into your feelings on any number of matters."

Eleanor could not help but admire this adroit answer. It suggested a compatibility between them without offering any specific information. Miss Gissop had taken the rope offered to her and rather than jump through hoops or tie herself up in knots, had fashioned a tightrope that she had delicately navigated without a wobble.

She picked up Miss Gissop's reference and scanned it for a moment. "Sir Stuart Crane mentioned that you looked after his sister very well, but I notice that you were only with her for a year."

Miss Gissop sighed. "Was it only a year? It felt much longer."

"Oh dear. Was Miss Crane difficult to please?" Eleanor asked in a sympathetic tone.

Miss Gissop gave a conspiratorial smile. "Only after midday." She leaned forwards and dropped her voice. "She was quite addicted to strong drink but would not touch a drop until then."

Not by the flicker of an eye did Eleanor display the disappointment she felt at this answer, but she was indeed dismayed. Miss Gissop had fallen at the final hurdle; intelligent and humorous she might be, but if she had also been discreet, she would not have breathed a whisper about her former employer's failings.

The hope that the trail of visitors to his house in South Audley Street might go unnoticed by Lord Haverham was dashed when he returned home a little earlier than was his habit. He came into the house as Miss Gissop departed it. After a quiet word with the butler, he strode into the morning room, a frown between his eyes.

"I hear you have had a busy afternoon, Eleanor," he said. "You had not mentioned that you were looking for another companion, and I must say that I cannot see that you have need of one whilst you are under my roof and have Diana to keep you company."

Lord Haverham's natural expression tended to be serious, but Eleanor saw both bewilderment and hurt lurking in his hazel eyes.

She crossed the room to him and laid a hand upon his sleeve. "Do not be cross, Frederick. I did not think it worth mentioning the matter until I had found a suitable candidate for the post. I have been happy living with you, but I cannot do so forever. I find London suits me very well and am considering purchasing or hiring a property of my own here, but you must see that I cannot set up my own establishment without a companion."

As she had expected, her cousin was clearly upset by this notion.

"Four and twenty is far too young to be setting up your own establishment, my dear," Lord Haverham said. "It would look very odd. You should rather be looking about you for a husband."

"Why? One of the things I most admired about the culture in Constantinople was that women were allowed to have property and wealth in their own right. I am fully aware, however, that I am extremely fortunate to have the means to support myself in this country."

"If you mean to tell me that Constantinople is full of ladies who have set up their own establishments in preference to finding themselves a husband, it will be the first time I have heard of it."

"Well, no," Eleanor admitted. "It is just that all their property and wealth does not automatically fall into the hands of their husbands as is usually the case here. There is as much if not more pressure upon them to marry. It is true that they could not understand why I had not yet wed, but I cannot and will not believe that a female's position in this world must be defined as a mother and wife only."

Lord Haverham stared at her in some bemusement. "From everything you have told me, Eleanor, it seems you were perfectly happy looking after your father as I imagine your mother would have done had she been alive."

"Yes, I was," she said, a little wistfully.

"Then, although you are not in the first flush of youth, you have the advantage of already possessing the qualities and experience that a gentleman of refinement and taste must value in his spouse. You did not mind running a household as a daughter, so I cannot see why you should object to running one as a wife, and I think it extremely unnatural that you should not wish to be married or a mother."

"You misunderstand me, Frederick," she said, her grave tone belied by the hint of laughter in her eyes. "I meant only that in Constantinople, although in some ways the ladies had more rights than women generally do in England, their role was still defined by them being wives and mothers to countless children. It is not that I do not wish to *ever* be a wife or a mother, it is just that I have a choice, and I would use it wisely. Papa and I had a very fond relationship, a deep understanding of one another, and he allowed me a great deal of freedom. If I could discover another gentleman with whom it might be possible to share a similar relationship, I dare say I would be very happy to marry him."

Lord Haverham looked a little relieved.

"I have not discovered such a gentleman, however," Eleanor continued, "and I would consider it a very poor bargain to cede both my fortune and my independence to one who only wished for a wife to provide for his comfort and furnish him with heirs."

"But what else should he wish for?" her cousin asked, bemused. "What is it you expect of a husband, Eleanor?"

"He should wish for an intelligent companion with whom he can converse on any and all topics concerning him. As for myself, I would require a man who is prepared to at least listen to his wife's counsel, to consider her wishes, and conduct himself in a way that she could be proud of."

Lord Haverham gave a bark of laughter. "Is this all?"

"Not quite. I would also expect him to grant me the freedom to travel, with or without him. I am very fond of travelling, you know. I met Lady Hester Stanhope in Constantinople and liked her very much. It was unfortunate that she avoided British circles whenever possible. She found us a dull set." She sighed. "She left for Egypt afterwards, I believe."

Lord Haverham's frown deepened as he said abruptly, "Eleanor, you must not mention her name in polite circles. You can do yourself no good by claiming her acquaintance; she is quite disgraced. As for the type of husband you wish for, well, you will never find such a man."

"No, I fear you are right," Eleanor said regretfully. "It is why I interviewed three prospective companions today. But it appears that my expectations there were also quite out; they were none of them suitable."

Lord Haverham's expression gentled a little and when he spoke it was in a more moderate tone. "You have had an unusual upbringing, Eleanor. You have spent most of your formative years trotting about the globe with my uncle, and it has bred in you an alarming amount of independence. But trust me when I tell you it will not do for you to set up home with only a hired companion, at least not in London.

"You are welcome to remain with us for as long as you choose, my dear. I have noticed a marked improvement in Diana's spirits since you came to stay at Standon. As you no doubt discovered, she can become quite moped when we are in the country. You have also done me a service by going about with her in Town to a host of events that I would have found little enjoyment in. On top of this, although I should not perhaps admit it, I have never known our household to run quite so smoothly since you came to us."

Not wishing to be at loggerheads with her extremely correct cousin, who had been so very kind to her, she smiled noncommittally and said, "Well, we shall see. Nothing is set in stone as yet."

The truth of the matter was that she was becoming increasingly tired of the burden of responsibility Frederick seemed very happy to lay about her shoulders. She knew he did not like to be forever at a ball, musical party, or a rout, but Diana's behaviour and frequent mood swings were giving her increasing cause for concern. She had put her flirtatious behaviour down to naturally high spirits after being so long buried in the country when they first came to Town, but she had been disturbed to find she could not discover her at Lady Battledon's ball last week, and suspicious when she had suddenly appeared, her colour heightened and her eyes bright, with Lord Sandford trailing in her wake. He had carried on past Eleanor, but not before he had sent a satirical glance in her direction.

When she had questioned Diana about her absence, she had given a trill of laughter and said, "It is so hot and stuffy in here, Eleanor, that I must admit I stepped onto the terrace for a breath of air, but you need not worry, several other people had also done so."

She had known it would be useless to question Diana further and so let it pass, telling herself that she would ensure she kept a closer eye on her in future. She was really quite fond of her cousin and would not have him made a laughing stock if she could prevent it.

As Lord Haverham made to leave the room, she said, "Come with us to Almack's this evening, Frederick. Although I am happy to accompany Diana, I am sure she must prefer your escort."

"Nonsense, Eleanor," he said brusquely. "You know I can't abide the place. I am sure Diana can have no need of me; I have never yet known her to have a dance free. Besides, I am already engaged with a party of friends this evening."

The stubborn set of his mouth discouraged her from pressing him further. As the door closed behind him, she sighed. At least she need have no qualms this evening; Diana knew that any untoward behaviour at Almack's would have far-reaching consequences. Fully aware that her conduct was being observed by the patronesses who ensured that strict notions of propriety ruled the assembly rooms, Diana would not put a foot wrong.

And so it proved. Only Diana's occasionally down-turned mouth and the frequent glances she sent in the direction of the door, hinted that she hoped for someone's arrival.

Freed of any worry, Eleanor was thoroughly enjoying herself. She was an accomplished dancer and never found herself without a partner. It had only just turned eleven o'clock when Diana sought her out.

"It is all so insipid, and I find I have the headache. Would you mind very much if we went home?"

Eleanor smiled at the two gentlemen who were even now approaching to take them to supper, made their excuses, and ushered Diana out of the room. It was not until they were in their carriage that she said, "If you had hoped to see Lord Sandford at Almack's, you were foolish, Diana. I doubt very much that any of the patronesses would allow someone of his reputation entry."

"But he is a marquess!" she protested.

"They would not care a jot for that," Eleanor said, a hint of approval of in her tone. "I would go so far as to say that they would take some enjoyment in refusing someone of his rank entry."

Diana pouted. "If you ask me, they think far too much of themselves, and some of them are positively spiteful. It does not seem fair that they should be allowed to ban anyone they take exception to."

Only a year separated the two ladies, but the difference in their experience and characters created a yawning chasm between them that was sometimes difficult to bridge. Thus far, all the compromises had been made by Eleanor; she had accompanied Diana wherever she had wished to go, listened to her witter on for hours about topics she had very little interest in, and patiently coaxed her out of the darker of her uneven moods.

But the gratitude that she felt towards Diana for accepting her into her household without question was wearing thin. Her bright blonde curls, flawless complexion, and forget-me-not blue eyes, coupled with an air of naivety, made her appear younger than her years. This childish quality was genuine, for Diana was still very much the spoilt child. First pampered by her parents, and now spoilt by her husband, it was perhaps not surprising. But it was becoming ever clearer to Eleanor that if she did not try to open Diana's eyes a little, she would find herself in a great deal of trouble before long.

"You know very well that all the patronesses do an excellent job of ensuring that Almack's is a safe place for young ladies to find suitable husbands, Diana. I can find nothing at all to object to in Lady Cowper or Lady Jersey, and Countess Lieven is rumoured to be an excellent political hostess. I admit she is a little haughty, but she has a keen intelligence that I admire."

"Then perhaps you should follow her example and find a husband who is interested in politics and become a political hostess yourself," Diana said, a little crossly.

"But I have no such ambition, besides, any gentlemen I have met with such leanings have either been already married or far too old. I notice that you did not deny that you hoped to see Lord Sandford."

A faint colour infused Diana's cheeks. "And why should I not wish to see him? He is by far the most amusing gentleman of my acquaintance."

"He is also the most disreputable gentleman of your acquaintance," Eleanor said dryly.

Diana shrugged. "I am not a little innocent, Eleanor, but a married woman. I am sure it is not at all unusual for a woman who has been married for some years to enjoy a flirtation with another gentleman."

"Not if she is discreet," Eleanor said, "and in your case, only if it is merely a flirtation. Frederick dotes on you, my dear, but his fondness for you would not survive a scandal. You have not yet presented him with an heir, after all."

Diana was not nearly as up to snuff as she imagined, and her eyes widened in shock and then filled with tears. "Make a scandal? Not yet presented him with an heir? Eleanor! You surely cannot think that I would, I would—"

"No, my dear," Eleanor said softly. "But it is not what *I* think that counts. You know how quickly rumours can fly about Town, whether they are true or not. If as you claim, you are only enjoying a light flirtation with the marquess, perhaps you have no need to worry. But if you are going to allow him to steal a kiss on a darkened balcony, he might be forgiven for thinking that you will allow him further liberties."

Diana said nothing and hunched a shoulder. Eleanor was not unhopeful, however, that her words might have some effect. She could quite see, of course, why Lord Sandford appealed to Diana. He was handsome, expert in the art of flirtation, and possessed that slightly dangerous quality that thrilled certain young ladies; in effect, he was everything that staid, dependable Lord Haverham was not.

Diana was, Eleanor believed, fond of her husband. Indeed, why should she not be when he showered her with gifts? She did not think that Diana had any serious intentions towards Lord Sandford but was merely enjoying the thrill of being the object of his attentions. Eleanor placed no dependence on that gentleman behaving as he should, however. If only Frederick would indulge Diana as much with his attention as he did with his presents. It was no wonder she was seeking approval and appreciation from another gentleman.

CHAPTER 3

Although Miles kept his own rooms when he was in Town, his family home was only a short stroll away in Berkeley Square. This arrangement allowed him the freedom to come and go as he pleased without his parents or the servants knowing of his movements, whilst giving him all the convenience of somewhere close by to stable his horses and curricle.

After a leisurely breakfast, he made his way there, intending to enjoy a morning ride before visiting his mother, who he knew rarely rose early when she was in Town. He had underestimated Lady Brigham's eagerness to see her only son, however. When he entered the stables via the mews behind the house, his groom grinned and said, "Her ladyship sent down a message half an hour ago, my lord; said she would appreciate it if you would visit her before you go out. She's in the morning room, I believe."

"Thank you, Tibbs," he said, swivelling and crossing the small courtyard in a few hasty strides.

Lady Brigham jumped up and flew across the room to embrace him the moment his foot crossed the threshold of the morning room.

"Mama," he laughed, putting her from him and straightening the delicate wisp of lace atop her dark, curling hair that served as a cap. "What scrape have you fallen into?"

"Do not be absurd, Miles," she said, smiling. "I no longer fall into scrapes as well you know. Whatever made you think that I had?"

"The urgency with which you wished to see me. I expected you to still be abed."

She threw him a look of mock severity. "I have been expecting you in Town any time this last month, Miles. I was most put out that you did not come to see me yesterday but instead sent the briefest note informing me that I would have that pleasure today. I came to your rooms immediately, but you had already gone out."

"You should not have done so," he said, his dark brows slashing downwards.

"Oh, do not talk such fustian," Lady Brigham said impatiently. "You are my son, after all."

"But there are many other lodgings in the street, some of which are occupied by gentlemen of questionable reputation!"

His mother gave a gurgle of laughter. "Miles! I am well past the age of attracting the attention of libertines!"

Miles sighed. "You are still pretty as a picture, Mama, and you know it!"

"It is very kind of you to say so," she said, grabbing his hand and pulling him to a sofa. "I wished to see you before you went for your ride and fell in with friends who would no doubt tempt you to Jackson's boxing saloon, Manton's, or some other place that gentlemen like to frequent. Now, let me look at you."

She raised a hand to his hair and said rather solemnly, "You look very severe, my dear. You are still extremely handsome, of course, but what made you cut your hair so close? When you were a child you had as mad a riot of curls as me."

"But he is no longer a child, my dear."

Both heads turned to the doorway. Lord Brigham had entered the room unheard. Somewhere in his late fifties, he still cut an impressive figure. He was tall, well-built, and dressed with taste and elegance. The aquiline cast of his countenance hinted at his noble lineage and the grey which peppered his dark hair served only to make him look more distinguished.

"I rather like your new look. It suits you, Allerdale."

Miles stood and went to shake his father's hand. "How are you, sir?"

"Very well," the marquess said, a faint smile touching his lips. "I am pleased to see you; it will be a relief not to hear your mother say, 'I wonder when he will come?' several times a day."

Miles grinned ruefully. "I would have come before, but there was so much to do, and I wished to see out the lambing first."

"Yes, Janes wrote that you had thrown yourself wholeheartedly into all aspects of estate business but had become particularly interested in the farms. I was very impressed by his report. You may certainly consider any obligation you feel towards me to have been fulfilled."

"Thank you, sir," Miles said. His lips twisted into a grimace. "You need not fear that I will embarrass you whilst I am in town."

"I am suffering no such apprehension, Allerdale, and will even allow that you have earned a respite after all your hard work; enjoy yourself a little. Whilst this seeming transformation in your character is laudable, it is also slightly alarming. I only wished you to curb some of your excesses, not change your character completely."

"I should think not," Lady Brigham said, crossing the room with a light step and natural grace. "Speaking of enjoyment, Miles, there was another reason why I wished to see you so urgently. We are holding a ball next Tuesday and I did not wish you to become engaged with a party of friends on that particular day."

This time the smile Miles offered Lady Brigham did not quite reach his eyes. His mother had clearly not forgotten his obligation to her.

"I shall not do so, ma'am."

"Well, now that is settled, I must go and finalise some of the arrangements. You can have no idea of how much I still have to do. It would be much easier if you would take up your rooms in the house, Miles, then I would be able to consult you so much more easily on a number of matters."

"Good God!" he said. "What do I know of arranging balls?"

"But, Miles! I am holding the ball for you! Not that I have said as much to anyone for I was not at all sure that you would be here. It is a shame that you have already missed half of the season, but I have gathered together everyone who is worthy of your notice under one roof in an effort to make things as easy for you as I can. I know how tedious you find it to always be doing the pretty at a round of polite parties. If you won't take up your rooms here, at least come to dinner tonight so we can discuss some of the young ladies I have invited."

"Although I hate to disappoint you, Mama," Miles said firmly, "I am afraid I am already engaged for the next few days."

Lady Brigham's large dark eyes opened to their fullest extent. "I knew how it would be! I have not seen you for months and yet you cannot spare me one evening. It is too bad of you!"

Miles' expression softened as he took her hand. He was on the point of capitulating when help came from an unexpected quarter; his father had always been his fiercest critic and generally did everything in his power to ensure his mother was not made unhappy.

"That is enough, Julia," Lord Brigham said gently. "I am sure Allerdale has many friends to catch up with. Content yourself with the knowledge that he will be at your ball. As I have already said, he has earned the right to enjoy himself a little."

"Oh, very well," Lady Brigham said, offering her son a contrite smile. "I am sorry, Miles, I do not mean to be hounding you. Will you at least come to dinner on the night of the ball? There will be so many people attending the event that we are only going to serve a buffet-style supper in a quite informal arrangement, and you will need a good dinner before it begins.

There will only be ourselves, your aunt Frances, and your cousin Charles. They come up to Town on Monday and will be staying with us. As you know, Bassington can't abide London and refuses to keep a house here."

"Yes, I do know. Charles has availed himself of my sofa on more than one occasion and I shall certainly come to dinner," he said. "I have not seen him for at least two years, and I have always liked him."

"Yes, he has always been full of mischief which no doubt explains it," Lord Brigham said dryly. His expression grew serious. "But I am glad you will have the opportunity to see him. He has been granted a short leave to visit his family, but his regiment went straight from Ireland to Belgium and he will follow them at the end of next week. Wellington is desperate for more men and who can blame him with so many of his old campaigners still in America? I am sure none of us knows when Napoleon will strike, but he will not remain quietly in Paris, that is certain."

"I am so thankful that you are not in the army, Miles," Lady Brigham said earnestly. "Poor Frances is to be pitied. She will not know a moment's peace until Charles is safely home again, not that she shows her worry to the world, but how can it be otherwise? A mother's nerves must always suffer in such a case."

Lord Brigham, who knew his sister to be one of the most placid, good-humoured women of his acquaintance, very much doubted this assessment of Lady Bassington's nerves. If she had any, he had certainly never discovered them. She was mother to four children, two girls who were as easy-going as she was and had happily married local gentlemen without even putting her to the trouble of bringing them to Town, and two sons, the eldest of which possessed the bluff good humour of his parents and had recently married the daughter of one of Lord Bassington's closest friends. That left only Charles, who was by far the liveliest of them all, but even when he had inevitably fallen into a number of scrapes, his mother had only laughed and said she wished she had half his energy. Lord Brigham did not contradict his good lady, however.

Miles did not hesitate to do so. He gave a shout of laughter. "I have no doubt that you, Mama, would suffer a great deal if you had a son in such a position, but Aunt Frances would find it far too fatiguing to worry about things that might never happen!"

"Frances is extremely fond of Charles," Lady Brigham said, a little reproachfully.

"Lord, yes," Miles agreed, "she is fond of all her children as long as they don't require her to exert herself!"

"I think you are very severe, Miles. Is she not exerting herself by coming up to London with Charles? She hardly ever does come to Town, you know."

"She's probably been driven out by her new daughter-in-law," Miles said grinning. "I would lay odds she is turning the house upside down. You must know that Aunt Frances is the most shocking housekeeper, leaves everything to the servants, and can never be brought to see that the curtains are too faded or the carpets sadly worn!"

"Horrid boy!" Lady Brigham said on a gurgle of

laughter. She reached up and kissed his cheek. "I shall leave you to your ride."

When she had gone out of the room, Lord Brigham flicked open his snuffbox with practised elegance and took a small pinch. "I am fully aware that you promised your mother to find a bride this season, Allerdale, but do not offer for anyone just to please her. You know how enthusiastic she is when some idea takes her fancy, but she would not like you to be unhappy."

"I know it, sir," Miles said.

"Neither would I," Lord Brigham said softly.

A rueful smile twitched his lips as he saw the flash of surprise in his son's eyes. "You would have been quite justified in reminding me that I tried to force your hand in the matter of your marriage only last year. I am impressed that you have not flung that fact in my face."

"You meant it for my own good, sir."

"I am happy that you know it, but I was mistaken. I had not fully realised quite how unhappy you were. Do I take it that you have stopped blaming yourself for the death of your friend and are no longer quite so blue-devilled?"

Miles had not expected such an open conversation, it laid bare wounds only recently healed, but he cleared his throat and said, "When Somerton did not blame me for the death of his brother, the guilt slowly faded. As for being blue-devilled, how could I be when I have had so much to do? If I do find someone I feel I could marry, would you allow us to live at Murton, sir? I have enjoyed being in charge of an estate."

"The idea is not without merit," Lord Brigham

conceded. "Of course, you would need to find a bride who would not object to living in the wilds of Yorkshire."

"Murton is hardly in the wilderness, sir. York is no very great distance, after all."

Encouraged by his father's frankness, he said, "How did you know Mama would suit you?"

The ghost of a smile flicked Lord Brigham's lips. "I was not at all sure she would," he admitted softly. "But the thought of her not being in my life was insupportable. She never bored me, you see, as so many girls did."

"I shouldn't think she did," Miles said feelingly. "You were too busy extracting her from scrapes!"

"Yes," his father admitted. "But she fell into them in all innocence and it was my pleasure to extract her from them. Now, are you going for that ride, or would you like to come with me to Whites? I own I wouldn't mind hearing of your experiences in Yorkshire from your own lips, and there will be no fear of us being interrupted there."

"Yes, sir," Miles said promptly; this was not an offer often extended to him. "I shall go for my ride later this afternoon."

CHAPTER 4

Eleanor added the last neat stitch to the rose satin ribbon on her bonnet, glanced at the sketchbook which lay open beside her, and reached for one of the silk flowers that lay scattered at her feet. She set it at a jaunty angle and pinned it in place.

"Much better," she murmured.

The door to the morning room opened and Diana stepped through it.

"I don't know why you go to all that trouble," she said. "I thought your bonnet very pleasing as it was."

"It was passable, I grant you," Eleanor agreed. "But so ordinary. You are so beautiful that you look ravishing in whatever bonnet you wear, which is why Madame Griffon gives you such a generous discount. I, on the other hand, am not so fortunate and must contrive to be a little different."

Pleased by the compliment, Diana smiled and came further into the room. "I think you are very pretty, Eleanor. If you did not like the bonnet, why did you buy it?"

"No doubt I am a fusspot, but I can never find just what I like. It is why I prefer to purchase my bonnets from less exalted persons and furbish them up myself."

Diana picked up the sketchbook and examined the various hats that Eleanor had designed.

"I must say, these are very good. If ever you lose your fortune, you could set up as a milliner. I would certainly purchase your hats."

Eleanor laughed. "Thank you, but I sincerely hope that day never arrives. I suspect that creating designs to suit my own preference and having to do so for others in order to survive, would prove to be two very different things."

Diana replaced the sketchbook, sat down, and said with a cheerfulness that was not entirely convincing, "Yes, of course. I was only funning. Besides, Frederick would never allow you to demean yourself in such a fashion."

Eleanor merely smiled and waited for Diana to voice whatever was troubling her. She attached the flower with a few carefully placed stitches and removed the pin. Satisfied, she laid down her bonnet, bent, and began to restore the remaining flowers and odds of ribbon to her sewing basket.

Diana slid onto her knees and began to help her. When everything was safely stowed, she did not immediately rise but grasped Eleanor's hands and raised eyes that were unusually pensive to meet her gently questioning gaze.

"Frederick informed me that you are looking for another companion. Do not leave us, Eleanor! It is so pleasant to have someone to talk to; I was so lonely before you came."

"Were you?" Eleanor said softly. "I am sorry to hear you say so. Did Frederick not keep you company before I came?"

"Yes… no… what I mean to say is that I saw him of course, at breakfast and at dinner, at least, but he was always so busy." She released Eleanor's hands and sank back on her heels. "He is so kind, so generous…" Diana touched her fingers to the topaz butterfly brooch she wore, "Frederick gave me this only yesterday, and a pair of earrings to match."

"It is lovely."

"Yes. But he is not interested in the things that concern me, you see, and I have no understanding of his affairs."

Eleanor rose to her feet, bringing Diana with her. "I have seen how things are between you. There is affection on both sides, I think, but you are making a sad mull of it between you."

Diana bristled. "Whatever do you mean? I have always done my duty by him and try to be a good wife. My mama warned me not to hang upon his sleeve or show too much sentiment, and I do not. You have seen for yourself that I never plead with Frederick to accompany us anywhere."

"Then he can hardly be blamed for not comprehending that you wish he would sometimes escort you," she said gently. "And as for not understanding his affairs, how could you if you have never asked him to explain them to you?"

Diana's eyes widened. "Do you think he would explain them to me?"

"Perhaps," Eleanor said. "If he really believed that you were interested in them. He might even then return the compliment and show more interest in yours."

Uncertainty and then contrition flitted through Diana's eyes. "Even if you are right, I do not wish you to leave us. If it is because of what happened the other evening – with Sandford – I did not expect or desire him to kiss me. I pushed him away and told him he must not. It is only because I do not like to be scolded that I pretended I did not care."

Eleanor could not help but be touched by Diana's wish that she would not leave her, but her sympathy did not reach so far that she would jeopardise her own happiness.

"I am pleased to hear it, my dear, but it is not that which caused me to advertise for another companion."

"Then what was it?"

"I have been used to running my own household, or at least that of my father which amounts to the same thing—"

"That would explain why you are so good at it," Diana said. "You must know that I am quite happy to allow you to take over the running of ours. You are so much better at it than I."

"That is very kind of you," Eleanor said, not quite able to keep a hint of irony from her voice. "But you would do better to learn from me while you can, Diana. I have been used to a great deal of freedom you see and find I cannot meekly submit to the role of dependant in someone's household."

"But we are not just anyone, Eleanor," Diana

protested. "We are your family, and we love you dearly."

Realising that there was very little chance of someone who had had such a conventional upbringing as Diana understanding her position, Eleanor changed tack.

"And I am very fond of you both, I assure you. If, as Frederick assures me, my plans are quite out of the question, I will have to think again. But I do not wish to do so today. The sun is shining, and although there seems to be quite a breeze blowing, I am sure it will be a warm one. I find myself tired of being indoors; do say you will come with me for a walk in the park."

"Of course, I will," Diana said, brightening.

As Hyde Park was only a very short stroll from South Audley Street, it was not long before they were smiling and nodding at a variety of acquaintances. Eleanor sent Diana a sideways glance as a curricle drawn by a showy pair of horses came towards them. Lord Sandford slowed as he drew near, but Diana, who had been excited and shocked in equal measure by his kiss, merely offered him a cool nod and quickened her steps.

"You see, Eleanor, I mean to be perfectly well behaved from now on. Oh, I think I see Lady Langton and her sister ahead. Do let us join them."

Eleanor had no very great opinion of Lady Langton, whom she found frivolous and empty-headed, but she made no demur, pleased at Diana's seeming resolve to keep Lord Sandford at arm's length.

"Eliza!" Diana called, as they came up behind them.

Lady Langton looked over her shoulder revealing

a pair of sparkling blue eyes. They were quite her best feature, apart from perhaps her smooth, unblemished complexion. She was generally considered pretty but her nose was a little too long and thin for her to deserve the tribute of being called a beauty. Perhaps it was this attribute that gave her voice a rather nasal quality.

"Diana!" she squealed, grabbing her friend's arm. She spared a quick nod for Eleanor before rushing on, "What a lucky chance that I have met you today, for I have several snippets of information that I am sure you will wish to know."

As the park was crowded, there was no room for four ladies to easily walk abreast. Eleanor fell behind with Miss Farrow, Lady Langton's younger sister. She shared the nose and was quite as silly as her sibling, but unfortunately for her, did not share her sister's other attributes; her eyes were set a little too close together, and her complexion was sadly prone to redness. Although Lady Langton dutifully took her sister about with her and introduced her to the many connections her marriage had afforded her, two seasons had resulted in no offers of marriage for Miss Farrow.

"Eliza is ridiculously excited about Lady Brigham's ball," Miss Farrow said in hushed tones. "Have you received an invitation, Miss Edgcott?"

"Yes. Even Lord Haverham is to attend which surprised me, for he is not fond of balls. Will I see you there?"

Miss Farrow's titter did not disguise her bitterness. "No, I have not been honoured with an invitation, and

I am sure I do not care, even if it is the first ball Lady Brigham has held in years."

"Is it? I had not realised, but that perhaps explains why Lord Haverham has agreed to attend."

"Most likely," agreed Miss Farrow. "Lord Brigham is very well respected according to Langton. But that is not why Eliza is looking forward to it. She is far more interested in his son, Lord Allerdale. Apparently, it is almost as rare for him to attend a ball these days as it is for Lady Brigham to give one, but he can hardly fail to do so when it is his mother who is hosting the event. I do not know him, but Eliza saw him with a party of friends at the theatre last season and thinks him very handsome."

Both ladies came to a halt as a high poke bonnet rolled across the path in front of them. Eleanor picked it up and brushed the dust from it. She thought it very stylish and not quite in the common style. The crown was cream, with two brown ribbons creating a striped effect, the wide brim was also brown, and a spray of delicate lilac flowers completed the pleasing colour palette.

She looked up and saw a young lady with wide anxious eyes and glossy golden ringlets hurrying towards her. She smiled and went to meet her.

"Is this yours?"

"Oh, yes. Thank you. I had tied the ribbon too tightly and when I undid it, the wind whipped it from my head!"

"I do not think it has suffered any damage," Eleanor said, handing it to her. "It would have been such a shame if it had for it is a very fetching creation. Would you mind telling me where you purchased it?"

The girl smiled shyly at her. "Not at all. I buy all my hats from Mrs Willis. Her shop is in Cranbourn Alley, off Leicester Square."

Just then a short, plump lady dressed in a startling dress largely distinguished by green and yellow stripes that made her look as wide as she was tall, rushed up to them.

"Emily! What are you about to go running through the park? I am sure this kind lady must think you a regular hoyden!"

"Not at all," Eleanor said. "I think I too would run after such a hat!" She gave the young lady a reassuring smile. "I can see my friends waiting for me and so must leave you."

"Yes, of course," Emily said. "Thank you again for your help."

As she walked the short distance to her party, Eleanor heard the lady she assumed to be Emily's mother say in rather exasperated tones, "How are you ever to make friends, Emily, if you will not even make a push to learn people's names or give them yours or your direction?"

"But it would be so forward of me," the girl said in trembling accents.

Eleanor felt sorry for the girl and might have returned and introduced herself if Diana had not rushed up to her and taken her arm.

"Eleanor! You must not go about talking to strangers in the park!"

She laughed. "Why? Neither of the two ladies in question looked at all dangerous."

"They do not need to be dangerous for them not

to be fit persons for you to know," Lady Langton interjected. "I would lay odds that they were *cits.*"

Rarely had Eleanor heard such scorn poured into one little word. She felt a spurt of annoyance; she had frequently entertained English merchants at her father's table and had little patience for such assumptions of superiority, especially when they came from someone as inane as Eliza Langton.

"Have you ever visited Mrs Willis' shop in Cranbourn Alley, Diana? I believe it is off Leicester Square. That is where the young lady found that delightful bonnet."

"I do not believe I have."

"Ha!" Lady Langton said. "Then they are definitely cits. I would not be surprised if that young lady had purposefully lost her hat in the hope that she might make the acquaintance of one of her betters."

Eleanor was about to question this view of the situation when she heard herself being hailed. Turning, she saw two intelligent, dark eyes set in a sharp face, regarding her. She hurried up to the barouche.

"Good afternoon, Countess Lieven."

"Oblige me, Miss Edgcott, by joining me for a turn about the park."

There was no question of refusing. "Certainly, ma'am. I will just inform Lady Haverham of my intention."

"You must certainly go," Diana said. "I shall be perfectly safe with Eliza."

Lady Langton pulled a face. "Rather you than me. She scares me to death."

The three ladies began to amble along the path again, their heads together as they shared the latest tidbits of gossip. Eleanor returned to the barouche and swiftly climbed in.

Countess Lieven raised a fine eyebrow. "Perhaps I am being conceited, Miss Edgcott, but I feel sure that my company must be more interesting than that which you have left. Ninnyhammers, all of them!"

"You should not say so, ma'am, as one of them is related to me," Eleanor said, but with a smile.

"Only through marriage," the countess said, unabashed. "Haverham has far more between his ears, as do you, I think. I never met your father, but I have heard only good reports of him."

"Yes, he was a fine man. I am, of course, pleased to bear you company for a short while. Indeed, I am glad of this opportunity to have some private conversation with you, for I can think of no one better to consult about a matter of propriety. Would it be wrong of me to set up an establishment of my own in Town?"

"Would you have an elder relative, perhaps an aunt, living with you?"

"No, but I would hire a companion."

"I do not think that would do at all; you are far too young. Are you unhappy in your cousin's house?"

Eleanor's heart sank. She would not wish to act in a way that would cause anyone to think such a thing. "Oh no, but I have been used to a different life—"

"You have lived many years abroad and are feeling a little confined by the English ways. This I understand. It has come to my ears that you have turned down more than one offer of marriage, for which I do not blame you in the least. But have you considered that you will be granted a deal more freedom as a married lady if you choose wisely? Even the ladies in Constantinople – who, I believe, generally only mix with their own sex – probably have some influence over their husbands and sons."

"Yes, that is true," Eleanor admitted.

"You could do far worse than attaching yourself to someone involved in diplomacy, or who is likely to be in the future; it is a world you are familiar with after all. Come to my salon the day after tomorrow; there is someone I would like you to meet."

Eleanor was fully aware of how honoured she was to receive this invitation and so accepted gracefully.

"By the way, where did you get that hat? It is something above the common."

"Originally from Madame Lafayette's in Bruton Street, but I have redesigned it in my own style."

"You have a certain flair, Miss Edgcott. It is certainly far superior to Madame Lafayette's designs, and she is no more French than I am English! There is a rumour going about that she is going to shut up shop. I am not surprised; she has not moved with the times and that, you know, is fatal in all matters of fashion."

Two gentlemen on horseback passed the carriage. Countess Lieven smiled at the fairer of the two, but only nodded frostily at the other. Eleanor looked up quickly and nodded at Lord Carteret before allowing her eyes to quickly sweep over the other gentleman, but he was gone before she could form any firm impression apart from that he was dark. She felt a strange tingling at the base of her neck and an urge to turn around and look at him more closely. She firmly ignored it.

"Do you know Lord Carteret?" Countess Lieven asked.

"Yes. I have met him on a few occasions."

"And what did you make of him?"

"What should I make of him?" Eleanor said, surprised. "He is all politeness, his manners are very polished, but he possesses a reserve that makes it difficult to know him."

"That is true. From what Lady Jersey has told me, it is all Lady Haverham's fault."

"Diana's? In what way?"

"He fell in love with her or thought he did; I still find it hard to believe that someone of his not inconsiderable understanding should fall for someone as bird-witted as she, but then more than one sensible gentleman has been blinded by a pretty face. She turned him down in favour of Haverham. I have nothing at all to say against Haverham; he feels just as he ought on a number of topics, but one cannot deny that he is rather dull. I am not at all surprised that his wife's head might be turned a little by the Marquess of Sandford."

Eleanor paled. "Has that rumour already begun to circulate? There is nothing serious between them, I assure you. In fact, there is nothing at all between them beyond a little gentle flirtation."

"No rumour has yet reached my ears," the countess conceded. "I speak only from my own observations. I believe I have a little more astuteness than most. If you tell me Lady Haverham has indulged in nothing more than a gentle flirtation, I choose to believe you. But you may believe me when I tell you that Sandford does nothing gently. In plain words, he is a rake. Any intentions he may have will certainly be dishonourable and he is far from discreet. For some reason, Miss Edgcott, I like you and would not wish you to suffer by association if Lady Haverham's reputation becomes tarnished."

"No! It will not come to that," Eleanor said quickly. "I will ensure that it does not. Only today Diana snubbed him."

"Good. Let us hope that she will continue to do so."

Uncomfortable, Eleanor turned the subject.

"You seemed to disapprove of Lord Carteret's companion."

"You are very observant, but I would rather say that I have not yet approved of him. Lord Allerdale is the son of the Marquess of Brigham, a man who is certainly worthy of my esteem. Unfortunately, his son seems to take more after his mother; I hear she used to be extremely volatile. I believe there is an Italian somewhere on her side of the family which perhaps explains it. I do not say that Lord Allerdale is as bad as Lord Sandford, but he has acquired the reputation, however, of being rather wild. The latest on dit is that he is a reformed character, but as I am almost certain that it is his mother who put that rumour about, I do not set much store by it. She is no doubt hoping that he will choose a bride this season and is attempting to allay the fears of the mamas who still have daughters to dispose of."

"I always like to judge people for myself," Eleanor said. "I shall be at Lady Brigham's ball next week and so have that opportunity."

"Yes, so shall I," Countess Lieven said. "I daresay

it will be a sad crush, but everyone who is anyone will be there, as well, no doubt, as every girl of marriageable age."

"Not every girl," Eleanor said gently. "I know for a fact that Miss Farrow has not been invited."

"That is something, I suppose," the countess said dryly.

∽

"Oh dear," Lord Carteret said. "Judging by the Countess Lieven's icy stare, I do not think you will be making an appearance at Almack's any time soon, Allerdale."

Miles laughed. "If only that were true. My mother is friends with Sally Jersey so I doubt there will be any difficulty."

"Did you notice the other lady in the carriage?"

"I only had time to observe a dashing bonnet and a pair of large brown eyes."

"That was Miss Edgcott."

"Then if Countess Lieven has taken against me, I should think that any chance I may have had of fixing my interest with Miss Edgcott is already dashed."

He did not seem overly concerned by this likelihood and his gaze became suddenly fixed on one of the paths that approached the carriageway. "Talking of dashing bonnets," he said, "who is that delightful creature over there? She is a piece of perfection."

"I have no idea, old chap, which leads me to suspect that she does not move in the first circles. And before you are carried away by her rosebud lips and guinea gold curls, might I suggest you look at her mother?"

"Why? It is not the mother that I am interested in."

"Her vulgar appearance aside, you might consider that the beauty may well take after her when she is older, at least, that is the advice my mother gave me years ago."

"Really? Then I am surprised you offered for Diana Ramshorn; her mama was quite stout as I recall."

Lord Carteret's lips twisted into a bitter smile. "I did not say I took her advice."

As he spoke, the young lady stumbled, let out a screech, and clasped a shapely ankle.

"And this is yet another instance when I am not about to take yours, Carteret. A gentleman cannot ignore a lady in distress."

But even as Miles moved into a trot, a curricle flashed by him causing his highly-strung thoroughbred to skitter across the road and rear. A phaeton coming in the other direction was forced to come to an abrupt halt in front of him.

By the time he had his mount under control and had appeased the temper of the driver of the phaeton, who did not hesitate to rain down curses upon him, the curricle had taken up both the unknown beauty and her mother and was disappearing off into the distance.

"Damn Sandford. He should know better than to drive at that pace through the park."

"But he was coming to the rescue of the damsel in distress," murmured Lord Carteret.

Miles' dark brows snapped together. "If he has ever come to anyone's rescue, it is the first I have heard of it! He is more likely to ruin her! Whatever was her mother thinking?"

A cynical gleam came into Lord Carteret's eyes. "Is your temper up because you are concerned for the young lady's virtue, or because Sandford has stolen a march on you, Allerdale?"

He did not wait for a reply.

"I can think of only two reasons why his escort was acceptable to her. The first is that she has no idea of his reputation and is merely grateful for his help in delivering her daughter safely home. The less charitable interpretation, but the one I think most likely to be true, is that she knows exactly who he is and hopes to turn him to advantage. She may, of course, hope he will offer marriage, but depending on her circumstances, may settle for something less honourable. As you are about to turn respectable, my friend, and would no more offer for the child than Sandford will, I cannot see that either scenario can be any concern of yours."

Miles' eyes flashed, but when his companion merely raised a challenging brow, he grinned ruefully.

"I do not know why I bear with you, Carteret!"

"Was I wrong?"

"No, damn you! You rarely are! But if that pretty little thing is to become someone's mistress, she would do better to accept the protection of almost anyone but Sandford. I have heard that he does not treat his inamoratas at all well, either during their arrangement or when he severs it."

"I expect the girl will have very little say in the

matter. Her mother must have spent a great deal to turn her out in style and she will wish to recoup her investment. Now, Allerdale, might I suggest we pay a visit to Jackson's or Angelo's? You may then rid yourself of some of your spleen."

"Angelo's," Miles said decisively. "I have a greater chance of bettering you with a sword than with my fists!"

"Not unless you keep a firm rein on your temper," his friend said gently.

CHAPTER 5

Eleanor and Diana dined alone on the evening of the Countess Lieven's salon. Lord Haverham had gone to Newmarket, excusing himself by pointing out that it would be the last meeting until July, but had promised to be back in time for Lady Brigham's ball.

Diana picked at her food and had very little to say for herself. This strange mood of abstraction had been upon her since their walk in the park.

Sensing the impending storm, Eleanor eyed her warily. "I will stay if you wish. I can easily send a note of apology to Countess Lieven."

Diana shook her head, unable to speak for the tears that welled in her eyes despite her efforts to blink them away.

Eleanor looked at the footman that hovered in the background.

"You may leave us, Stanley."

When he had left the room, she said, "You have

been in low spirits for the past two days, Diana. Come, tell me what is troubling you."

The tears fell faster, and Diana buried her face in her napkin. Eleanor placed her fork on her plate and waited, hoping that a good cry might alleviate Diana's melancholy. When she finally stemmed the flow, Diana said, "No, I am just being stupid. You cannot decline an invitation to one of the Countess Lieven's salons; they are very much sought after this year, although not by me. From all I can gather, the talk is all about politics. Dull stuff. But then, you, I suppose, are used to talking of such things."

"Not really. My role was rather to entertain my father's fellow ambassadors, his staff, English merchants who traded out of Constantinople, or English visitors who were passing through. They did not generally talk of their work in my presence, although Papa did sometimes share some of his frustrations in dealing with the Turkish officials, and he often asked my opinion on the people we met. He always said that I had a good instinct where people were concerned."

Diana sniffed and blew her nose. "At any rate, I am sure you will find the evening more stimulating than I would. And I dare say you will find it far more interesting than my company."

The last words were uttered on a wail of self-pity, and Diana once again fell to a bout of weeping.

It was some time before Eleanor could calm her, and when she did, a tale of woe poured from Diana. The source of her unhappiness seemed to come from several quarters, but its chief cause appeared to be her husband's inattention – she was sure he would not care if she lived or died, apart from the fact that she had not yet presented him with an heir – but even that could be easily remedied if she caught some fatal disease or was run over by a carriage, for then he could remarry and his new wife would in all likelihood be dutiful enough to present him with a son before they had been wed a year.

Eleanor patiently pointed out to her that Frederick had never, to her knowledge, expressed any dissatisfaction that Diana had not yet produced an heir, that he would be hard pressed to find anyone as beautiful, and that although he did not always show his affection, she was sure that in the event of her death he would sustain a blow from which he might never recover.

"Do you really think so?" Diana said hesitantly.

"I am sure of it."

Diana crumpled the napkin that she still held into a ball and threw it onto the table. "But it is not just Frederick. I am quite tired of the… the fickleness of people. I used to be very good friends with Lord Carteret, you know, but now he barely acknowledges me—"

"How can you expect him to remain friendly with you when you broke his heart?" Eleanor said gently.

It was not to her credit that for a moment Diana looked a little cheered by this thought. It was only a momentary lifting of her spirits, however.

"If he had truly loved me, he would still wish to be my friend. And then there is Sandford."

Eleanor raised a brow. "Stealing a kiss was certainly a liberty, and to attempt it in such a public place showed a deplorable lack of consideration for your rep—"

"It is not only that," Diana said peevishly. "He must have taken another turn around the park when you were with the countess because he passed us again, this time with that… that *person* whose hat you retrieved."

"No!" Eleanor said, surprised. "Alone?"

"That vulgarly dressed creature was with her," Diana acknowledged.

"Perhaps he knew them," Eleanor suggested.

"Eliza said that she was probably his m-mistress and I think she was right," she said on a sob. "If you could have seen the gloating look Eliza gave me, for she was quite jealous that Sandford was making up to me, you know. I had not thought her so spiteful. The only person who truly loves me is my little Lucinda, and I have not seen her for so long she will most likely have forgotten me when we return to Standon."

Eleanor, who was by nature practical, said, "Then why don't you send for her?"

"How can I? You know she had that horrid cough just before we came away, and Doctor Lampton said that on no account must I bring her to Town for the air would not be good for her."

"Yes, of course, how silly of me," Eleanor said, a little sharply. "Then perhaps we should return to Standon. I have no objection. We could go tomorrow if it pleases you."

Diana seemed at a loss to know how to answer this doubler, but after a moment made a recovery.

"No, I do not think that is possible. I would like it of all things, of course, but it would not be fair on you or Frederick. And then there is Lady Brigham's ball on Tuesday; I am sure none of us would wish to miss it. I at least have the consolation of knowing that Miss Ryder will take very good care of my little daughter."

Eleanor knew Diana's nature to be shallow and so was not surprised by this response, but any impatience she might have felt at this orgy of self-pity was ameliorated by the knowledge that Diana was genuinely suffering a crisis of confidence. Although she did not feel it was her place to interfere between her cousin and his wife, she could see that she was going to have to take a firmer hand with Frederick when he returned.

It was inevitable that she arrived late to the Countess Lieven's salon. As she was announced she saw her hostess coming towards her with a man who had a pleasing, if serious, countenance. The dark shadows under his eyes made him look a little haggard and although his skin remained smooth, his hair was already well on the way to becoming grey.

He bowed to her and said, "It is unfortunate, Miss Edgcott, that my affairs prevent me from staying any longer, but I hope I shall have the opportunity to speak with you again. Your father is sadly missed, especially now when I have need of good men experienced in diplomacy."

Before she could make any sort of reply he had left the room. Countess Lieven raised a brow.

"I was beginning to fear that you would not come, Miss Edgcott."

"I do apologise for my being so late," Eleanor said calmly, aware of the edge in her hostess's voice. "It is not my usual habit, I assure you, but I was unavoidably delayed. Was that who you wished to introduce me to? Who was he?"

"It is a sad state of affairs, Miss Edgcott, when you do not recognise the foreign minister of your own country."

Eleanor coloured. "I have not had the pleasure of making Lord Castlereagh's acquaintance."

"No? Well, he is rather taken up with world events just at the moment. I do hope that you are not one of those who has some sympathy for Napoleon?"

"I am not. Whilst he is free, he must always be a danger I should think."

"I am pleased that you have the wit to see it, Miss Edgcott. It is a constant source of surprise to me that he still has supporters in this country and that there are others who think there remains a peaceable solution to be found." She nodded towards a corner of the room. "Earl Grey is here tonight; he is one who believes it, should you wish to discuss the matter with him."

"But I do not wish to discuss it at all, ma'am. I do not know enough about the intricacies of the situation and so am not qualified to do so."

A small smile twitched at the countess's lips. "A wise decision. He can be very persuasive, and I would not wish you to be bamboozled by his eloquence."

"But if you do not agree with him, why is he here?"

"Because I like to keep up with all sides of an argument. Just because I do not agree with him does not mean that I cannot appreciate his ideas. Besides, things change all the time in politics, and it is not wise to alienate people who may one day hold more influence than they do at this present moment."

Eleanor had heard that Countess Lieven was not

at all shy of alienating people but smiled. "I am sure you are right, ma'am."

The countess then took her by the arm and led her about the room, introducing Eleanor to a bewildering array of people she did not know. They did not stay with anyone long enough for her to do more than exchange polite pleasantries until they came to a handsome gentleman with white-blond hair and humorous, light green eyes.

"Allow me to introduce Mr Nicholas Pavlov to you, Miss Edgcott."

The gentleman bowed gracefully. "I am pleased to make your acquaintance, Miss Edgcott."

She smiled at him in her usual friendly fashion, and said, "But you sound like an English man!"

"That is because my mother was an English woman," he explained. "I grew up speaking French and English in equal measure, and I completed my education at Oxford before returning to Russia."

"My husband and I have been trying to persuade Mr Pavlov that these circumstances make him ideal for a career in diplomacy. He has agreed to work for my husband in an unofficial capacity for a few months, and we are hopeful that by the end of that time we will be able to recommend him for a more official position, if he wishes it. Oh, I see Lord Grey is ready to depart, do excuse me."

"And what is it that the countess wishes *you* to do, Miss Edgcott?" he asked with a twinkle.

"Wishes me to do?" she said, nonplussed.

"I mean no disrespect to our hostess," he said, "but I believe the countess' invitations are generally given out with some object in mind, whether they are socially or politically motivated."

"Well I can think of no way in which I could be of use to her in either case," Eleanor said. "*Are* you interested in a career in diplomacy, Mr Pavlov?"

"It is not why I came again to England," he said. "It was my English grandfather, Mr Fallow, who insisted I finish my education in this country and provided me with an allowance whilst I did so. He was a modest landowner from Cheshire who unfortunately had too many daughters to provide for. My mother chose to be a governess, but after one particularly unpleasant situation she replied to an advertisement placed by my father, Count Pavlov, and went to Russia."

"And he fell in love with her, how romantic."

"Perhaps. But it resulted in him being ostracized in St Petersburg, and he was forced to retreat to his country estate."

"Was that so bad?" she asked. "Did he not like the country?"

"Not all year round," he said. "Russia is not unlike England in that respect; the nobility only moves to their country estates in the summer. He bore it well enough, and now my mother is dead, he and my half-brother are being welcomed back into the fold once more."

"But not you?"

"No. I must always be a reminder of what is seen as my father's mistake. Not wishing to be a hindrance to either him or my half-brother, I decided I would try my luck in England. I got to know my grandfather a little when I was here before, and I liked him. I hoped to know him better, but I am too late; he died six months ago, and my uncle has stepped into his shoes. He does not seem overly keen to develop closer ties with his half-Russian nephew. I think he is afraid I will be a drain on his resources."

He did not seem unduly concerned over this development, but Eleanor was aware of a feeling of sympathy towards him. His words about his mother had been matter-of-fact, but she had seen and recognised the pain in his eyes.

"And would you be a drain on his resources?"

"No. My father is not rolling in riches, but he is funding my visit. However, if I decide to stay, I will have to find some sort of employment."

"It seems that you already may have done so. That is, if you wish to serve in the diplomatic service. Do you?"

He grinned, wryly. "You are not easy to sidetrack, Miss Edgcott. Countess Lieven is very patriotic and does not wish to lose me to my English relatives; she thinks I may still be useful to Russia. She has taken an unaccountable liking to me."

Eleanor looked thoughtful and then suddenly laughed. "Oh, I see it all now."

"Do you?" Mr Pavlov said agreeably. "What is it you see?"

"I think, sir, that the countess may be trying to organise more than your career. I, you see, am a diplomat's daughter and have spent many years abroad. I returned home only last year when I lost my father."

The flash of surprise that shot through his eyes told her that he had not been primed in any way for this meeting.

"You think she is matchmaking?"

"I am sure of it," Eleanor said. "You have already told me that you are not very well off, sir, but I have been left very comfortably circumstanced. If Countess Lieven has your best interests at heart, I suppose I would seem a very suitable prospect for you."

"You are very frank, ma'am," he said.

"Yes," she agreed. "I think in this instance, it is best. I do not know about you, sir, but I do not like to be a pawn in anybody else's game."

"No more do I," he agreed.

Eleanor raised a sceptical brow. "No? You have twice evaded informing me whether or not you wish to be a diplomat and so I take it that you do not. Yet you have allowed the Lievens to persuade you to explore that possibility."

A look of admiration came into his eyes. "You are astute, Miss Edgcott. I will match your frankness for although I am not at all sure why, I feel I can trust you. I have a particular reason for wishing to stay in London for the present and so it seemed both practical and diplomatic, if you will, to accept their offer."

Eleanor smiled; she instinctively liked Mr Pavlov. "So, it is they who are the pawns? I will not ask you what your reason is for I sense that it is private, and you need not fear that I will give you away; I have no reason to do so, after all."

"Thank you," he said bowing. "We are about to be interrupted, ma'am. May I take you for a drive in the park next week? It might be in both our interests to at least appear to be playing the countess' game."

"I would be perfectly happy to drive with you in

the park, sir," she said truthfully, "and not because it is part of anyone's game."

He smiled and moved off. Eleanor turned, her own smile growing as she saw a tall, beautiful lady approaching her.

"Georgianna! I did not see you in this crowd! I am delighted to find you here."

"And I you, Eleanor. The talk is all of Napoleon and the inevitability of war. Somerton is deep in a conversation about the likely efficacy of both our troops and those of our various allies. You may call me a traitor, but I can only be glad that he is no longer serving his country, even if *he* is not."

"Is he not tempted to re-join his regiment?"

"Very. Only the joint persuasion of his father and myself have thus far held him back." Georgianna smiled gently. "But whatever now happens in Europe, I feel certain he will not do so."

Eleanor's eyes widened. "Are congratulations in order?"

The glow in her friend's eyes answered her.

"Yes," Georgianna said softly. "But it is not generally known as yet. I know I can trust you not to breathe a word; only Somerton, Marianne and now you know of it. I have even forbidden Alexander to inform his father just yet, for the duke would be bound to insist that I return home to Rushwick Park. He very much wishes for a grandchild."

"I will not, of course, but there is a glow of health and happiness about you that might give you away."

"No, why should it?" Georgianna said. "My maid informs me that I can expect to feel languid, horribly sick, and suffer from unpredictable mood swings."

"Oh, I see. I do not know of such things, but I am very glad you have not suffered any of those symptoms; it seems a shame that such an exciting event should be accompanied by them. How is Marianne? The last time I spoke with her she was writing to both the prince regent and Lord Liverpool about those poor animals in the menagerie."

"She has received a reply from the latter informing her that although they cannot be moved to an outside park due to the danger that they might escape, their living conditions and diet will be looked into."

"In other words, she has been fobbed off," Eleanor said dryly.

Two engaging dimples peeped in Georgianna's cheeks as she said, "That is because Lord Liverpool, or rather one of his secretaries, does not know Marianne. If she does not see any improvement, she will make herself a nuisance until she does."

"I hope you are right, for I quite agree with her sentiments. Will you be at Lady Brigham's ball on Tuesday?"

"I most certainly shall," Georgianna confirmed, a glint of amusement in her eyes. "Her son, Lord Allerdale, is the godson of my aunt, Lady Hughes, and a friend of mine."

"Now that *is* interesting," Eleanor said, an inquisitive gleam in her eyes, "for Countess Lieven informs me that he is known for being rather wild, although I believe the rumour is that he has changed his ways."

Georgianna laughed. "I hope he may have, but I do not place any dependency on it. He may well try if his mama has indicated that she wishes him to. He loves her dearly and would do anything for her, but I doubt that she has; she can never be brought to see that he has any faults."

"But you said he was your friend, Georgianna, and so he cannot be so very wild."

"He can be very amusing and good company, and I do not believe him to be a bad person but watch out if he loses his temper!"

"Did he do so with you?" Eleanor asked, agog with curiosity.

"Yes," Georgianna admitted, her eyes softening as if she were remembering a fond memory. "But ask me no more; I would not colour your opinion of him."

They had been walking slowly about the perimeter of the room but paused as they came up to two gentlemen. Lord Somerton's forehead had been furrowed and his face serious, but he broke off his earnest discussion as he spied his wife. He raised an eyebrow, and a look that hovered somewhere between concern and adoration softened his golden eyes.

"Have you had enough?"

Georgianna smiled at him and then the other gentleman.

"I will admit that I am a little weary," she said. "But only because I am sure Lord Brigham will not sink me beneath reproach by repeating my words to the countess. Have you met my friend, Miss Edgcott, sir?"

He bowed. "No, I have not had that pleasure. How do you do, ma'am?"

Eleanor inclined her head and said, "I am very well."

Lord Brigham was well aware of the speculation surrounding Miss Edgcott, as he was also aware of the bets currently being placed at his club on which lady would win his son's favour, not that anyone speculated upon this subject to his face.

"Will I have the pleasure of seeing you at our ball, Miss Edgcott?"

Eleanor's smile was perfectly serene, but her eyes laughed. "You certainly shall, my lord. Who am I to miss the most anticipated event of the season?"

Lord Brigham looked at her keenly for a moment and then his rare smile dawned.

"I have the feeling, Miss Edgcott, that you do not care a fig for our ball."

She laughed. "Well, no. But I have been to so many in such a short time, you see, and although they are all very pleasant, they do sap one's energy, which is a shame, for there are so many other interesting things to concern oneself with."

"What a refreshing perspective. Come, Miss Edgcott," he said, offering her his arm. "Walk with me and educate me as to what could be more important to a lively young lady than a ball."

CHAPTER 6

Captain Charles Bassington of the 13th Light Dragoons sprawled at his ease in a chair in his cousin's sitting room, his careless attitude not quite at one with his smart regimentals.

Miles strolled in and said in the voice of one about to face his doom, "Will I do, Charles?"

"You look very dapper, Miles, but for heaven's sake wipe that scowl from your face or it will all be for nought! You don't have to make any decision tonight, after all, and I hope you won't; it don't do to rush into these things. Flirt with every pretty girl in the room and enjoy yourself; it's what I intend to do."

"It's what you always do!" Miles said dryly. "But as you usually have to flit across the channel not long afterwards, you can hardly be accused of raising false hopes in any young lady's breast."

"True," Charles acknowledged. "But I am being serious for once; forget that you are supposed to be finding a bride. You will find it far easier to like a girl if you are not trying to ascertain if she is suitable wife material at the outset."

Miles had been tugging at the sleeve of his close-fitting coat, but stilled, a memory from last summer flashing vividly in his mind. His godmother had come to stay at Brigham with Georgianna, and Lady Brigham had held a dinner for their neighbours. Viscount Maudley, who held himself in very great esteem, had ruthlessly questioned Georgianna on her accomplishments as if attempting to determine if she was worthy of his attention. A grin twitched his lips as he remembered how she had neatly turned the tables on him before giving him a ruthless set-down.

"That's better," Charles said, rising to his feet in one fluid motion. "It's not like you to be such a miserable fellow and I have seen you bring more than one little beauty around your thumb, after all. You can be very charming when you choose to be."

"Yes," Miles admitted, "but the beauties you speak of, were none of them at all respectable!"

Charles laughed. "Don't I know it; I remember that little dasher…" he paused and shook his head. "No, I will not taunt you with memories that must now be laid to rest. Come on, or we will be late for dinner, and I promised your mother that I would have you in Berkeley Square in good time."

A sardonic gleam, which Charles found far too reminiscent of Lord Brigham, came into his cousin's eyes. "You wound me, Charles. I had thought you sought me out for the pleasure of my company alone."

"And so I have, as well you know, but if in following my own inclination I can also bask in the approval of my aunt, all the better!"

"Toad-eater!" Miles said, holding the door open.

"No, that's coming it too strong, old fellow!"

They quickly fell into their old way of bantering each other and so were oblivious to the admiring glances they attracted from more than one occupant of a passing carriage as they made their way to Berkeley Square. Both were tall, with broad shoulders and handsome countenances, but where Miles was dark, Charles was fair, his hair a mixture of blond, gold, and red tints.

"What a dutiful son you are, Miles," Lady Bassington said, not troubling herself to rise as they came into the drawing room.

"Aunt Frances." Miles strode over to the handsome woman who reclined on a sofa, her feet resting on a footstool. He bent and kissed her.

"Please, do not get up."

She patted his cheek and gave a low laugh. "Impudent boy! I have no intention of doing so! It is so wearing to always be getting up and down whenever anyone enters the room."

He grinned down at her. "I quite understand. I expect you are saving your energy for the ball. No doubt you will find it deplorably fatiguing."

Lady Bassington might be indolent, but she was by no means dull-witted. She chuckled. "Not at all. I shall enjoy watching you navigate your way through the hopeful young gals on offer."

As no hint of maliciousness laced her words, and her eyes held a wealth of understanding, Miles only smiled and said, "You may give me an assessment of my performance."

"You may be sure I will, and of the gals you choose to dance with."

Lady Brigham tutted. "This talk of your performance is ridiculous. You do not have to act a part, Miles, just be yourself. Any young lady who cannot appreciate you for who you are is not worthy of your consideration."

"I quite agree with you, Julia," Lady Bassington said. "Miles certainly needs an intrepid lady."

Miles laughed. "No, Mama, do not rise to the bait. You know how much Aunt Frances enjoys teasing you."

Over dinner, Lady Brigham launched into a recital of the various ladies he might like to invite to dance.

"Miss Crabtree is only the daughter of a baron, but she has a respectable dowry, or if you do not like her, there is Lady Selena Sheringham, who is very pretty and will inherit a fortune that her great aunt left her when she either marries or comes of age. It is a shame Lady Barbara Philpot has already accepted an offer from Lord Buntingdon, for she is quite breathtaking, and then there is Miss Edgcott. I spoke with her at Lady Battledon's ball and found her very engaging, and rumour has it that she is very well provided for. But if you don't like any of them—"

"Julia," Lord Brigham said gently, "I think you have said enough. You would not wish to influence Allerdale, I am sure. Let things take their natural course this evening."

Miles threw his father a grateful look.

"My head is spinning, Mama. All the names you mentioned have already flown out of my head, apart from the last one, and I am sure that will soon follow."

"Miss Edgcott? Yes, well, I do not hold out so much hope in that direction. She does not appear to wish for a husband; she turned down Ormsley, you know, and with his wealth and good looks, he has had a succession of girls thrown in his path by hopeful mamas. I was surprised to hear he had offered for Miss Edgcott as he is very starched up and she is, after all, only the daughter of a baronet and a lively girl; I would not have thought that would have suited him at all."

"At least that is one lady, then, I may cross off my list."

"Do not be so hasty, Miles," Lady Brigham said. "She has not met you yet, after all. We are not looking for you to make a great match; we only wish you to be happy. If you like Miss Edgcott, I am sure we would not object; her birth is respectable."

Lady Bassington's deep, lazy voice sounded, its slow measured tones in sharp contrast to Lady Brigham's bright, bubbly speech. "You talk as if Miles has only to click his fingers and he can marry who he pleases, Julia."

"Well, and why not? There are very few gentlemen with as good prospects, and he is more handsome even than Ormsley."

"You are prejudiced, Mama," Miles said with a fond grin. He turned to his aunt, "I may have been arrogant enough to believe it at one time, ma'am, but I am no longer."

"Oh? Why is that?"

"Because, Aunt, I have already been turned down once."

Charles had been allowing the talk to flow over his

head whilst he applied himself to a substantial dinner but at this, he raised his head, his eyes alight with curiosity. "You don't say? Who was this girl who had so much sense?"

"Charles!" protested Lady Brigham.

"It is not the place of a gentleman to tell you," Miles said, his tone stern but his lips twitching.

"Quite right," his father said in the soft, silky voice which always dampened Charles' exuberance.

The subject was allowed to drop.

The ballroom filled quickly, and Lady Brigham was fully occupied greeting guests for some time, but she did not fail to bring Lady Selena to her son just as the set for the first dance was forming.

He agreed with his mother's assessment of her, she was indeed pretty, and he thought she had a singularly sweet smile. Lady Brigham had failed to inform him, however, of her extreme shyness. She rarely raised her eyes to his, and murmured only *yes*, *no*, or *I'm sure I couldn't say*, in response to his attempts at conversation. Miles did not wish for a wife who would try to rule the roast, but neither did he wish for one that could barely string a sentence together and jumped whenever he spoke.

He was relieved when the dance came to an end. He had barely returned Lady Selena to her mother and exchanged a few pleasantries with Lady Sheringham, a formidable matron with a calculating eye, when Lady Brigham appeared by his side with Miss Crabtree in tow. His lips tightened and the swift glance he sent his mother made his exasperation clear. However, when he bowed before Miss Crabtree, he had wiped all signs of annoyance from his countenance.

He at first thought her a little dab of a thing but when they came together in the dance, and he asked her how she was enjoying her season, she surprised him by raising eyes that were full of merriment.

"I wonder how many times you shall be forced to ask that question this evening? You are behaving with great restraint, Lord Allerdale, but you do not fool me. I know exactly what you are thinking."

"I doubt it," he said dryly.

She smiled knowingly. "Oh, I think I do. You are wishing yourself anywhere but here. Am I right?"

She won an answering smile from him. "Now how can I answer that, Miss…?"

He realised with some mortification that he had forgotten her name.

"Crabtree." She threw the words over her shoulder with an understanding smile before she skipped away from him.

"Forgive my wretched memory," he said, offering her his most charming smile when they came together again.

"Of course, I will," she said promptly. "When I first came to Town, I suffered from the same affliction. It is so tiresome to be bludgeoned into dancing with a host of people one does not know, or who one does not particularly wish to know. I am in the same predicament, you see."

Miles found himself warming to Miss Crabtree.

"I was not bludgeoned into dancing with you, and I am very pleased to know you, ma'am."

"Were you not?" she said with a twinkle. "You were, at least, left with very little choice. It would have been shockingly rude of you not to ask me to dance when it was perfectly plain that is what your mama intended."

"I am perfectly capable of being shockingly rude, I assure you."

"That's better," she approved. "It is also tiresome to be forced to talk polite nothings all evening."

"But you don't!" he said.

"Not with you," she said. "Did I not say we are in the same predicament or has your wretched memory struck again?"

He laughed. "No, it has not. Did you not wish to come to Town, Miss Crabtree?"

"No," she said. "But my father would insist. I finally gave in when it became clear he would not be happy until I did. In his eyes, I am his adored only child and so perhaps he can be forgiven for thinking that I am beautiful and worthy of an earl or even a marquess. And do not think I am fishing for compliments, because I am not. I know I am nothing at all out of the ordinary and I also know exactly what I want, and you may be sure I shall get it."

"I believe you," he said, his eyes alive with amusement. "What is it you want?"

"Mr Shaddon," she confided. "He is the son of our local magistrate, who is only a squire. He is not particularly handsome, although I find his countenance very pleasing, and he is not at all fashionable, but that don't concern me either."

"And is Mr Shaddon devastated at having you torn from him?"

Miss Crabtree's eyes crinkled as she laughed. "I

cannot imagine him being devastated by anything! He is a very stoical sort of gentleman, and usually has a great deal of sense, but on the subject of my coming to Town he became quite buffleheaded!"

"Is that a word, Miss Crabtree? I do not think I have heard the term before, although I think I understand you."

"Well, if it is not, it should be. The clunch agreed with my father that I should come. He said that he was not worthy of me and that he would not marry me until I had had the opportunity to do better."

Miles bowed and kissed her hand as the set came to an end.

"It has been a pleasure, Miss Crabtree, and I wish you very happy with your Mr Shaddon."

Although Miles had enjoyed his time with Miss Crabtree, he did not intend to allow himself to be cornered by his mother again. He made for the opposite side of the crowded room but pulled up short when he spied one of the most beautiful ladies he had ever encountered. Her figure was nicely rounded and elegant, her neck long and graceful, her profile perfection. When she turned her head towards him as if aware of his scrutiny, he saw her bone structure was of the sort that would guarantee she would age gracefully.

Lord Carteret's voice murmured in his ear. "Exquisite, isn't she? But Lady Barbara is already taken; Buntingdon was there before you."

Lady Barbara's long curling lashes dipped over her eyes in a coy manner, but not before Miles had seen an invitation in them.

"But she is not yet married," he said, swiftly closing the distance between them.

As he bowed before her, a waltz struck up.

"May I have the honour of dancing with you, Lady Barbara?"

"I am afraid you are too late, sir," she said, regretfully. "My betrothed asked me to reserve this dance for him."

Undeterred, Miles took her arm and led her towards the couples who had already taken their places. "It is Lord Buntingdon who is too late," he said. "For the dance is about to begin and he is nowhere to be seen."

As his arm encircled her waist, she glanced up at him from beneath her lashes. "He will not like it. I only hope he does not call you out."

"I hope he may," he said with a grin. "For when there is an obstacle in one's path, I find it best to remove it."

Her eyes widened. "*Is* he an obstacle in your path?"

He had expected her to laugh and take his words in the light-hearted spirit in which they had been given and could not help but compare her studied innocence with the more open manners of his last partner. But as he could not withdraw his words, he gave her the answer he knew she wished to hear.

"How could it be otherwise when he has claimed the season's brightest star?"

When she neither objected to his flattery nor attempted to deny that she was worthy of such a comparison but accepted his compliment as if it was her due, for some reason her beauty dimmed.

"Yes," she said in a forlorn little voice, "it is a shame that we did not meet before... before I made my choice. We make a striking couple, don't you think?"

Miles's eyes hardened. He had intended to flirt outrageously with the beautiful Lady Barbara, and if she had uttered her words with a laughing insincerity he would have continued to do so. But there was no hint of playfulness in her words. To have shown her hand so plainly, to belittle Buntingdon by making it clear that she would not have accepted him if she had known that the son of a marquess would be in the offing – for it could only be that which made her regret her decision – gave him a disgust for her.

Gentleman enough to not wish her to see it, his eyes lifted from hers. They came to rest on a couple who were dancing as if oblivious of everyone about them, their eyes locked on each other, their mouths curved in a gentle smile, and their adoration for each other patently apparent. His parents were defying convention and behaving in a shockingly vulgar manner by dancing together in such a way, but they would surprise no one. They always danced one waltz together at every ball they attended if it was on the programme. He suddenly wished for the music to end, feeling as if he were somehow unworthy to share the floor with them.

"Lord Allerdale?"

Lady Barbara's voice was petulant, and her mouth pursed. Miles suspected she was unused to her admirers' attention wandering whilst in her presence.

As the last few notes of the waltz were played, Miles released her and offered an elegant bow.

"Forgive me, but I caught sight of another striking couple, my parents, who are still very much in love. They have reminded me that I should not have robbed the man who has been fortunate enough to win your affection of this particular dance but satisfied myself with admiring your beauty from afar."

He escorted her from the floor and nodded at the earl, whose eyes narrowed at their approach. Lord Buntingdon was a haughty man of large fortune, some ten years his senior, and known as a great collector of beautiful objects.

"Allow me to offer you my congratulations, sir," Miles said, with a pleasant smile. "And to beg your pardon for stealing the dance that should rightfully have been yours, but you were nowhere to be seen and I do not think you can blame me for wishing for one dance with the most beautiful creature in the room."

"I quite understand, Allerdale," he said coldly. "It took me a little longer than I had anticipated to wend my way through the crush of people. I hope you enjoyed your dance, for you will not be granted another."

Miles correctly interpreted his words to mean *ever* rather than just this evening, but as he did not wish for another opportunity, he accepted this with good grace, bowed, and moved off.

Lord Carteret fell into step beside him. "Already playing your games, Allerdale?"

Miles gave a weary smile. "Do not concern yourself, Carteret, there was no game I wished to play."

"Oh? Do not tell me Lady Barbara was impervious to your charm?"

"My charm was of secondary importance to my

future prospects. I think she may be regretting her decision to marry Buntingdon; he is a cold, one might almost say sinister character, after all. I think she hoped that I might fall for *her* charms and somehow rescue her."

"You do not fancy the role of knight in shining armour?"

"It would hardly suit me," Miles said dryly. "Besides, I do not like to play other people's games."

"I am pleased to hear it," Lord Carteret said softly. "Buntingdon is a deuced fine shot if it came to a duel."

"I would not cause such a stir," Miles said, "have I not promised my father to behave in a more circumspect manner?"

"Ah, I am pleased you have remembered it, old fellow. It saves me from bringing your ire down on my head by reminding you of it."

Miles did not consider this comment worthy of a response, and at that moment caught sight of Charles among a small group of people.

"Come," he said to his friend, "I am sure Charles will wish to speak with you."

CHAPTER 7

Lord Haverham returned home in good time for the ball, and Eleanor ran him to ground in his study before he went up to change.

"I am pleased to have this opportunity for some private conversation with you, cousin."

He eyed her a little warily as he encountered the look of determination in her eyes.

"Oh? Nothing wrong is there?"

"Well, do you know, Frederick, I rather think there is." She laughed as his brows descended. "Do not look so worried, cousin, it is nothing that cannot be easily remedied."

Lord Haverham's frown did not immediately lift, some instinct warning him that his comfort was about to be disturbed.

"Is it Diana?"

"Yes, it is Diana. It is a shame she is so beautiful. Only Lady Barbara Philpot and Lady Somerton can perhaps equal her."

Lord Haverham's eyes gentled. "She is a jewel past price, isn't she, Eleanor?"

"Undoubtedly," Eleanor promptly agreed.

"But why should you say that it is a shame she is so beautiful? I am very proud to have such a beautiful creature for my wife."

"Of course you are, Frederick, and I imagine that when you courted Diana you complimented her often and spent a great deal of time in her company."

"Yes," he admitted, "how else would I have won her affection and interest when she had so many other admirers?"

"You have a very splendid stable at Standon," Eleanor said meditatively.

Lord Haverham's eyes shot up. "What the deuce has that to do with anything?"

"Oh, nothing at all," Eleanor said airily. "But please, humour me for a moment. When you choose a horse, what do you look for?"

"Its pedigree, its proportions, oh, many things."

Eleanor smiled. "Very good. And once you have purchased the horse, do you ride it or allow your stable hands to do so?"

"Of course I ride or drive it!" Lord Haverham said. "I do not purchase my horses for the benefit of anyone but myself, although I do allow my servants to exercise them of course."

"Yes, naturally you do; you can, after all, trust your servants to take the greatest care of what is yours."

Lord Haverham began to see the light.

"Eleanor! You cannot be comparing Diana to a horse!"

Eleanor laughed. "It does sound ridiculous when

you put it like that, Frederick, and I hope you will never tell her I did so, but if you think about it, you will, I am sure, see my point."

Frederick pulled back his shoulders and glared at her, clearly offended. "You are saying, I suppose that I take better care of my horses than I do my wife."

"Well," she said gently, "if you do, I am sure you do not mean to. But most of the beauties I have encountered, with the exception of Lady Somerton, remind me of highly-strung horses; they are used to being admired and if they are not handled in the right manner, they can become rather wayward or unhappy. And when one is as beautiful and naïve as Diana still is, it is not always wise to leave them unprotected when surrounded by people who may owe you no loyalty."

A look of dawning horror darkened Lord Haverham's eyes. "Are you saying, Eleanor, that my wife has gone beyond the line of what is pleasing with another man?"

"No, Frederick, I am not saying that. But if it is generally believed that you are not keeping a watch on so desirable a creature, you cannot be surprised if other gentlemen, some of questionable reputation, make up to her."

"Who has made up to her?"

"Lord Sandford has shown her a great deal of interest recently."

Lord Haverham's eyes snapped together. "Sandford? How could you let such a wastrel make up to Diana? Only last year he had an affair with Lady…" he paused, "do not tell me Diana has encouraged him?"

Eleanor went to her cousin and laid a hand on his arm. "She is still an innocent, Frederick. Since I explained to her how undesirable, not to mention damaging, his attentions might be, she has treated him only with the coolest civility. But she would not have been as susceptible to his charms if she had felt as valued as she should be."

Lord Haverham looked down at his cousin, a stunned, bemused look in his eyes.

"Diana has never mentioned to me that she wished me to accompany her anywhere. You may be sure I would have done so if she had requested me to."

"I know she has not. Her mother warned her not to hang upon your sleeve and probably spouted a great deal of other nonsense. She told me that she had been very lonely before I came, that you did not share an understanding of each other's concerns."

"But why would I bother her pretty head with the business of estate management or the latest bill in parliament? She wouldn't understand the half of what I told her. She's not as needle-witted as you, cousin, nor would I wish her to be."

"Perhaps not," Eleanor agreed. "But she would feel more valued by you. Do you know that she feels badly about not providing you with an heir as yet, as if she is failing you somehow? The thought quite sinks her spirits at times."

"Eleanor, I have never uttered a word of censure on that subject; there is time enough, after all."

"It is what I told Diana." Eleanor sighed. "It would be much better if you would talk honestly with each other about things, you know. Now, I must get ready for the ball. Please, consider all I have said, Frederick, but do not speak to Diana of Sandford, or anything else we have discussed."

Lord Haverham looked confused and exasperated. "Make your mind up, Eleanor. In one breath you ask me to talk with Diana, and in the next tell me not to!"

"I mean you should talk more from now on but not report our conversation to her," she said. "Pay her some attention this evening. Dance at least once with her and at other times make time to seek her out and ask her if she is enjoying herself."

The result of this conversation was most promising; not only did Lord Haverham compliment his lady on her beauty when she came downstairs but treated her with a gallantry Eleanor had not previously witnessed. Diana blossomed under these attentions, and Lord Haverham not only led her into the first set of the evening but also claimed her hand for the waltz.

Diana laughed when he did so, and said, "But, my lord, how unfashionable we will appear, to dance twice before supper is even served."

"I do not care a fig if we appear unfashionable, Diana," he said firmly. "And I do not choose to watch another gentleman claim so intimate a dance with the most beautiful lady in the room."

A delicate bloom of colour brushed Diana's cheeks and her eyes sparkled with unshed tears. "Frederick," she said softly, "oh, Frederick. You do care."

As Eleanor's attention was at this moment claimed by a gentleman she did not know, she did not hear her cousin's response. A handsome man in regimentals bowed gracefully before her, an engaging smile upon his lips.

"May I have the pleasure of this dance, ma'am? We have not been introduced but as this is a private ball, I think we need not concern ourselves with this small detail. Captain Charles Bassington at your service."

Eleanor inclined her head and dipped gracefully into a small curtsy. "Miss Edgcott, and I would be delighted to dance with you, sir." She returned his smile. "But only because you are fortunate enough to wear a blue uniform, if it had been red, it would have clashed with your hair, you know, and that could not have added to my consequence."

Charles laughed. "It was, of course, the clincher when I was deciding which regiment to join."

Eleanor laid her hand on his sleeve and allowed herself to be led onto the floor, immediately determining that he was a charming scapegrace.

As his arm snaked about her waist, his eyes glanced over her head and he smiled. She looked over her shoulder and saw Lord Brigham lead his lady onto the floor.

"How lovely," she said.

"Yes, isn't it? My uncle is generally the epitome of dignity and decorum, but he never fails to waltz with my aunt at a ball."

"I think it is charming," Eleanor said. "I will never understand why, once one is wed, it suddenly becomes not the thing to show one's affection for your spouse; it is nonsensical."

"I do not think my cousin, Allerdale, would agree with you, ma'am," he said grinning.

She followed his gaze and saw him gazing down at Lady Barbara Philpot.

"Her betrothed is looking daggers at the pair of them!" Captain Bassington said, cheerfully.

"If Lord Buntingdon does not like it, he should have ensured that he was there before your cousin."

"Are you a romantic, Miss Edgcott?"

She smiled. "I do not think so, but I have dealt with enough young employees of my father – he was a diplomat – to realise that so many misunderstandings are caused by a lack of communication."

"Are we talking of romantic misunderstandings or diplomatic ones, Miss Edgcott?"

"Both," she said. "I imagine it is the same in the army; where would you be without a reliable source of information and line of communication?"

"Nowhere, ma'am," he acknowledged.

"Well, that is what I have always thought. It is, of course, different in your case, but where do these ideas originate from, that dictate what we should and should not talk openly about in polite society?"

Charles raised his brows in mock horror. "But, ma'am, if there were no such rules, the lines that have been clearly and carefully drawn in the sand for hundreds of years would become muddied!"

"Yes," Eleanor said with a wry smile. "I expect you mean the lines drawn between the roles of men and women in society. Just think how awkward it would be if a lady asked her husband what he did all day, and he had to explain his exact movements."

Charles laughed. "That would not do at all, Miss Edgcott, for either sex, I imagine."

"Perhaps not," she agreed. "Will you be involved in the fight against Napoleon?"

"Undoubtedly," Charles admitted, sobering for an instant. "I have been involved in it for years."

"I wish you well," Eleanor said softly. "And hope you come through it unscathed."

As the dance reached its end, Charles bowed and kissed her hand. "I will endeavour to do so, ma'am."

He led her from the floor. "Who shall I return you to, Miss Edgcott?"

"My cousin, Lady Haverham, if you please."

"I see her," he said. "I had the pleasure of dancing with her earlier."

"Yes, I know," she said dryly. "I was standing by her side when you asked her. I was eclipsed by her beauty, no doubt."

Charles glanced down quickly, his eyes sheepish, but relaxed when he saw the impish light in her own.

"You are a very unusual woman, Miss Edgcott, and I sincerely regret that I will not have time to know you better."

"I hope that you will have the chance, sir, when you have routed our enemy."

As Lord Haverham and Charles exchanged greetings, Diana turned to Eleanor and whispered in her ear. "It has been an age since Haverham was so attentive, I had forgotten how pleasant it is."

Eleanor smiled. "I am glad."

Lord Haverham turned back to them and bowed over Diana's hand. "Would you mind very much, my lady, if I disappeared to the card room for a short while? I find that after dancing with you, I have no appetite to dance with anyone else just at this moment. I will come back after the next set to take you in to supper."

Eleanor hid a smile; she had had no idea that Frederick could be this charming and was not surprised when Diana made no demur.

"Bassington! How come you to be in Town at such a time?"

Charles clasped the hand offered to him and shook it vigorously. "Somerton! How are you, old fellow?"

"Under the cat's paw!" he said, smiling. "Let me introduce you to my wife."

Charles bowed before Georgianna, a glimmer of appreciation in his eyes. "I will be off to the continent by the end of the week, but I begin to understand, Somerton, why you shall not. It is a pleasure to make your acquaintance, Lady Somerton. If I do not return, I will at least have the consolation of having witnessed such beauty before I breathe my last."

Georgianna did not seem at all impressed with this sally. She raised one finely shaped brow and said, "If that is all your consolation, sir, I suggest you take great care that you do return. Your last memory should not be that of a woman you have met in passing, but of one you have spent many years admiring."

Lord Somerton grinned. "Your cajoling ways will not work with my wife, Bassington."

He bowed to Diana and Eleanor, "Good evening, ladies."

Lord Somerton was easily the tallest man in the room, and as he rose from his bow, his lips twisted into a crooked smile. "Here comes the sacrificial lamb."

Diana and Eleanor turned to see to whom he was referring, but it was not until Lord Allerdale was almost upon them that they saw him emerge from the crowd.

"He does not look very pleased," Diana whispered in Eleanor's ear. "His frown is quite demonic; he is certainly not like a lamb."

"No, more like a wolf in sheep's clothing," Eleanor murmured. "But I am not at all sure he is frowning; his eyebrows are so thick and dark that they give him a naturally stern expression, don't you think?"

He passed very close to Eleanor as he reached out to shake Lord Somerton's hand, and the air about him seemed to vibrate with a powerful, masculine energy. He was very striking but she thought his features a little too harsh to be deemed handsome precisely. His dark eyes had a keen intensity about them, and his square chin was rather too firm, hinting at a strong will and stubborn character. But when he turned to Georgianna, a gentle smile softened his face, and she thought him very handsome indeed, dangerously handsome!

Diana suddenly gasped beside her. Eleanor looked at her with an understanding smile, assuming she too had been impressed by this transformation, but it was not Lord Allerdale who had caused her reaction. Diana had paled and her wide eyes were turned in another direction altogether.

Eleanor followed her gaze and saw Lord Sandford sauntering towards them, his gaze fixed on Diana, and a lazy smile on his lips. He had the air of a predator about to claim its prey.

"I do not wish to dance with him," Diana hissed.

"No, you must not," Eleanor agreed.

Any good that she had done this evening would be undone if Haverham came from the cardroom and saw them dancing together, but she could not quite see how she was to prevent it. Yet another of society's nonsensical rules was that a lady could not refuse to dance with a gentleman unless she had a very good excuse and was prepared to forgo dancing for the rest of the evening. She groaned inwardly as she suddenly caught sight of Countess Lieven and saw that she too was watching Lord Sandford's approach.

"It is not like you to look so stern, Miss Edgcott."

She pinned a smile on her face, "Lord Carteret. I do apologise, I did not see you."

He bowed rather stiffly to Diana, who nodded with icy politeness. Lord Sandford had reached them, and Lord Carteret made as if to move aside.

"Wait!" Eleanor said quickly, colouring a little as he raised his brows in enquiry. "Have you forgotten that you are to partner Lady Haverham for the next dance?"

Diana gasped again, her startled eyes flying to Lord Carteret's. Eleanor held her breath, but her faith in his gentlemanly manners proved not to be misplaced. He bowed and offered his arm to Diana, his face impassive.

Lord Sandford did not miss a beat but bowed before Eleanor.

"May I have the pleasure, Miss Edgcott?"

As Lord Allerdale was leading Georgianna onto the floor, and Lord Somerton and Captain Bassington were deep in conversation, she was left with no choice. She laid her fingers lightly on his sleeve and allowed herself to be led towards the line forming for the country dance.

"You are very busy on Lady Haverham's behalf, Miss Edgcott," Lord Sandford said coolly.

Eleanor did not pretend to misunderstand him. "I acted only with her best interests at heart, sir. The same cannot be said of you, I think."

His green eyes reminded her of a cat's and at that moment they held a malevolent quality.

"I am pleased you are so charmingly unsubtle," he said softly. "It allows me to answer you in the same style. It is not wise, Miss Edgcott, to interfere in my affairs."

Eleanor read a barely veiled threat in his words but as they had reached the line of dancers, she said nothing. When the figure of the dance brought them together, she murmured, "My interference was hardly needed, sir. Diana wished for nothing more than a flirtation. You took a serious misstep when you kissed her; she neither expected nor wished for you to do such a thing."

She forced herself to smile as they skipped around two other dancers. When he next took her hands, he said, "I am rather more experienced than you, ma'am, and you may believe me when I tell you that Lady Haverham was ripe for the plucking."

Eleanor raised an eyebrow, unshaken by his crude words. "I will allow that you may have had some excuse to think it, sir, but *you* may believe *me* when I say you were mistaken. You also showed a complete disregard for her reputation by behaving as you did in such a public place where anyone could have stumbled upon you."

"I take my opportunities when and where they present themselves," he said, unabashed.

Eleanor's cheeks were aching with the effort of keeping a smile fixed on her lips. She opened them a fraction and spoke through her teeth. "Then I will ensure that you are not presented with any opportunity to come near Lady Haverham again, sir."

She let go of his hands and stepped hastily away from him. She felt herself stumble into someone and quickly turned, her dress bunching awkwardly around her legs as she did so. There was a sound of fabric tearing and she looked down to see a black pump set upon the lace flounce of her gown. She glanced up into two dark eyes the colour of warm chocolate, their expression one of mingled apology and amusement.

"Forgive me, Miss Edgcott. I do not know how I came to be so clumsy."

A slow, wide smile spread across her face. "Do not concern yourself, sir. It is easily done."

"I will help you pin it up," Georgianna said, "it is always so difficult to see if you have it straight without another pair of eyes."

∾

Miles stepped away from the line of dancers and it reformed seamlessly behind him, his eyes watching their progress through the room. He had come to Miss Edgcott's aid at Georgianna's request, as she had been convinced that her friend was not enjoying herself. Although he had initially felt some reluctance to meet the lady in so awkward a manner, he could not now regret that he had done so. There had been humorous understanding and gratitude in her intelligent eyes. Carteret had been right; she was not unattractive. Her hair was cut boyishly short, but it clustered in a wild riot of curls about her elfin face in a decidedly feminine manner. Her mouth was unfashionably wide, this fault exaggerated when she smiled, but it only added to her air of mischievous charm.

"I do not believe I have ever known you to suffer from clumsiness, Allerdale."

"No, it is unaccountable and deuced humiliating, Sandford; I had not yet been introduced to Miss Edgcott."

"Consider yourself fortunate," the marquess said. "She is an interfering busybody."

Miles merely raised an eyebrow.

"It is I who should have been dancing with Lady Haverham, not Carteret, but Miss Edgcott claimed that he had already asked her to dance." He gave a bitter laugh. "They both seemed most surprised."

"Be careful, Sandford," Miles said softly. "Lord Haverham is here tonight, and I would not like any hint of trouble or scandal at my mother's ball."

"I am fully aware of it, old chap. He was entering the card room as I left it. He has kept an unusually close eye on his wife this evening and I have not been able to get near her, and when I finally saw an opportunity to do so, Miss Edgcott ruined all."

"I had thought another lady might have caught your attention," Miles said. "Did I not see you take someone up in your curricle the other day?"

"Yes, but she is at present playing the pretty innocent, and as I am hardly likely to find her at a society ball, I must find my amusement where I can."

"Just make sure your amusement does not inconvenience any of our guests, Sandford, Lady Haverham and Miss Edgcott included. Now, if you will excuse me, I must go to my mother; I can see her beckoning me."

Lord Sandford's lips twisted into a sneer. "Of course you must; you are still tied to her apron strings, after all."

The marquess was so incensed at having his plans thwarted that he had overlooked Miles' temper, but he was forcibly reminded of it as that gentleman took a step closer to him, his eyes glittering. Sandford half raised his arm as if to ward off a blow, but no such indignity awaited him. He did, however, find it taken in such a strong grip that he was sure he would find a series of small bruises the size of fingerprints on his forearm in the morning. Before he could protest, he found himself being propelled forwards.

"Smile, Sandford," Miles said softly. "I wish everyone who sees us to think we are enjoying a private conversation."

"What are you doing?" the marquess asked.

"I am escorting you from the premises, dear fellow. I cannot think why my mother invited you."

When he put that question to Lady Brigham a few minutes later, she looked surprised. "I thought he was a friend of yours. Was I wrong? I am aware he is not quite the thing, but he is still invited everywhere, and I thought it only fair that you should have your particular friends about you this evening."

"He is rather an acquaintance, Mama, and one that is quite capable of causing trouble."

"Oh?" she said, her eyes alight with interest. "Has he done so?"

Miles saw Lord Haverham escorting his wife

towards the supper room. She was looking up at him, a happy smile upon her lips.

"No, thanks to Miss Edgcott's quick thinking, he was not given the opportunity to do so. Now, what is it that I can do for you?"

"I was going to ask if you would take Miss Bantam in to supper, but I have already found her another escort. What trouble was it that Miss Edgcott averted?"

"I hate to disoblige you, Mama, but I do not intend to disclose that information to you. You are an angel, but you are not always in command of your tongue!" His words were softened with a smile.

Lady Brigham did not look at all angelic as indignation flashed through her eyes, but she was silenced by the arrival of Lady Bassington.

"Miles, I am quite parched and cannot see Charles anywhere. Stop putting your mama all on end and take me in to supper."

"With pleasure," he said, offering her his arm and joining the throng of people heading for the supper rooms. He grinned fondly down at her. "I imagine gossiping with your friends is thirsty work."

She chuckled. "Rudesby! Very few of my friends are in Town and talking about a host of people you know nothing about is tedious, but I have been adequately entertained."

"I am pleased to hear it, Aunt. Who entertained you?"

"You. I have been observing you closely; your interests are far nearer to my heart than anyone else's here, after all, apart from Charles' of course, but he is still too much of a flibbertigibbet to settle down yet."

"And dare I ask what conclusions you have drawn from your observations, Aunt?"

"You terrified Lady Selena, but that is hardly surprising; she is a shy little mouse. She lives not far from us you know, at Sheringham Court. I did wonder if she might do for Adolphus, but Bassington pointed out that he would need someone with a bit more rumgumption about her, and I will admit that Caroline has more than her fair share of that."

Miles laughed. "I told Mama that it was she who had driven you from the house. Has she been disturbing your peace by turning everything upside down?"

"Lord, yes," Lady Bassington said without rancour. "But I'm quite happy for her to furbish things up a trifle if it keeps her occupied. But I will not be sidetracked, Miles. I could see you were amused by Miss Crabtree and she by you."

"Do not get your hopes up, Aunt Frances; she is merely going through the motions and is determined to marry a country squire."

"Perhaps it is just as well, for I do not think she would do for you; she is not nearly pretty enough to hold your interest. I noticed you chose Lady Barbara as your next partner. I will admit she is extremely pretty."

"Surely you mean beautiful?"

"No, she falls short of beauty; even the most perfectly drawn face requires a spark of something to render it beautiful. Lady Somerton is most definitely a beauty. You were wondrous great with her; it is a pity she wouldn't have you."

He frowned. "Mama should not have told you."

"Oh, do not blame Julia. I worried the bare bones of the story out of her but even then, she refused to give me the name of the young lady you abducted. But there is a lack of restraint between you two that hinted at shared adventures. I thought you did very well to tread upon Miss Edgcott's gown, by the way; I did not like the look of her partner at all. I am glad you got rid of him. Now *she* has a very animated countenance."

Miles laughed down at her. "Aunt, how on earth have you been able to observe me so closely in such a crowded room?"

Lady Bassington patted her reticule. "Forward planning, Miles. I have my opera glasses with me and chose a chair with a good view of the dance floor. Now, introduce me to Miss Edgcott; I noticed Charles enjoyed her company very much. She is just over there with Lady Somerton and some other sweet-faced chit. They make a pretty picture, don't they?"

Miles glanced at the three dark heads that were crowded close together. "They seem to be enjoying a private conversation, Aunt."

"Nonsense. You can't have a private conversation at a ball."

CHAPTER 8

Eleanor had had the good fortune to meet Lady Somerton and Lady Cranbourne at her first society party soon after she arrived in Town. Although they were a few years younger than her, they had hit if off immediately, which was not perhaps surprising for they were all enjoying the delights of London for the first time and had soon discovered that they shared a quick intellect and an irreverent sense of humour.

She had found neither of them to be tittle-tattles and so, when Marianne gently enquired as to the cause of the awkwardness between Eleanor and Lord Sandford, she leaned towards her friends and explained the situation to them in a hushed voice.

"I know him to be a dreadful flirt," Georgianna said. "He tried to flirt with me when he first met me. I gave him short shrift, and then Cranbourne, who knows all about him, had a word in Somerton's ear and he never came near me again."

"I expect Lord Somerton warned him off; I do not

think there are many men who would wish to get on the wrong side of your husband," Eleanor said. "It is a pity that I cannot ask him to do the same for Diana, but I do not think it fair on Haverham for you to say anything about it to him."

"I will not, of course, but it is a pity you have such scruples for I am sure he would do so if I asked him," Georgianna said.

"Thank you, but it would not do, and I cannot say anything more to my cousin. I do not wish to upset all the progress that has been made between Frederick and Diana this evening."

"There is no need for you to do so," Marianne said. "I have a plan."

Georgianna groaned. "Do not listen to her, Eleanor. Marianne's plans nearly always go awry, especially if there is an animal involved. Thus far, a dog, a cat, and a fox have all got her into a scrape."

Eleanor smiled. "Do tell."

Marianne laughed. "Another time. I cannot imagine that any animals will be involved in this plan. We do not need a man to keep Lord Sandford away from Diana, Eleanor. All we need do is coordinate which events we shall be attending and between the three of us we should be able to keep him away from her."

"It might well work," Eleanor said slowly. "Three pairs of eyes are certainly better than one. We will make him very angry between the three of us, however."

"Pooh!" Marianne said. "What can he do in a public place, after all? And it may well be that once Lord Sandford realises we are on your side, he will give up chasing Lady Haverham, for he will wish to upset Cranbourne as little as he would Somerton. My husband may not be as large as Somerton, but he is known to be an excellent practitioner of the art of boxing."

"I see Lord Allerdale is bringing someone over to us," Georgianna said quickly. "Let us meet in the park tomorrow to coordinate our calendars."

"I cannot," Eleanor said. "I have a prior engagement. Would you ask Diana? Then you can mention which events you are attending and suggest how pleasant it would be if she did also. She would like that; I think that she is beginning to realise that Lady Langton is not quite the friend she thought her."

"Yes, of course," Georgianna said. "And if you are not engaged tomorrow evening, perhaps you would both like to join us at the play. It is something by Milton and has been well received, I believe."

"Thank you."

All three ladies rose and made a little bow as Lady Bassington came up to them, their confidences at an end.

Once Lord Allerdale had introduced Lady Bassington, she waved him away.

"We will do very well without you, Miles."

"Very well, Aunt. I shall go and procure some refreshments for you."

"Good boy," she said, lowering herself into the chair next to Eleanor. "Take your time; I believe I will not die of thirst in the next ten minutes or so."

Miles' smiling eyes swept over the small group. "Do not be fooled by my aunt's sleepy exterior," he said. "Nothing passes her by."

"Do not worry, girls. I shall not try to wheedle out of you whatever it was you were all discussing." Lady Bassington looked at Eleanor. "But if it was about Sandford, let me reassure you, Miss Edgcott, that you will not need to endure his company again this evening."

Eleanor smiled. "No, I do not think he will seek me out again tonight."

"Gave him a set-down did you? Good girl. He has a sort of sneering arrogance that I cannot like. It seems Miles did not like it either for he persuaded Sandford to leave whilst you were pinning up your gown."

"Oh? How did he do that, ma'am?" Eleanor asked.

"I'm not perfectly sure," Lady Bassington admitted, easing her opera glasses a short way out of her reticule. "These can only tell me so much and unfortunately I cannot lip read, but Sandford certainly said something to anger him."

"Then I am not surprised Allerdale persuaded him to leave," Georgianna said, a small smile playing about her lips. "He can be quite ruthless when his ire is roused."

"You would know, of course." Lady Bassington chuckled as Georgianna stiffened. "Do not worry, child, I may be nosy, but I am not a gossip."

"I am becoming increasingly desirous of hearing what happened between you," Eleanor said.

Lady Bassington looked surprised. "I apologise, Lady Somerton, it seems I am not such a knowing one as I had supposed. You all seemed on such friendly terms that I thought Miss Edgcott would know all."

"I have not told her yet, ma'am, as I did not wish to prejudice her against Lord Allerdale. I did not think it fair for her to know his bad points before she had seen his good ones."

"Very commendable of you," Lady Bassington said. She raised a questioning eyebrow. "Have you discovered any good points, Miss Edgcott?"

"I have barely exchanged two words with Lord Allerdale, but the kind attentions he has shown you, ma'am, his friendship with Lady Somerton, and his timely intervention during my dance with Lord Sandford, not to mention his subsequent dealings with the man, have certainly done him no harm in my eyes."

"Then you had best tell your tale, Lady Somerton, before he returns," Lady Bassington said dryly. "I feel Miss Edgcott should know who she is dealing with."

"But I am not dealing with him," Eleanor pointed out. "And I am certainly not on the catch for him or anyone else."

"As you have already turned down Ormsley, who I wouldn't know from Adam but have heard is very eligible, I do not doubt you. Now, do you wish to know Lady Somerton's story or not?"

And so Eleanor learned the story of Lord Allerdale's gambling debt of the summer before and his father's insistence that he marry and settle down almost immediately. Her eyes widened as she heard of a spurned offer of marriage, an abduction, and a trip to the border. A look of deep appreciation came into them as she discovered how Georgianna had escaped from a locked room, was pursued, and finally delivered safely back to Brigham by a sheepish Lord Allerdale.

"I do not think he would have done it," Georgianna said, "if the gentleman who had cheated at cards had not sent a letter to his mother, hinting at Allerdale's imminent loss of face and honour and suggesting she take a hand in the affair. That enraged him; he does not like to see his mama upset and feared she might sell an heirloom or fall into some sort of scrape trying to extract him from his. And I fanned the flames of his temper by the scathing way I spoke to and of him."

Lady Bassington, who had been much entertained by the full story of Miles' failed abduction, looked at Georgianna approvingly, before regarding Eleanor intently.

"You do not seem very shocked, Miss Edgcott, although you have listened to a tale that would not appear out of place within the pages of a novel!"

"I am not easily shocked, ma'am," Eleanor said with a smile. "And Lady Somerton told her story with a dry amusement which somehow robbed it of its serious nature, and there was a happy ending, after all. Does Lord Allerdale frequently lose his temper?"

"He has never done so when he has been under my roof," Lady Bassington said. "But he is very protective of his family and particular friends. And then, you know, gentlemen often behave in very odd ways when they are in their cups. Charles told me once that there is no one better to have in your corner if you are in a tight spot. I believe Miles has saved his bacon on more than one occasion when they have been on a spree."

"It is what Cranbourne told me when I asked him about Lord Allerdale," Marianne said. "Although he would not explain to me what situation he was in that made him need his help. I expect it was something quite disreputable for I believe my husband was not a pattern card of respectability before he met me."

"In my experience, gentlemen who have always been a pattern card of respectability are dead bores," Lady Bassington said. She sighed. "My son, Adolphus, is a prime example. I'm very fond of him, but there's no getting away from it; he is undoubtedly a slow-top."

"At least he can never have caused you a moment's anxiety," Eleanor said, amused.

Lady Bassington laughed. "Oh, none of my brood do that. Charles is the only one who might do so, I suppose, but he seems to lead a charmed life. He's been in so many battles I've lost count, but he always seems to come out of them with only the most trifling of injuries."

Lord Allerdale, Lord Somerton, and Lord Cranbourne just then came up to them, laden down with refreshments. Once Lord Allerdale had put the glass and plate he held onto the table, he offered his arm to Eleanor.

"Lord and Lady Haverham wish you to join them, Miss Edgcott. Allow me to take you to them."

"Of course," she said, rising quickly to her feet, her wide smile dawning as she looked down at Lady Bassington. "I have enjoyed your company, ma'am."

"The pleasure was all mine, child," that lady said, taking Eleanor's free hand for a moment and pressing it lightly.

"Has my aunt been routing out all your secrets, Miss Edgcott? I do not know how she does it, but she has a way of extracting information from a person without them really being aware that she is doing it, if she can rouse herself enough to do so. She is very like my father in that respect."

Eleanor looked up at him and wished she hadn't. His lopsided smile made her catch her breath, but she paused only for a moment before saying, "What secrets could I possibly have, sir?"

"I have no idea, Miss Edgcott, but you have led such an interesting life that I am sure you must have some." He grinned wickedly at her. "Save the next dance for me and I will try to discover them."

His flirtatious smile countered the effects of his more natural one, and Eleanor found herself able to reply with perfect calm. "I will certainly dance with you, sir. I am very grateful to you for coming to my rescue earlier but do not hope to discover anything shocking or you will be disappointed."

"Eleanor," Diana said, coming towards them. "I really do not wish to curtail your pleasure, but would you mind very much if we left after supper? I find myself a little tired."

Eleanor felt a little disappointed at these words but saw that Diana was indeed looking pale.

"As you wish." She glanced at Lord Allerdale. "I am sorry, sir, but our dance will have to wait."

"Until next time, then," he said, bowing. "I hope you are not sickening for something, Lady Haverham."

"I am sure I am not," Diana said, smiling prettily at him. "Please thank your mama for a splendid evening."

It was only a short carriage ride to South Audley

Street and as they entered the house, Diana begged Eleanor to come to her room before she retired for the evening.

Lord Haverham cleared his throat. "I thought I might pay you a visit, dear. That is, if you are not too tired."

Diana blushed. "Oh, yes, of course, please do. You wish to discuss the ball, no doubt. I will not keep Eleanor very many minutes."

Diana dismissed her maid and clasped Eleanor's hands. "Dearest cousin, thank you."

"Whatever for?" Eleanor said. "I did not mind leaving early. I could see you were a little fagged."

Diana embraced her. "You are always so kind, so thoughtful. But it is not that, or at least not just that. I meant for saving me from Sandford. I have been such a fool. I had not realised quite how much Frederick cared, you see, but tonight he said such pretty things to me. He even said that he was pleased I had not yet produced an heir, for he was not yet ready to share me with anyone else, not even another child." She gave a tinkle of laughter. "He admitted that he was a little jealous every time I danced with another man. Do you think that is why he does not often accompany us to balls?"

"Perhaps it is," Eleanor said, silently congratulating her cousin on his address. "I hope your dance with Lord Carteret was not too unpleasant?"

"Although I did not think it at the time, I am even grateful to you for that. It was a little difficult, at first, but I felt so grateful to him for not humiliating me by claiming that you were mistaken or some such thing, that I thanked him and said I was sorry that he had been put in so awkward a position. I explained that you were only trying to protect me from Lord Sandford."

"And how did he respond?"

Diana coloured. "He looked surprised and asked if I *wished* to be protected from the marquess. I think he may have seen that unfortunate event at Lady Battledon's ball, in fact, I know he did, for he told me. He looked so cold and haughty that I almost ran from the floor, but he saw my distress and then suddenly smiled so sweetly at me, in the way he used to, that I managed to gather myself. I ended by telling him all and how shocked I had been, for I was, you know, and he said he quite understood, and I must not fear he would breathe a word about it."

"How very gentlemanly of him," Eleanor said. "Perhaps you will both go on more comfortably now. You may expect a note from Lady Cranbourne or Lady Somerton tomorrow. I believe they are to invite you to go for a walk or a drive in the park."

"Me?" Diana said surprised. "But they are your friends."

"Yes, but I have agreed to go for a drive with Mr Pavlov tomorrow. I met him at the Countess Lieven's salon, and they said they would invite you in my place."

Diana looked pleased. "That is very kind of them. I must say that Eliza has become very tiresome recently. She found a few moments this evening to speak with me and was very unkind about Miss Crabtree. She called her a little country nobody and said she had laughed herself into stitches when she had seen her dance with Lord Allerdale. She said that if she thought her smiling and simpering ways would catch the son of a marquess she must have windmills in her head. It was all jealousy of course."

"That was not well done of her," Eleanor said. "She is a spiteful little cat. Lady Langton has probably never spoken to Miss Crabtree, but I have and can tell you that she is a very pleasant girl. She has no interest in fixing her interests with anyone in Town. She has already fallen in love with a country squire's son and is determined she will have no one else."

"I did not know that," Diana admitted. "But she helped me when I lost an earring in the retiring room at some ball or other, and I also thought she was very pleasant. It must have been at least half an hour before she found the earring and returned it to me."

"She was probably hiding from any potential suitors; she often does so. Good night, my dear."

Eleanor did not immediately go to bed but sat wrapped in a dressing gown on the window seat of her chamber, looking out over the moonlit garden. She smiled as various vignettes from the ball came to her. She had also noticed Lord Allerdale's dance with Miss Crabtree and thought that rarely had she seen that lady so relaxed with a partner. He too had shown to advantage as he had on more than one occasion that evening. But she was not fooled, the sight she had had of Lord Allerdale before he smiled at Georgianna had shown her a glimpse of a more forbidding character, and the story Georgianna had told when it was stripped to the bare facts could not show him in a good light.

His masculinity and winning smile may have won a response from her, as it probably had from dozens of other ladies, but when she passed under review her list of requirements for a husband, she could hardly believe that he would fulfil any of them. That strong chin did not suggest a man who would listen to his wife's counsel; he had not even listened to Georgianna until she had hit him over the head, and she certainly did not think she could rely on him to conduct himself in a way she could be proud of if his temper was up. It was to his credit that he had almost certainly prevented an ugly scene between Frederick and Lord Sandford by not giving that scoundrel another chance to come near Diana, but he might just as easily have caused one between himself and Lord Buntingdon by dancing the waltz with his beautiful betrothed.

She sighed. It was at moments like these that she particularly missed her father. She had always enjoyed discussing with him the various characters who had been at a dinner or a ball more than the events themselves. She smiled as she wondered what he would have made of Lady Bassington. She was not at all sure whether that lady had been matchmaking or not. If she was, she had a strange way of going about it. Surely she would not have wished to have Lord Allerdale's less than savoury escapade described to her if she was? No, she could not have been, and Eleanor was glad; she had liked the unusual lady and would not like to have disappointed her.

She suddenly laughed. She would no more suit Lord Allerdale than he would her. She also had a strong will and was of a managing disposition. She had told him she had no secrets, but she had a plan forming that she was sure no titled gentleman would approve of, including her cousin. She put the ball from her mind and instead considered the several things she wished to achieve during the coming day.

∽

Miles returned to his aunt in time to hear Marianne describing how Cranbourne had proposed to her after she had fallen down a muddy bank whilst attempting to rescue a fox cub.

"I was bedraggled and filthy," she laughed, "and yet he said I looked delightful!"

"And so you did," Lord Cranbourne said, a small intimate smile playing about his lips.

Lady Bassington sighed. Although all her children apart from Charles had contracted very happy marriages, there had been very little romance attached to any of them. Despite, or perhaps because of this, she enjoyed coaxing the story of their courtship from anyone she suspected of having formed a love match.

Miles shook Lord Cranbourne's hand and said softly, "I am glad you seem so happy."

"There is no *seem* about it, Allerdale, I *am* happy. And I am pleased that you look in much better form than when I saw you last year. Somerton has told me of what troubled you then and what passed between you. He is a good man."

"Yes, and a far better one than I will ever be," Miles said. "He treated me much better than I deserved."

"Perhaps," Lord Cranbourne said. "But I do not think he would have done so if he had not seen some good in you."

Miles staggered a little as a huge hand suddenly

clapped him on the shoulder. "I hadn't realised you were Bassington's cousin, Allerdale. I am glad that I did not murder you, after all, he seems fond of you and I wouldn't have liked to upset him. He's a rapscallion but a damned fine soldier. How did you get on in Yorkshire?"

"I liked Murton very much," Miles said. "I learned a great deal."

"I'm glad to hear it. You certainly look the better for it. Cranbourne and I have been persuaded to play cricket for Lord Balderston's XI, but he is still a man short. Care to join us?"

Miles had formed a few vague plans for how he intended to spend his time, but cricket had featured in none of them, and he only liked to partake in sports he knew he could excel at.

"I haven't played for years," he said apologetically.

Lord Somerton was not so easily put off.

"The match is not for a few days yet, Allerdale, and there are a few practice sessions arranged so you will have time to hone your skills."

Lord Carteret had just then come up to them. He laughed. "You don't want him, Somerton. Allerdale had a good eye for the ball when we were at school, but any bowler with any brains soon discovered that if he pitched the ball a little wide often enough, he would soon lose his temper. Once that happened, he would attempt a wild swing and find the bails at his feet."

"Ah, but it is no longer permitted to bowl wide," Lord Somerton said.

"It doesn't matter, they'll find another chink in his armour, you may be sure. I tell you, you don't want him. He's a liability. Not that I should be warning you, for I am playing for the opposing side."

Miles' eyes narrowed. "I will certainly play, Somerton. And I will bet you a monkey, Carteret, that we will win."

"Done," the viscount said, putting out his hand.

Miles shook it and saw an amused glint in his friend's eye.

"You goaded me on purpose, Carteret."

"Quite right," he said, grinning. "It will do you good and keep you out of mischief, but as I took advantage of my close acquaintance with you, we will reduce the bet to ten guineas, I think."

Miles intercepted a knowing look between Georgianna and Somerton and scowled. "I see you two have also been plotting. I have no intention of getting into any mischief, you know."

Georgianna raised her brows. "You must forgive me if I have no very great faith in your intentions."

Lady Bassington's deep laugh sounded. "I think I may extend my visit. I had not expected it to be quite so amusing."

Miles turned on his heel and stalked off, inwardly seething. How dare they group together and treat him like some callow youth who needed steering away from the dangers of Town? There was nothing he did not know about them, after all. Did they really think he was likely to indulge in the sort of riotous dissipation that would lead him into trouble when he was pledged to find a bride? As he reached the double doors of the ballroom, he realised Carteret was close on his heels.

"I do not need a watchdog, Carteret. I am going to have a quiet drink in the library."

"I'll join you. I have had quite enough of dancing for one evening."

Something in his friend's voice gave Miles pause. His expression gentled. "Diana?"

"Yes... no... I was not best pleased with Miss Edgcott, but the dance served its purpose."

"How so?"

"For one thing, I discovered that she is not quite the designing hussy I had painted her, which was, of course, a relief, for one does not like to admit that one's judgement had been so glaringly abroad."

"And what was the other thing?" Miles asked, crossing the library and pouring them both a brandy.

Lord Carteret did not immediately answer but looked pensively into the empty grate of the fireplace. When Miles handed him his drink, he cupped his hand around the glass and swirled the amber liquid gently.

"She is much the same as ever she was," he said slowly. A wry smile twisted his lips. "It is I who perhaps needed a watchdog tonight, old fellow. I very nearly caused a scandal."

"No. I cannot believe it. You are always in complete control of yourself. I envy you in that respect."

"It is true, nevertheless. For a moment when I looked into her eyes, I was transported back to when we first met." Lord Carteret gave a cynical laugh. "What a greenhorn I was then, and for a moment I was a greenhorn again. Would you believe I confronted her with what I had seen the other night?"

Miles crossed his legs and leaned back in his chair, his anger gone as swiftly as it had arrived. "I am surprised, certainly. It is not like you to be so maladroit."

"I know it, and I very nearly overset her composure. She was on the point of running from the floor, I am sure, when I remembered myself."

The gentle smile that had so affected Miss Edgcott graced Miles' face. "I am glad you did. Can you imagine the fodder you would have given to the gossips?"

"Indeed. And Diana would not have deserved it. She has been unhappy and so was easy prey for Sandford. But she did not expect or wish for him to take things beyond the line. That is why I suggest she hasn't changed. She is still a little innocent."

"She did not appear unhappy tonight."

"No. Haverham has been very attentive. I would hazard a guess that Miss Edgcott might have had a hand in that, and I am glad. Diana is like a flower that will surely wilt if not showered with enough compliments."

"How very wearing," Miles said. "I should not wish for such a bride."

"No, neither would I." Lord Carteret frowned. "That is the other purpose the dance served. It is hard for me to credit that I thought myself madly in love with her. She will always only see the world through the lens of how it affects her. I do not mean that she is unkind, only that she will always be unable to fully understand or interest herself with anything that does not directly concern her. I thought that I would like to protect her innocence and shield her from every ill wind that blew, but it is just such treatment that has moulded her. She is a stunted flower, a bud half-opened that will never fully unfurl its petals, and I would not have been able to respect such a creature in the end."

"Do you think respect so important?" Miles said.

"I think it of the utmost importance. On both sides of the equation. You only have to look about you, Allerdale, to see a host of marriages that are nothing but a sham. As long as appearances are kept up, both parties feel quite at liberty to treat each other in what I cannot help but think a contemptible manner behind each other's backs. Can you imagine either of your parents behaving in such a way?"

"No. But theirs was a love match."

"Perhaps it is the same thing," Lord Carteret said thoughtfully. "At least, I do not think you can have one without the other."

"You may be right," Miles said, pushing himself to his feet. "But I do not aspire to such dizzy heights. Now, I must return to the ball or I will be in disgrace."

"You go ahead, old fellow," Lord Carteret said quietly. "I will finish my drink and then take my leave."

"Again, I envy you," Miles said dryly. "I can feel my hitherto delightfully untrammelled existence slipping inexorably away from me."

"That is why your friends are closing ranks about you, my dear fellow. You are like a cornered rat, and they, you know, have a tendency to bolt or bite."

CHAPTER 9

Eleanor awoke to a bright, sunny day ready to explore new and exciting possibilities. Seeing Marianne had reminded her that she had not yet visited the alley that bore her friend's name. Eleanor was feeling increasingly hemmed in, and when they had returned last evening, she had felt decidedly in the way. As long as she could keep Lord Sandford away from Diana, she felt sure that she would soon have very little need of her. It was time to think again of her future.

She hopped out of bed, humming softly to herself.

"Good morning, Miss Eleanor. You seem mighty perky this morning. What mischief are you plotting?"

Eleanor smiled at the stern face of the maid who had known her all her life. "None at all, Linny."

The maid's eyes brightened with hope. "Then, might it be a gentleman that has put you in this happy mood? Perhaps someone you met at the ball?"

"No, it is not. But I am plotting our future."

"I knew you were up to some mischief."

"Linny! What mischief have I wrought since we came to England?"

"None that I know of," the maid admitted. "But I remember the time you were cross as crabs because you wanted to see some mosque or other and they wouldn't let you in. You gave young Mr Wantage your measurements and persuaded him to have a suit of men's clothes made for you and went with him to view it."

"Yes, Hagia Sophia, and I enjoyed it very much."

"You wouldn't have enjoyed it if you had been caught. I dread to think what would have happened to you! And you can't deny that your father nearly sent Mr Wantage packing when he discovered it."

"But he didn't."

"No. You could always bring your papa around your thumb. And then there was the time you went to visit a *harem* and swapped your clothes with one of the ladies there."

"Linny! You talk as if it was a disreputable place. It was no such thing! It was the most protected place I ever visited, and the ladies were so hospitable, so warm and welcoming. As for the dress and veil, Papa said I looked very well in it."

"He would! At least he made you promise not to wear it abroad."

"Yes, that was a shame. I could have passed unnoticed in the streets."

"And why would you have wished to if you weren't planning some mischief? I told him as much and he listened to me for once."

Eleanor sighed. "I do miss him, Linny."

"Of course you do," her maid said gruffly. "Which

is why you should be looking about you for a husband. He would want you to be looked after."

Eleanor threw off her momentary sadness. "I am perfectly capable of looking after myself. Now, I am going shopping this morning and will need you to accompany me. I do not expect Lady Haverham will be up for some hours yet. Besides, I may need a second opinion. You may have some old-fashioned notions, Linny, but you have very good taste."

"You'll want your nankeen half-boots then if we're to be traipsing about the streets all morning."

"Not necessarily," Eleanor said casually. "We are going a little further afield and will take the carriage. I believe there is an interesting shop to be found off Leicester Square."

"I may only have been in London a handful of weeks, but I know that isn't one of the more fashionable places to shop. What are you up to?"

Eleanor threw her a rather saucy smile. "I shall not tell you until I know if my idea might work."

"I knew it," the maid grumbled, heading for the dressing room. "You're up to mischief for sure."

If the fine houses that lined the square were no longer occupied by the haut ton, neither maid nor mistress found anything to complain of when the carriage set them down. The area was clean, the people appeared perfectly respectable, and a pleasant garden was set in the centre. Eleanor was delighted to discover the Linwood Gallery housed in Savile house, and they enjoyed a pleasant half-hour there, marvelling at the reproductions of paintings entirely created through needlework.

"They are wonderful," Eleanor murmured.

"I wouldn't have believed that anything so fine could have been produced by embroidery alone," Linny admitted. "To think of the hours and hours each one must have taken." She frowned. "Do not tell me that you have some cork-brained notion to attempt something similar, Miss Eleanor. You have a knack with a bonnet, I will allow, but you haven't the skill for this."

Eleanor laughed. "No, my ambitions are much more modest."

It was only a short distance from there to Cranbourn Alley, which branched off at an angle from the north east corner of the square. It was narrow and a little dark, but the windows on each side were full of hats, bonnets, feathers, muffs, shawls, and many other nick-nacks designed to tempt the shopper in.

Those displayed in the first shops they came to were not of the highest quality, and they had gone no more than a few steps into the alley when a lady, who was not of the first stare, stepped from a shop doorway and tried to entice them in.

"I can see you're a woman of some taste, miss. That bein' the case, you should know that you will not find anything more reasonably priced than in Mrs Bainbridge's establishment."

"Don't you listen to her, miss," came another voice from a little further down the alley, "if it's cheap trumpery you wish for, then go in by all means, but if it's something of quality you are looking for, it's Madame Flaubert's that you want."

"Let us go," Linny whispered.

Eleanor looked at her, the light of battle in her

eyes. "After visiting the grand bazaar, Linny, this is nothing."

She regarded both ladies with a cold stare. "I prefer to make my own decisions. Now, I would thank you to step out of our way. I will certainly not visit either of the shops you mention if you bother me again, and what is more, I shall lay a complaint against you for harassment."

Her last words affected her accosters powerfully. They immediately stepped back into the establishments they had been promoting.

"If you ask me," Linny hissed, "they are selling more than hats in those shops! No wonder they didn't want you reporting them to the constable!"

"Well, never mind," Eleanor said. "I admit I am a little disappointed, but we will just take a quick glance…" she paused, a growing delight in her eyes as she gazed at the objects on display in the window they had just come to. Not a speck of dust or smudge of grime obscured her view of the pretty bonnets within.

"Now, tell me what you think of these," Eleanor said.

"They are a touch above the rest, that is certain," Linny admitted.

"You are mistaken. They are *vastly* superior to not only the other shops here but also to anything I have yet encountered in London. Why, I could purchase at least three I see immediately and not wish to modify them in any way."

She went quickly into the shop. A modest lady, with a plain face and a calm demeanour, came towards her. Eleanor judged her to be about the same age as herself.

"Good morning, my lady," she said, eyeing Eleanor's bonnet with some appreciation.

Eleanor was surprised to discover that her voice was well modulated and genuinely refined.

"Mrs Willis?"

"Yes," the lady said, looking pleased. "Has someone recommended me? Do tell me who, for I shall be sure to offer them a discount on their next purchase."

"I would certainly do so if I knew her name. I met her in the park. She was a pretty girl…" Eleanor broke off, laughing. "That will not help you at all, I am sure many pretty girls frequent your establishment. I will describe the bonnet, that I am sure, you will remember."

When she had done so, Mrs Willis smiled. "Then it was Miss Finchley that you met. She is a sweet girl, and I must admit that I am surprised you are the first to come on a recommendation from her, for she must set off to advantage anything that she wears."

"Yes, she is quite lovely, but a little shy, I think."

"Yes, her aunt usually does all the talking."

"Her aunt? I had assumed she was with her mother."

"No, she was orphaned only last year and her aunt took her in."

"Well, I am extremely glad I did meet her, for your bonnets are everything I hoped they would be. It is so rare that I find anything I like, you see."

Mrs Willis looked surprised. "But the one you are wearing is very fetching."

"Thank you. But I furbished it up a trifle."

"You have a very good eye, ma'am."

"Miss Edgcott," Eleanor said, holding out her hand. "Is there someone who could mind the shop for you for a little while? I would very much like to have a private word with you."

"Certainly, Miss Edgcott. Milly is trimming bonnets in the backroom. If you come this way, I will send her out and we can be perfectly private."

Eleanor smiled at her maid and handed over her reticule. "Have a good look round, Linny, and feel free to purchase anything you feel I might need."

Some half an hour later, Eleanor left the shop very satisfied with what she had discovered.

"Well, miss?" her maid said. "And what kept you talking for so long?"

"Oh, we were just exchanging ideas," Eleanor said. "I feel very sorry for Mrs Willis. She only moved to her premises a little over a year ago, and she said the alley has gone sadly downhill since then. Two of the shops have changed hands and have cut their prices and hired those girls."

They were just crossing the road when Eleanor caught sight of Miss Finchley coming out of a linen draper's shop. She hurried over to her, a friendly smile on her face.

"Good morning, Miss Finchley. I must thank you for giving me Mrs Willis' name and direction. She was very pleased to be recommended and you can expect a discount on your next purchase for your trouble."

A tremulous smile hovered on Miss Finchley's lips. "Oh, thank you, Miss—"

"Miss Edgcott. I think you must be braver than you look, Miss Finchley, if you can navigate your way through the ladies who try to drag you into their shops."

"They don't bother with us anymore," Miss Finchley said, raising two troubled eyes. "My aunt is quite formidable, you see."

"I imagine you might be grateful for that every time you shop in Cranbourn Alley."

"Oh yes, I am happy that she is *then*, if only..." She broke off and cast a quick glance at the sharp-faced maid who hovered a few feet behind her.

"I think we should be getting back, miss," the maid said. "Lady Crouch gave me strict orders that I was to take you straight home after you had fetched the material for your new cloak."

"Yes, yes, of course, Hoby." She turned back to Eleanor, tears starting in her eyes. "It was very pleasant to—"

"Do not hurry off so soon," Eleanor said, taking the girl's arm.

She glanced coolly at the maid. "I am sure Lady Crouch will not object if Miss Finchley takes a turn about the square with me. I heard her saying only the other day that she wished her niece to widen her acquaintance in Town."

The maid's mouth tightened, but she merely said, "Yes, ma'am."

Eleanor sent Linny a meaningful look, and she fell into step with the maid and began to chat with her.

"Although I am sure they have our best interests at heart, servants who have known one a long time can become quite proprietorial, can't they?" Eleanor said conversationally.

"Hoby is my aunt's maid," Miss Finchley said in a

soft voice. "I never had one of my own, although we did have a general maid. My aunt asks Hoby to wait on me also, but I do not think she likes it above half."

"Oh dear," Eleanor said sympathetically. "That cannot be comfortable for you."

"No," Miss Finchley admitted. "I am not very comfortable, although I am fully aware of how kind it was of my aunt to take me in."

"We have much in common," Eleanor said. "I too lost my parent a little over a year ago, and my cousin and his wife asked me to come and live with them, although I do not think I had seen my cousin above twice in my life, and then only when I was a child."

"It was the same with me," Miss Finchley said. "I hardly knew my aunt. She fell into disgrace with the family, although I have never discovered precisely why. She made a respectable marriage to a baronet, but my father would have nothing to do with her. Perhaps it was because Sir Roger was so much older than her. That is why it is so particularly kind of her to have taken me in, especially as she is not at all well off. It is the shabbiest thing, but now that she is widowed and Sir Roger's cousin has inherited, she has been put into the meanest little cottage on his estate and is left with only a meagre jointure to live on." She suddenly looked uneasy. "Here I am rattling on like a regular gabble-grinder as my papa used to say. I should not have said so much, but you are so very easy to talk to, Miss Edgcott."

"Oh, do not give it a thought. You have said nothing at all out of the way, after all. What did your papa do?"

"He was an apothecary." Miss Finchley smiled

wistfully. "In Westmorland. We had a quaint little shop and lived above it. I used to tend the herb garden with Mama."

"What happened to them?" Eleanor said gently.

"They both died of a fever. They had helped so many others, and yet could not save themselves." Her voice trembled. "Please, ask me no more. It is too painful to remember."

"I quite understand. Forgive me."

They had by now almost completed their trip around the square. Miss Finchley impulsively took Eleanor's hands.

"Oh, no! There is nothing to forgive. It has been so pleasant to feel I have a friend."

"You may consider me your friend, Miss Finchley. You may find me at Lord Haverham's house in South Audley Street." She reached into her reticule and withdrew a card. "Here is my direction."

"Thank you," Miss Finchley said.

Eleanor returned home with much to think about. She was far too well bred to have shown it, but the knowledge that Miss Finchley's aunt had married into the gentry whilst her niece was an apothecary's daughter had surprised her. Miss Finchley seemed the most genteel of the two by far. She felt sorry for the girl. She clearly missed her parents and was not happy. She frowned as she recalled that Lord Sandford had taken Miss Finchley up in his carriage. She hoped very much that Lady Crouch was not trying to promote a match between them, for however far that lady had married above her station, she felt certain that the marquess would not marry so far beneath his.

She was also puzzled as to how Lady Crouch

could afford to dress Miss Finchley in such fine style if she was so purse pinched. Lady Langton's suggestion that they walked in the park in the hope of meeting desirable acquaintances now seemed more than likely, but Lady Crouch's position as widow to a baronet had clearly not granted her entrée into any select circles. She did not believe Lady Langton's other suggestion for a moment; there was a sweet innocence about Miss Finchley that did not suggest that she was anyone's mistress, and Lord Sandford had not yet given up his pursuit of Diana.

Eleanor shrugged off these thoughts as she entered the house. When Clinton informed her that his lordship had already gone out and her ladyship was resting, her mind returned to her own business. She went into the library and sat herself at the desk. She pulled a sheet of paper to her, dipped her pen in the ink standish, and began to write a letter to her solicitor. She quickly covered the first sheet and reached for another, not wishing to mar the clarity of her missive by crossing her lines.

When it was finished, she folded it neatly and rose. She could, of course, ask Frederick to frank it for her, but there was every possibility that he would ask her why she needed to consult her solicitor. Not wishing to disturb the harmonious atmosphere that she felt sure would pervade the house today, she asked the footman to deliver it.

When, sometime later, she entered the drawing room in a neat carriage dress of Pomona green, she discovered Diana sitting on a sofa, a small, contented smile on her lips. Eleanor thought that she had never seen her look so beautiful. It was not the rather splendid white satin pelisse she wore, or the matching hat with a plume of feathers in celestial blue that wrought this impression, although they suited her to perfection, but the soft bloom in her cheeks and the happy glow in her large blue eyes.

"Have you had a good day?" Eleanor asked her.

Diana blinked as if waking from a pleasant dream. "Oh, yes. Although it has been a shockingly lazy day."

"Why shockingly?" Eleanor asked. "You must have needed just such a restful day for you look to be in high bloom."

"I feel very well, it is true," Diana said. "Did you find what you required on your shopping expedition?"

"Indeed, I did, and then I wrote a long letter, and now I am ready for my drive with Mr Pavlov, as you see."

"You always like to be busy," Diana said. "You never rest as I do in the day."

"No, but my constitution is a little more robust than yours, my dear."

Clinton came into the room. "Lady Somerton and Lady Cranbourne await your pleasure, my lady."

Diana rose gracefully to her feet. "I shall be there directly, Clinton. Thank you."

The eyes she turned to Eleanor had a hint of mischief in them. "How provoking. I wished to catch a glimpse of this Mr Pavlov. Is he your latest admirer?"

"No, I don't think he is," Eleanor said reflectively. "He is rather a new friend."

Diana lost interest. "Oh, I see. Well, enjoy your afternoon."

Eleanor was not at all sure she would. Mr Pavlov had seemed bright and amusing when she first met him, but today he seemed pre-occupied and distant, and after they had exchanged a few pleasantries, he lapsed into silence. He at first drove towards Hyde Park but when they came to the entrance, he turned his horses and drove away from it.

"Are you taking me home already?" Eleanor asked. "Has five minutes more in my company convinced you I can be of no use to you after all?"

He glanced down at her, his eyes reminding Eleanor of a troubled sea. "Forgive me, Miss Edgcott. I am poor company, I know. It suddenly struck me that I could not bear to join the throng of people in the park, to have to put on a display of urbane politeness, and perhaps see… see people I would rather not. Would you mind if we just drove about Town for a while?"

"Not a bit. But I thought we had established a certain honesty between us at our first meeting, yet I do not think you are being perfectly honest now, sir. Are you afraid to come across someone in the park, or are you afraid that someone in the park will see you with me?"

He smiled ruefully. "And at our first meeting, I said you were acute! Both!"

"Ah," Eleanor said, smiling, "then it is a lady who has induced this strange mood of abstraction in you. She is I assume, the reason you wish to remain in London at present?"

Mr Pavlov's countenance sobered again.

"Yes, I had thought… but I was mistaken… or at least I think I was…"

Eleanor laughed. "I may be acute, but I cannot help you with so little to go on, you know."

"I am not sure anyone can help me," he said.

"Try me," Eleanor said, encouragingly. "I do not like to see you so downcast."

He glanced down at her, the glimmer of a smile in his eyes. "Why do I have the feeling that you will badger me until I do unbutton my lip, Miss Edgcott?"

"I shall not," Eleanor said gently. "But might I suggest that your troubles may not weigh so heavily upon you if you share them? You do not need to mention names, after all."

"Very well," he said, before falling again into a ponderous silence.

Eleanor looked about her and realised she was in a part of town she did not recognise. She leant forwards to see past Mr Pavlov as they passed a pair of tall gates that opened onto a large courtyard surrounded by elegant buildings.

"What is that place?"

"The Foundling Hospital," he said absently as if his thoughts were far away.

She would have liked to discover more about the institution they had just passed but sensed this was not the time.

"Mr Pavlov?" she said gently when he still made no attempt to unburden himself. "Perhaps it would help if you started before you met this lady. Did you come straight to London after visiting your uncle?"

"No. After my uncle made it clear that he did not want me hanging around his neck, I went to visit my mother's sister. My mother had spoken fondly of my aunt Jemima and both her welcome and that of her husband was all I could have wished it to be. They have never been blessed with children and said that they would give me a home and that I could help Uncle Silas with his business. He is a successful coal merchant with warehouses in Newcastle."

"You felt such a position beneath you, perhaps?"

"No, but I knew my father would not approve. He had given me a letter of introduction for the Lievens and I thought I should at least make a push to follow his wishes, but to be honest, I know more about farming than I do about diplomacy. Then I met a girl in the park, no, *an angel* in the park, not long after I arrived in Town. At first, it was her beauty that drew me to her, but it was her modesty and the gentleness of her nature that made me fall in love with her."

"And does she not return your regard?"

"I thought that she might. We had very little opportunity for private speech whenever I called on her, but the way her hand trembled in mine when I greeted her, the gentle look in her eyes when they rested on me, encouraged me to think she looked favourably on me." He frowned. "But it seems I have fallen out of favour. She has not been at home to visitors the last few times I have called, and when I rode in the park in the hope of seeing her, her aunt pretended not to have seen me and hurried away with her."

"And did the lady you love pretend not to see you?"

"No. That is why I am still not entirely certain of where I stand. She sent a look of apology over her shoulder."

"I see," Eleanor said thoughtfully. "And what is it that has caused you to fall out of favour, do you think?"

"My circumstances," he said flatly. "Her aunt seemed impressed that I was the son of a count, at first. But when she eventually enquired a little more closely into my circumstances, she turned cold. I can hardly blame her; I am not in a position to easily provide for a wife."

"But you are not without patronage or prospects. If your uncle Silas is prepared to take you in as one of his family and train you up in his trade, might they not also accept your wife into their home? Or is their house too small?"

"No. It is quite grand. But the fact remains they are in trade. And the aunt of Miss F—, I mean the girl who has captured my heart, is a lady." He grimaced. "In name at least. I am fairly certain that she married above her station, but as she has rented an uncomfortable house in Castle Street, I must assume that she is not very plump in the pocket."

Eleanor looked at him intently. "I believe it is Miss Finchley you have fallen head over heels in love with, Mr Pavlov."

He looked at her in some surprise. "You know her? Then you will understand. Is she not the sweetest lady?"

"Oh, yes," Eleanor agreed. "I had some conversation with her only this morning."

"How did she seem, ma'am?" he asked eagerly.

"She seemed as downcast as you," Eleanor said with a small smile. "Perhaps I now understand why."

Mr Pavlov latched onto her words like a drowning man clutching at a stick. "Could it be… dare I to hope… that is, do you think she might feel our separation as much as I?"

"That I cannot yet tell," Eleanor said truthfully. "But she was certainly twitching about something. And I must say, that if you can achieve a good position in your uncle's business, I cannot think that your circumstances would make you at all ineligible. Miss Finchley is the daughter of an apothecary, which does not put her out of your reach."

Mr Pavlov's green eyes brightened for a moment, "I had not realised…" he paused, his hands tightening on the reins. "Then I can only assume that Lady Crouch has higher ambitions for Miss Finchley. This knowledge cannot help me."

"But I may be able to," Eleanor said. "I shall pay a call on Miss Finchley and see if I may have some private speech with her. If I find she returns your feelings, I will see what I can do. There is something in Lady Crouch's past that put her in disgrace with her family, if I can discover what it is, you might find yourself in a firmer bargaining position."

"I would not wish to gain Miss Finchley because I blackmailed her aunt," he said, his voice dripping with disapproval. "It would not be gentlemanly to put pressure on Lady Crouch in such a way, nor would it be likely to recommend me to her niece."

"That is fine talk, Mr Pavlov, but it is not fighting talk," Eleanor said sternly. "What about the pressure I feel sure Lady Crouch is bringing to bear on her niece? Notions of gentlemanly behaviour like so many other things, are admirable as a general principal, but may not always be applicable in individual cases. Allow me to discover what the case is before you decide what it is right for you to do."

CHAPTER 10

Miles had spent an unexpectedly pleasant afternoon. He might be shockingly rusty at cricket, but the practice session had been enjoyable and unexpectedly amusing. Once he set his mind to something, he gave his all. The light-hearted ribbing he had received at the start of the session had been given in such a friendly spirit he had grinned at his own ineptitude, but it had only made him focus all the harder, and before they had called it a day, his natural co-ordination and aptitude in all matters of sport had ensured that he had vastly improved.

He left Lord's ground in such good humour that even the reflection that his mother had persuaded him to join her party at the theatre that evening could not blight his good humour, even though Milton's *Comus* with its theme of a virtuous female withstanding the attempt of a would-be seducer from luring her into vice did not particularly excite him.

He smiled and nodded as he saw Miss Edgcott

coming towards him, but she did not appear to have seen him as she turned away and smiled up at a gentleman he did not recognise. He was surprised to discover he felt a little piqued, almost slighted; he was certain she had been looking in his direction. He searched his memory but could not discover anything he had said or done that might have caused her to cut him. No, there was nothing, and on reflection, her eyes had had a rather fixed look about them, as if she were thinking deeply about something. He grinned. What a conceited fellow he was becoming. He was too used to the ladies of his acquaintance falling over themselves to claim his attention on the rare occasions he graced respectable society parties.

He had a feeling that Miss Edgcott was not of their ilk; she had certainly not seemed overly disappointed that they had been forced to postpone their dance. That too had irked him, he realised. It was the strangest thing, but when he had finally fallen into bed not long before dawn, instead of a welcoming darkness it had been her face, lit up by the pleased wide smile she had given him when he had trodden on her dress that he had seen. She seemed to have become a rather elusive itch that he could not quite reach. The sooner he had that dance and relieved it, the better; he was not the type to moon over females.

He returned to his rooms, changed, and sat down to an early dinner before strolling to Berkeley Square. The carriage pulled up in front of the house as he arrived.

"There you are, Miles," Lady Brigham said, coming through the open door and running lightly down the shallow steps that separated them. "I thought you were going to cry off like your father. He suddenly recalled a dinner he must attend."

"How very convenient," Miles murmured.

"Yes, wasn't it?" Lady Brigham said dryly.

"Well, I am looking forward to it," Lady Bassington said, following her down the steps on Charles' arm.

"I believe the last time I went to the play with you, Aunt, you fell asleep halfway through the first act."

"Nonsense, Miles, your memory is faulty; it was some years ago, after all. I was merely resting my eyes."

It was not until they were comfortably arranged in his father's box that it occurred to him that Charles was unusually quiet.

"It is not like you to sit at the back of the box, Charles," he murmured. "I am surprised you are not scanning the crowds to discover some beauty to search out in the interval."

"There is no point when I have no time to further my acquaintance with her," he said, his voice unusually flat. "I leave the day after tomorrow."

"That has never stopped you before," Miles said, surprised and a little concerned by this gloomy outlook.

"This time is different somehow," he said softly. "I have a strange feeling of impending doom."

Now Miles was seriously alarmed. Charles had always laughed off the dangers of a coming battle, his natural gay spirit and trust in his luck allowing him to preserve a devil-may-care attitude. He was sure that it was these traits that had helped his cousin come through so many dangers largely unscathed and he did not wish him to face his next battle without his customary armour.

"This will not do, Charles. I am afraid that the play we are about to witness is hardly likely to lift your spirits, but we shall escape before the farce and visit some of our old haunts. My father insists that I deserve to enjoy myself a little, but you deserve it so much more. Who knows when you will be in Town again, after all?"

Charles' smile was a little weary. "I was before you, old fellow. It was that line of thinking which caused me to slip away from the ball just before supper."

"I wondered where you had disappeared to," Miles said, a relieved smile curving his lips. "Got a little carried away, did you? Blue ruin?"

Charles nodded.

"You fool. It is not named that for nothing! No wonder you have a fit of the blue-devils. I withdraw my offer; a sound night's sleep is all you require to put you to rights. I expect you've still got a devilish bad head."

Charles laughed. "I cannot gainsay you, old fellow, but I'm damned if I'll sit here and let you of all people preach to me."

"Shh!" Lady Bassington said. "The play is about to start. And don't either of you think that sitting at the back of the box will enable you to disappear if you find it a dead bore. Charles looks as if he overindulged last night, and I do not wish you to lead him into trouble before he leaves for Belgium, Miles. Besides, I can see Miss Edgcott has joined Lady Somerton's party, Lady Cranbourne is there too, fine gals all of them. I shall expect one of you to take me to them during the interval."

"I think it is very unjust of you, Frances, to suggest Miles would lead Charles into trouble; he is far more likely to fish him out of it!" Lady Brigham said, bristling.

Lady Bassington chuckled. "Perhaps so. Now do hush, Julia. It is a rare treat for me to visit the theatre."

Her request for quiet seemed to extend to everyone but herself, and as the story unfolded, Lady Bassington frequently disturbed the peace with her verbal outbursts.

"Oh, they've left her alone in the woods, how foolish, now there will be trouble."

"How stupid of her to follow a stranger; he may be dressed as a villager, but you mark my words, he will be the villain of the piece."

"He is quite right of course, I am sure his inclinations are entirely natural, but not when he is trying to corrupt an innocent and must confine her in an enchanted chair. So underhand."

"Good girl! You stick to your guns! Don't drink any of that horrid stuff or you'll be done for. Where are those brothers of yours? Idiots, the pair of them!"

"Here they are at last! It is all very well for attendant spirits and river nymphs to free her, but I can't help but think that if some knight in shining armour was not to rescue her, it would have been better if she had managed it herself!"

Miles found these comments far more entertaining than the play itself and was so obliged to his aunt for enlivening an otherwise tedious evening, that it was he who led her into the saloon. It was a long gallery, dotted with plinths bearing graceful statues, with crimson covered benches set between them.

"Ah, this is better," Lady Bassington said, "I can breathe again. It is so terribly stuffy in there. It is to be expected, I suppose; although the theatre is large, there must be thousands of bodies crammed into it."

"Just so," Miles agreed. "That is a very elegant cane you have with you, Aunt. Do you have need of it?"

"Of course, I do. I guessed that the gallery would fill with people in a pig's whisper. Observe."

Lady Bassington released his arm and made her way towards the nearest bench, leaning heavily upon her stick. The two gentlemen who were lounging there, idly surveying the people emerging from their boxes, immediately rose to their feet, bowed, and moved off.

Lady Bassington sat upon the vacated bench and lifted a brow. "Forward planning, Miles."

"You are an unprincipled woman!" he said, looking down at her with a smile in his eyes. "Shall I go and find Miss Edgcott?"

Lady Bassington looked past him, lifted her cane, and waved it in the air. "No need, she has seen me."

Miles turned and saw her walking towards them arm-in-arm with Miss Crabtree. They were both lacking in inches, but Miss Edgcott's frame was slender and delicate in appearance, whereas Miss Crabtree's was stockier. They both smiled at him, a look of shared amusement in their expressive eyes.

He bowed before them, returning their smile. "Good evening, ladies. You look as if you are plotting something; should I be worried?"

Miss Crabtree laughed. "Do not be absurd, Lord Allerdale, but I am hoping that you will oblige me by appearing to be fascinated by my conversation for a few moments. I have explained to Miss Edgcott that you understand my situation and so would be sure to help me."

He glanced at Miss Edgcott and thought he saw a challenge in her eyes. He rose nobly to it. Turning to Miss Crabtree he said, "But I *am* fascinated by it. I can never guess what you might be about to say."

He was rewarded by a glowing look of approval from Miss Edgcott before she sat down next to his aunt.

"Do I take it that you are avoiding someone, Miss Crabtree?"

"Mr Everard. He is becoming most particular in his attentions, and nothing I can politely say to him appears to put him off. It must be my dowry, of course. He is talking with my father but he will not bring him over to me if he sees I am in conversation with you as he is only heir to a viscount."

"Whilst I am happy to be of service, Miss Crabtree, I think you underrate yourself," Miles said. "Who could not enjoy your frank conversation?"

"I am stupidly tongue-tied with most gentlemen," Miss Crabtree confided, "for if I ignored society's dictates and spoke what was uppermost in my mind, I would insult them greatly. That would not do, for it would upset Papa, but it makes it so difficult to put them off."

"You intrigue me. If you could be honest and tell Mr Everard what you think of him, what would you say?"

"That he is a pompous nodcock and incredibly tedious into the bargain!"

"You are severe, ma'am. Thank goodness for society manners! If a lady could really say what she thought of a gentleman to his face, think of the terrible wounds she could inflict on his consequence with her tongue! It would never do!"

"No, which is why I always search out a spot I might hide in at every function I attend. Papa is becoming quite exasperated with me, which only encourages me, of course."

"You hope to persuade him to take you home with such tactics, I suppose?"

"Yes, and I think it might just work."

"I hope for your sake, it does," Miles said with an amused smile. "It must be most uncomfortable to always be diving behind a curtain or screen in order to avoid someone."

"You can have no idea!" Miss Edgcott said, sighing. "It is so much easier for men, isn't it? You usually decide who you will or will not speak to, and if you are not enjoying yourself you can just walk out of the door and go and find something else to do."

"Not always," he said, looking over her shoulder.

"Can you see my papa?" she asked him.

"No," he said.

"Then he has probably returned to our box. I had better join him before his hopes are raised too far. Thank you for talking to me all this time."

Miles nodded as Georgianna, Lady Cranbourne, and Lady Haverham came up to him.

"Good evening, Allerdale," Georgianna said. "Did

you enjoy your afternoon of cricket? Somerton says you are shaping up nicely."

"Yes, I did, thank you. But I think I shall go and find Charles before I am corralled into doing anything else by you scheming females!"

"But, Lord Allerdale," Marianne said, "how else are we to get you stubborn creatures to do as we wish?"

"I can't imagine," he said dryly. "But as you managed to persuade one of the most confirmed bachelors of my acquaintance to marry you, Lady Cranbourne, I think I will treat you in particular, with extraordinary caution."

Marianne looked rather pleased by this but said, "You have no need to, you know, I am not at all subtle."

Lady Bassington moved along the bench a little and invited the ladies to sit down.

∽

"Are you feeling a little better now, Diana?" Eleanor said quietly, whilst Lady Bassington demanded of Georgianna a blow-by-blow account of the exact nature of the proposal Lord Somerton had made her.

"Yes," Diana said. "It was only when Lord Sandford directed his quizzing glass at our box that I felt uncomfortable. He stared at me as if he wished to eat me when we were in the park today too."

"That is understandable," Eleanor said. "Did I not tell you that you looked particularly beautiful?"

"Yes, but still… and then the play, or poem, or whatever it was, could have been written about him.

Not that he has ever tried to constrain me against my will, but I felt like the performance was a sign, almost a proof of his intentions. It is no wonder that I was unnerved, but you were quite right, Lady Somerton and Lady Cranbourne have not left my side, and Lord Sandford is in close conversation with Captain Bassington."

Eleanor followed her gaze. She was surprised to see a look of consternation on Captain Bassington's countenance; his nature had seemed so naturally sunny to her that it seemed odd. Her expression lightened as she saw a flash of pink behind the plinth they were standing next to. Miss Crabtree was hiding once again and her papa was striding down the gallery looking this way and that, his expression vexed. Poor Miss Crabtree was likely to receive a dressing down when she did emerge, but she certainly could not do so before Lord Sandford and Captain Bassington finished their conversation.

Lord Allerdale came to her rescue once again, although Eleanor was sure he was unaware of it. He approached them and Captain Bassington nodded at Lord Sandford and moved to meet his cousin. Lord Sandford watched him go for a moment and then also moved away. Miss Crabtree poked her head around the plinth and then emerged, standing for a moment as if she were admiring the statue it held. Eleanor watched her glance quickly at Lord Allerdale and his cousin, a pensive look on her face. She suddenly nodded and moved purposefully towards them, but she was intercepted by her papa.

Judging by the colour that came into Miss Crabtree's cheeks, he was indeed cross with her. So cross, in fact, that every time she opened her mouth to speak, he shook his head as if he would not let her. Finally, he took her arm and led her towards the end of the gallery where the stairs led down to the entrance foyer. It seemed they would not be staying for the farce. As they passed by, Miss Crabtree threw Eleanor a look which she could not quite decipher. Was it one of entreaty or apology?

"Oh no," Diana said, "Lord Sandford is coming in our direction."

"Do not worry, child, you may leave him to me," Lady Bassington said.

But Marianne and Georgianna were before her. They rose as one, linked arms, and sallied forth to intercept him.

"Who are they protecting, you, Miss Edgcott, or Lady Haverham?"

"Both, I suspect," she said softly.

"He is ruthlessly pursuing me," Diana said, dramatically.

Lord Sandford bowed and made to move past Georgianna and Marianne, but they simply stepped in front of him again. Marianne put a hand on his sleeve, gave him a blinding smile, and began to talk to him in an animated way.

"This is better than the play," Lady Bassington murmured. "I wish I could hear what she is saying to him."

"I have no idea," Eleanor said, a quiver in her voice. "But judging by his glassy-eyed look, nothing at all interesting."

When Marianne paused for breath, Lord Sandford again bowed, but Georgianna now laid a detaining hand on his sleeve. However, their ploy was ruined when Lord Cranbourne and Lord Somerton suddenly came up to them, both looking rather grim. Lord Sandford acknowledged them both, bowed, and began again to stroll in their direction.

"Walk with me a little, Miss Edgcott," Lady Bassington said.

"Do not leave me," Diana squeaked.

"Trust me," Lady Bassington murmured.

Eleanor rose and took her arm. Lord Sandford was looking straight at Diana, that predatory glint in his eyes again, but as he drew near, Lady Bassington shuffled sideways a couple of steps and put out her stick. He tripped and stumbled forwards, his arms cartwheeling in a most inelegant manner, before he crashed to the floor, almost at Diana's feet. She did not move, only her wide, startled eyes giving her more animation than the statue next to her. The hum of voices immediately around them stopped, and Lady Bassington's deep tones filled the silence.

"Oh, I am so sorry, sir. I stumbled and put my stick out to steady me. I did not see you. Are you injured?"

Lord Sandford pushed himself to his feet, his green eyes glittering in his white face, but aware of the many eyes that were upon him, he merely bowed, straightened his cravat, and walked hastily away towards the stairs, but not before he had sent Eleanor a look of burning resentment.

Eleanor looked at Lady Bassington, an expression of awe on her face.

"You were magnificent," she said.

"Thank you, dear. I wonder if my son and nephew will agree with you."

Eleanor saw Lord Allerdale striding swiftly towards them, his impressive eyebrows slashing downwards, and his gaze fixed on her. Captain Bassington followed close behind.

"Did Sandford offer you any unpleasantness, Miss Edgcott?"

"No, Lord Allerdale," she said, a slight shiver running through her as his intense dark eyes bored into her own.

"Then what did he do to upset you, Mama?" Charles said quickly.

"Not a thing," Lady Bassington said. "It was just an unfortunate accident."

Eleanor did not think that either gentleman was convinced.

"Then I shall take you back to our box before you can create any more havoc," Charles said.

Lord Allerdale remained for a moment.

"Is he still bothering Lady Haverham?" he said gently.

"You know of it?" Eleanor said, surprised.

"I am a particular friend of Lord Carteret's."

"Oh, yes, of course. Diana told him all about it." She frowned. "He promised not to breathe a word."

"He only spoke of it to me, ma'am. He knew it would not go any further. I am surprised Sandford is still pursuing her if she has told him she is no longer interested. Has she done so?"

"No. *I* have done so, but Diana cannot bring herself to speak to him. He has become some sort of ogre in her mind, and she even compared him to the villain of the play. But surely he must realise that she is no longer interested."

"Not necessarily so, Miss Edgcott. I believe Lady Haverham gave him every encouragement, perhaps innocent of the passions she would arouse in his breast. He might not believe that her feelings have changed, but only that you are trying to keep him from her. It would be better for all concerned if Lady Haverham told him herself. If either of you find yourselves on the end of any unpleasantness you may trust me to deal with him."

Eleanor could not completely hide her astonishment at this kind offer.

"You look surprised, Miss Edgcott. Why?"

Eleanor cocked her head to one side, her wide smile slowly dawning, the light of mischief in her eyes. "You may have been born a gentleman, Lord Allerdale, but from what I have discovered, you have seldom behaved like one."

He cocked an eyebrow. "So, you know about that, do you? I am surprised Georgianna would be so indiscreet."

"She knew it would not go any further," Eleanor murmured.

The flash of annoyance she had seen in his eyes turned to amusement.

"Then we hold each other's secrets, ma'am, and must trust each other to keep them."

He took her hand and dropped a light kiss upon it. "I must return to our box. My cousin leaves for Belgium the day after tomorrow and is a little out of sorts. I must do what I may to perk him up a little, but perhaps you would consent to drive with me to Richmond Park once he has gone?" He grinned, wryly. "I give you my word, I shall not abduct you."

"In that case, I shall certainly accept your very obliging offer," Eleanor said. "I have not yet visited that particular park and very much wish to do so."

The farce passed in a blur for Eleanor as she considered what had passed between her and Lord Allerdale. Her instincts told her that she could trust him, and she realised that she liked what she had seen of him. He had a quick understanding, and if he also had a quick temper, she had not yet witnessed it. She had, she realised, made her provocative remark about him not always behaving like a gentleman to see if it would show itself, but any indignation he had felt had swiftly died.

An energetic person herself, she recognised the same quality in him. A thrum of masculine power that his elegant clothes and polite words could not hide, emanated from him. She could easily imagine that if his energies were not directed in some useful way, they might become destructive. She shivered a little as she contemplated what might happen if the volcano she sensed within him erupted; it would certainly scald everyone within reach, she was sure.

CHAPTER 11

When they returned to South Audley Street, Clinton informed them that two letters had arrived whilst they had been out. He handed one to each of them.

"Thank you, Clinton," Diana said. "Has my lord returned yet?"

"No, ma'am. I believe it is a political dinner he is attending, and he informed me it was likely to go on into the early hours. He said that you should not wait up for him."

"No, I shall not. I am suddenly feeling quite weary," she said softly.

"Up to bed with you then," Eleanor said, taking Diana's arm.

When they came to Diana's room, Eleanor kissed her cheek and bade her goodnight. Diana smiled sleepily and opened the door. She stood on the threshold for a moment and gave a gasp of delight.

"Eleanor! Look!"

Eleanor gently pushed Diana, who still stood

rooted to the spot, a little further into the room. The delicious scent of roses reached her before she saw the three vases filled with the blooms. A single lemon rose had been laid on her pillow and a card lay next to it. Diana ran forward and snatched it up.

"What does it say?"

Diana held it to her breast for a moment, colour rushing into her cheeks.

"I cannot tell you; it is a personal message."

"I see," Eleanor said, smiling. "I will bid you goodnight."

She closed the door softly behind her. Frederick had outdone himself. He was either a very fast learner, or he had discovered a hitherto unsuspected romantic streak. She had just climbed into bed, dismissed Linny, and reached for her letter, when Diana threw open her door, her face ashen.

"What is it?" Eleanor asked, dropping her letter and throwing off her covers.

"I was so happy," Diana said, tears trembling in her eyes. "But this could ruin all!"

She held out the missive, her hand shaking. Eleanor swiftly crossed the room and took it from her.

My dear Lady Haverham,

I had dared to hope that I had won your affection. When I felt you tremble in my arms, I was sure of it. Could it be that I was mistaken? I cannot believe that you would have bestowed your kisses upon me if your heart had not been engaged. You are not so fickle. I burn to hold you again but cannot come near you. Miss Edgcott appears to have become your jailor. I would set you free if I can.

Meet me tomorrow morning in the park, at eight o'clock. I shall look for you near the Grosvenor Gate. Come alone. Either we will discover a way that we can be together, or you will tell me that your feelings have changed. I will only believe it if I hear the words from your own sweet lips.

Do not disappoint me.
Sandford

Diana's eyes blazed with sudden anger. "If Frederick had been home… if he had read that letter… Oh, I cannot bear to think of it. And it is lies! I did not bestow my kisses on him, he stole one. And if I trembled, it was with fear and shock! How dare he write to me! How dare he put my happiness in such jeopardy."

Eleanor looked at the letter thoughtfully. "I understand your feelings, but you must remain calm, Diana. You did encourage him, if not to kiss you, then certainly to flirt with you. You must meet him. It seems he will not leave you alone until you do."

"I cannot!" she exclaimed, wringing her hands. "I am beginning to think him capable of anything."

"You will be quite safe, for you shall not go alone. I shall come with you, as your maid."

Diana gave a wild little laugh. "As if a maid could stop him if he wished to carry me off! Besides, he would recognise you."

"No, he will not, for I shall wear a veil. Neither will he carry you off, for I shall bring this."

Eleanor crossed to a set of drawers, knelt, and pulled the bottom one open. She rummaged under the garments laid there and pulled out a small, silver pistol.

Diana's eyes widened. "Eleanor! Whatever are you doing with a pistol?"

"Papa insisted I had one for my protection. And you

need not fear I do not know how to use it, for Papa taught me himself. I do not envisage that Lord Sandford would be so stupid as to try and abduct you in daylight, in a public park, and with a maid as witness, but if he does attempt anything so rash, you may be sure I will use it!"

"Think of the scandal!" Diana breathed.

"There will be no scandal," Eleanor said calmly, "for I shall not kill him, only warn him off. If you do not like the plan, then I suggest you tell Frederick the whole. I think him far more likely to believe your version of events than Sandford's."

Diana blanched. "No, Eleanor, no. Even if he claims he believes me, it will sow a seed of doubt in his mind. I believe he has fallen in love with me a second time, and I could not bear it if… if he should fall out of it again."

"Very well. The park it shall be. Frederick is hardly likely to be up at that hour after a very late night, and we will be back before he is any the wiser. I shall tell Linny the whole, for she is to be trusted, and your maid never disturbs you before ten so I cannot see any difficulty."

Eleanor went to the fire and threw the letter onto the flames. "There, it is gone, and so will Sandford be once you tell him that he was mistaken in your interest in him."

Diana seemed to gain some confidence as she watched the letter burn. She suddenly nodded. "You are right, Eleanor. I will be ready by half past seven, you may be sure."

Eleanor climbed back into bed and picked up her letter again. She glanced at the looping letters that spelled her name, idly wondering who would have sent her a letter at such an hour.

Dear Miss Edgcott,

I sincerely hope you read this tonight, for the matter is of some urgency and I do not know what to do for the best. I overheard a conversation this evening between Lord Sandford and Captain Bassington. Captain Bassington apologised to Lord Sandford for his actions of the evening before, he said that although he had been provoked by the insulting way Sandford had spoken of his cousin, he should not have knocked him down. He went on to say that they had both been jug-bitten and therefore the actions of neither of them should be judged as harshly as they would be if they had been sober. He asked Sandford to accept his apology and withdraw his challenge. Lord Sandford replied that he allowed no man to knock him down and refused to do so, but if Captain Bassington wished to reconsider his decision for the business to be conducted without seconds, he would be amenable to this wish. Captain Bassington said he would not risk the meeting coming to Allerdale's ears, or of reaching the horse guards, for duelling was frowned upon in the army. Sandford then said that he would see Captain Bassington at six o'clock sharp at Battersea Fields and that he had arranged for a doctor to be present.

Miss Edgcott, Lord Allerdale has been so kind to me that I cannot feel that it is right that he should not be warned of this duel. He cannot wish his cousin to put his life at risk because Sandford slandered him in some way. At the very least, he should have his support as his second! I told my father all, but he said that although it was not at all regular for such a meeting to occur without seconds, it was not my place to interfere and that I could not be expected to understand the gentleman's code of honour. He refuses to intervene in the matter. I have witnessed your friendship with Lady Bassington and cannot help but feel that you also would not wish this event to proceed.

I do not know why I feel that you will be able to do something, but my instincts tell me that somehow you will think of a way. I would send a note to Lord Allerdale myself, but Papa has strictly forbidden me to do so and I think I have tried him far enough.

Your friend,
Miss Anne Crabtree

No wonder Captain Bassington had looked so unlike himself. He, at least, had seen the foolishness of the whole episode, but it appeared that Lord Sandford was not the man to forgive a slight. What a pity he had not been injured by his fall this evening and so been unable to take part in the duel. Eleanor frowned as something occurred to her. How could he arrange a duel for six o'clock and then so confidently a meeting with Diana at eight o'clock? He must feel very certain of the outcome. Was he so arrogant or could it be that he intended to cheat in some way? The presence of the doctor made this seem unlikely, but then, he had been chosen by Lord Sandford and might be in his pay.

Eleanor slid out of bed, picked up her candle, and went to the small desk that was set beneath her window. She must do something for she had a horrid suspicion that she was ultimately responsible for what had happened. If Lord Allerdale had not trodden upon her dress, his subsequent conversation with Lord Sandford would not have taken place, and he would not have humiliated Lord Sandford by escorting him from the house. It was surely this event that had caused Lord Sandford to malign Lord Allerdale to his cousin. What was it that he had said to her earlier? *Then we hold each other's secrets, ma'am, and must trust each other to keep them.*

Although this was not strictly Lord Allerdale's secret, she felt sure that he would wish her to inform him of it and somehow knew he would consider she had betrayed his trust if she did not do so. She chewed her lip. She owed him no allegiance, and she was sure she did not care either way what he thought of her, but Miss Crabtree had asked for her help and she had liked Captain Bassington on sight.

Eleanor reached for a pen and hastily began to write. In a very few minutes she had recorded what she knew and her fears that Lord Sandford was not to be trusted. She folded the letter neatly, wrote Lord Allerdale upon it, and then wrote the word URGENT beneath, heavily underscoring it. She had just donned her dressing gown when a thought occurred to her. She somehow felt sure Lord Allerdale would have the power to stop the duel, but would he have the inclination? Would it not bring dishonour on Captain Bassington for him to do so? She sighed. His presence might prevent Lord Sandford from behaving in a less than honourable way, but it would not guarantee Captain Bassington's safety.

She returned to her table and hastily scribbled another letter, before seeking out Stanley and requesting him to deliver them both immediately.

∽

Unfortunately, Miss Edgcott was unaware that Lord Allerdale did not reside in Berkeley Square, and

Michael, the footman into whose hands her letter was delivered did not so much as glance at it before laying it on the tray in the hall. He had only been hired for the season and was still rather green, although he hoped his current employment would lead to greater things. He received a severe trimming down the following morning from the butler when he enquired as to the hour of its delivery, and was then sent immediately to Duke Street, with instructions to explain his dereliction of duty to Lord Allerdale.

Miles had followed his own advice and enjoyed a relatively early night. He continued to be a little concerned for Charles, however. When they had parted company after the play, his cousin had shaken his hand and clapped him on the back saying, with what Miles had considered rather forced cheerfulness, "Sorry if I've been a bit of a rum 'un, this evening, old fellow. I'm sure I'll be back to my old self tomorrow. Come and see me then, but not before ten; I think I'll enjoy the last lazy morning I may have for some time."

He had every intention of visiting Charles this morning, and if he did not appear to be his usual cheery self, he would prise from him whatever was truly bothering him. He intended to enjoy a good gallop in the park first, and as this could only be achieved at an ungodly hour of the morning, he had given Tibbs instructions to bring his horse to him at five thirty sharp. He had risen with the light and was just draining his cup of coffee when the white-faced footman was shown into the room.

"Good morning," he said, rising to his feet. "What on earth brings you here at such an early hour?"

"S-sir," he stammered. "I have two letters for you." He held one up. "This was delivered to Berkeley Square last evening, and I b-beg your pardon, but I didn't think anything of it and laid it on the tray in the hall. It wasn't until this morning that I discovered it was marked urgent."

Miles was suddenly filled with a sense of foreboding. He strode across the room and plucked it from the shrinking footman's hand. He tore it open and knew a moment's relief when he saw that it was not written in Charles' lazy scrawl. He shook his head as if to clear it; Charles would have known where to reach him.

He rapidly scanned its contents. "You fool," he said softly. "You complete and utter idiot!"

"I'm s-sorry, sir," the footman said.

"Not you," Miles snapped, his eyes flying to the clock on the mantle.

It had just turned half past five.

"Is Tibbs outside?"

"Yes, my lord," Michael said. "He was here before me."

Miles grabbed his riding crop, jammed on his hat, and hurried into the street. He nodded at his groom, swiftly swung himself into the saddle, and raced off.

Tibbs stood for a moment, looking after him.

"Now where's he off to in such a hurry?"

"I don't know," Michael said. "But when he read the letter I gave him, he called someone an idiot."

"Did he now?" Tibbs said, musingly. "Well, if he didn't give you a message or tell you what he was up to, he probably don't want anyone to know, so you'd best not repeat that to anyone or the fact that he rode off as if the devil himself were after him. If you were to worrit Lady Brigham, he'd have your liver."

Michael turned quite green. "I will only say that I delivered the letter and Lord Allerdale then went for his morning ride – if anyone asks that is."

"That's the ticket," Tibbs said approvingly.

By Miles' calculation, it should take a good forty minutes to reach his destination, but his horse was swift and he an excellent horseman, so it was not impossible that he would make it in time. He flew down Whitehall, the Admiralty and Horse Guards passing in a blur. People on foot and cart drivers alike, who were making their way across Westminster Bridge, stopped and stared at the dark-haired man upon the sleek horse that was so fleet of foot it seemed it had wings. They could be forgiven for thinking that the man did not ride as if the devil was after him but as if he were the devil himself, for his eyes burned with a strange intensity and he appeared oblivious to their presence, manoeuvring around them effortlessly without ever checking his speed.

Once across the bridge, Miles hugged the river as much as possible, passing Vauxhall without a glance and breathing a sigh of relief as he came at last to the hamlet of Nine Elms. He only hoped the poor condition of the wooden Battersea Bridge had discouraged them from going that way, or he would certainly not make it in time. He left the road and had ridden only a short distance across a flat stretch of common when he saw a carriage and a horse grazing, and beyond them, two figures stripped to their shirt sleeves. He groaned as the ring of steel on steel reached him. He was too late; they had already begun. At least Charles had had the wit to choose the sword over the pistol, for although it was just as lethal, if not more so, it would ensure that the engagement was a true test of skill. A shaking hand or an unfamiliar gun brought an element of luck into the situation that he could not like.

He dismounted a little way behind the carriage, careful not to distract the duellers. He felt a surge of relief as he saw no sign of blood on his cousin's white shirt. He soon saw that they were evenly matched. Both Charles' and Sandford's brows gleamed with a sheen of sweat, their eyes never leaving each other's as they attacked, parried, and counter-attacked in turn. Miles thought Charles had the slightly better footwork, but Sandford had an astonishingly flexible and quick wrist.

"It's a close-run thing," said a voice behind him.

Miles turned and saw a man still seated in the coach. Although his clothes were respectable, his eyes were bloodshot, and he held a small silver flask in a hand that trembled. Miles ignored him, disgusted, and turned back to the fight. This was the doctor Sandford had called on! If either of them needed his aid, God help them!

He held his breath as Charles suddenly quickened his footwork and forced Sandford into retreat. Sandford looked like he was tiring and seemed to realise it; he swiftly turned his wrist and attempted to cross his opponent's blade, but Charles closed first, and Sandford's sword went sailing through the air, whether due to the slickness of his hand or the force of Charles' thrust was anyone's guess.

"Stop this, insanity!" Miles yelled, his voice deep

and commanding. "I would not wish either of you to risk your lives over a drunken spat!"

Sandford wiped his hand on his breeches and picked up his sword.

"You will not interfere," he said, a little breathlessly. "You know the rules as well as I, Allerdale. Only when one of us cannot continue will this be over."

He suddenly turned and before Charles had time to read his intention, he closed on him again. Charles staggered backwards, raising his sword just in time to stop his opponent scoring a hit. Miles clenched his fists. If Charles did not kill him, he would!

But even as Charles recovered his balance, the sound of thundering hooves signalled an approaching carriage. It drew up and two burly constables jumped down.

Charles and Sandford were fighting in earnest but now in anger and did not seem to notice.

"Choose your moment carefully," Miles warned.

"I know my business, sir," said the man nearest to him.

When they next broke apart, the constable reached into his pocket and pulled out a pistol. Before they could close again, he fired into the air.

"Drop your swords, gentlemen," he said. "Duelling is against the law, as well you know. You are both under arrest."

"Good man!" Miles murmured.

"Damn you, Allerdale!" Sandford hissed. "You had no place to interfere."

"Oh, it was not this gentleman who informed on you," the constable said cheerfully.

"Then who?" Sandford demanded.

"I don't know precisely," he said, "but I believe it was a lady. Now come along, nice and peaceful like, for the magistrate is awaiting your pleasure."

Charles picked up his coat and came towards them.

"I'd rather you dropped that sword, sir."

"Keep them for me will you, Quarlberry?" Sandford said to the doctor as he passed his coach.

He threw Charles a look of unmitigated scorn. "Bleat about this morning's meeting, did you, to some female whose sympathy you wished to arouse?"

"Don't be an ape, Sandford. No sane man would mention an affair of honour to a woman. I mentioned it to no one but you, last evening at the theatre."

Miles met Sandford's narrowed stare with a hard look.

"If you are going to ask me a similar question, don't. You will get nothing out of me."

"Come along, sir," the constable said. "Things will only go harder for you if you make trouble."

Lord Sandford looked coldly at him. "Remove your hand from my arm, or I shall have to throw away this coat."

The constable did not release his grip but waved his pistol and grinned. "It's no skin off my nose if you do, sir."

Miles grasped Charles by the shoulder as he came up to him and said in a low voice, "You will no doubt be fined and bound over to keep the peace, come to my rooms afterwards, there is much I have to say to you."

CHAPTER 12

Eleanor's dreams were unsettled and vibrant. She was not prone to flights of fancy, yet the duel played itself out in various incarnations. She saw Lord Sandford striding out of a rising mist, a reckless grin on his face, but a cold, almost inhuman expression in his eyes. Captain Bassington came in the other direction, his sword hanging loosely by his side, his fair, wavy hair and blue eyes making him appear like an angel to Sandford's devil. Then the scene shifted, they stood some distance apart, pistols in their hands, with only the doctor to give the word or make some sign that the duel should commence. Before he gave that word, Sandford raised his pistol and fired. His opponent was thrown backwards, his hand clutching his chest, and when he raised it to his face, it was drenched in blood. But it was not Captain Bassington's pale face and unfocused eyes that observed it, but Lord Allerdale's.

Eleanor awoke, her heart beating rapidly in her breast, wondering for a moment if she had indeed put

Lord Allerdale's life in danger. A few moments' reflection restored her calm; she was not fully conversant with the gentleman's code of honour, but she was certain that it would not allow such a thing to happen. An overwrought imagination had led Diana to demonise Lord Sandford, but he had done nothing to suggest he would behave in such a wicked manner.

Eleanor rose and went to the window. She drew back the heavy curtains and blinked as the sun shone in her eyes. The outcome of this morning's events would already have been decided. The half-formed fears that had beset her the evening before now seemed foolish in the bright light of the day. She had thought it sinister that Lord Sandford had been so sure he would be free to meet Diana a bare two hours after the duel, but now it seemed far more likely that only his pride had prevented him from drawing back from the engagement and once it had been satisfied, the gentlemen would shake hands and there would be an end to it. He would hardly have arranged to see Diana in the park if his intention had been murder.

Linny tutted and fretted when she understood Eleanor intended to masquerade as Lady Haverham's maid.

"I don't hold with clandestine meetings. If it isn't just like you to take matters into your own hands rather than let his lordship deal with it. If anyone discovers your antics, your name will be mud," she said, but in a resigned tone, long acquaintance with her mistress leaving the maid in no doubt that anything she could say would have the slightest effect.

"No one will discover it. I shall wear the hat I wore

when I was still in mourning, the one with the black veil."

"That you won't," the maid said. "It is far too elegant. You shall have to wear one of mine. It will be easy enough to attach a veil and you had best take my long cloak to cover your dress."

As the servants were at breakfast, they managed to leave the house unnoticed. Diana wore a mulish look, her confidence still buoyed by her indignation over the manner of her summons. The park was quiet but not deserted. Although no one of fashion was strolling there, a lady with a small group of children about her could be seen walking in the distance, and beyond them, a few horses were being put through their paces. None of them, however, appeared to be coming in their direction. Eleanor put her veil back, feeling rather stifled by it. Linny had attached the thickest one she could find, and Eleanor could barely see more than two steps in front of her.

"Surely it must be eight o'clock by now?" Diana said, fretfully.

Eleanor took a small silver pocket watch from her reticule.

"Yes, it is ten minutes after the hour."

They strolled slowly along the wide avenue for some time but still no horseman or carriage moved in their direction.

"Oh! This is too bad of him!" Diana complained. "I have practised over and over precisely what I should say to him and now he has not come after all. I am hot, tired, and my feet ache. What does he mean by it?"

Eleanor resisted the impulse to tell her about the

duel; neither Captain Bassington nor Lord Allerdale would thank her for spreading the tale, and she would only make Diana's irrational fears worse. She damped down her own feeling of unease and said brightly, "Nothing, I am sure. He must have been unavoidably detained. Let us walk over to that stand of trees; there is a bench underneath one of them, and we can rest a little."

The dappled shade did not appear to bring Diana much relief. She sat with drooping shoulders, her eyes downcast, and was unusually quiet, her confidence seeming to ebb with each minute that passed. Eleanor presently checked her watch again and rose to her feet.

"It is nearly nine o'clock. I think we have waited long enough."

Diana did not move and when she spoke her voice was faint. "Eleanor, I do not feel well. I think I am going to be sick!"

Barely had she uttered the words when she leaned forwards and started to retch. Eleanor waited until the paroxysms that shook her body lessened, and then passed her a handkerchief to wipe her face.

"Take a few deep breaths, my dear."

"Yes, I am better now, I think," Diana said shakily.

Eleanor put an arm around her waist and helped her to her feet.

"You are trembling," she said softly, "you poor thing."

"Being sick always makes me tremble," Diana murmured.

The sound of horses galloping suddenly reached their ears. Diana groaned.

"I cannot speak to Sandford now. I can barely walk or speak," she whispered.

"It is not Sandford," Eleanor said, hastily pulling her veil down. "It is Lord Carteret. Thank heavens! He can take you home. Listen carefully, Diana. There will not be room for me in his curricle, but do not worry. No one will look twice at a maid walking alone through the streets. I doubt very much if Frederick will have emerged, but if he has, just say that we went for an early morning walk and you were taken ill. Oh, and tell Stanley to keep a look out for me, will you?"

They had been slowly limping towards the carriageway and Lord Carteret could not fail to spot them as the park was still bereft of company. Seeing that Diana was being heavily supported by her maid, he came to a swift halt, said something to his groom, and descended swiftly from the curricle.

"Lady Haverham! You are ill. Allow me to take you home."

"Thank you," Diana murmured, accepting his arm. "I am feeling a little faint."

"We might be able to cram your maid in with us," he said doubtfully.

Eleanor shook her head and said in a fair imitation of Linny, "Don't you worry about me, sir. I can find my own way."

With no more ado, Lord Carteret lifted Diana into his arms and deposited her in the curricle. Eleanor smiled behind her veil. He really did have lovely manners, yet there was a coolness about him that did not attract her. She sincerely hoped that Diana had not left any lasting impression upon his heart, for he deserved better.

She was not overly concerned for Diana as she felt fairly certain of the cause of her malady. Her frequent tiredness, recent mood swings, and now her sickness all suggested she was in a delicate condition. Her brow wrinkled as she considered how Frederick would react. Would he insist they return immediately to Standon? That would not suit her.

She paused when she came to South Audley Street. She had asked her solicitor to enquire into the truth of the rumour that Madame Lafayette was going out of business, and if so, to discover if the lease on her shop was available, but he had not yet replied to her letter. Perhaps she could learn something useful in her guise as maid. It would not cause any occasion for remark if a maid visited a milliner's shop on behalf of her mistress, and Bruton Street was only a few minutes away, so what harm could it do?

She walked carefully down Mount Street, skirted Berkeley Square, and soon arrived at Bruton Street, revelling in the freedom her disguise accorded her. She came to a stop outside Madame Lafayette's establishment, pulled her veil to one side, and observed the window display. Only a few tired looking bonnets and a selection of ribbons graced it and set between them was a notice stating that from this time forth no credit would be extended to customers. It seemed the rumours were true.

A barouche came to a halt behind her and Eleanor saw Lady Langton and Miss Farrow clearly reflected in the window. She hastily entered the shop and went over to a collection of shawls that were displayed on a table in the far corner.

"Can I help—"

Madame Lafayette broke off as Lady Langton and Miss Farrow entered the establishment.

"Good morning, Lady Langton."

Eleanor raised a brow at her tone. It was not rude, but neither was it particularly respectful, and she had dropped her affected French accent.

"It is not a good morning, Madame Lafayette. I am most displeased," Lady Langton said peevishly. "My new bonnet should have been delivered yesterday, and as it was not and I particularly wished to wear it today, I have had to come to you."

"Your bonnet was not delivered, my lady, because it has not yet been paid for. I have been run into the ground by late payment of bills and it has ruined me."

"But I have always paid my bills," Lady Langton protested.

"So you have, ma'am – eventually. I have your hat ready and I have changed the ribbons as requested. I shall hand it over as soon as I am paid."

"But I do not think I have that much about me, and I need the bonnet."

Eleanor had heard enough. Madame Lafayette would hardly speak to her customers in such a way if she was not going to shut up shop. But whilst Eleanor could well imagine that late payments of bills had contributed to her downfall, she felt sure that was not the main cause of her unfortunate predicament. Madame Lafayette had become lazy and her hats were overpriced and unimaginative. She put down the paisley shawl she had pretended to be so engrossed in and walked towards the door.

"Then I suggest you come back later, my lady."

"Wait! I shall see how much I have with me."

Lady Langton stepped back as Eleanor passed and she brushed against her.

"I beg your pardon, ma'am," she murmured.

As she opened the door, Lady Langton said in a harassed voice, "Oh! Now I cannot find my reticule. What did I do with it, Letty?"

Before Miss Farrow could reply, she screeched, "You, maid! Stop! You have stolen it."

Eleanor froze for a moment and then went quickly out of the shop. If Eliza Langton recognised her, the whole of London would soon know that she had been going about alone dressed as a maid.

Lady Langton followed her into the street. "Stop her!" she screeched at her driver. "She has my reticule!"

Eleanor picked up her skirts and began to run, but the combination of her panic and the darkness of her veil caused her to bump into someone and she stumbled and fell. She was still lying face down in the dirt when she heard the coachman's voice say, "No, milady, I've got it. You left it on the seat, and I thought I'd best look after it for you."

"Oh," Lady Langton said. "How silly of me. But why did she run if she had nothing to hide?"

Her voice, which had but a moment ago been that of a harpy, was now gushing and girlish.

"Lord Allerdale! How kind of you to stop her, but it now appears that I was quite mistaken. I feel terrible. Is the poor girl injured, do you think? She does not appear to be moving."

Eleanor could not move; not only was she winded but her veil had become detached from one side of her hat in the fall. Despite her awkward situation, she felt a rush of relief flood through her as she heard Lord Allerdale's voice.

"I did not intentionally stop her, ma'am, she ran into me. And if she is not injured, it will be no thanks to you," he said in biting tones. "What reason did you have to accuse her?"

"She brushed against me, and then I could not discover my reticule. It was a simple mistake to make."

"It was a foolish mistake to make," he corrected her, going down on one knee beside the prone body. "You may carry on with your day, ma'am. I shall see to this poor lady."

Eleanor felt herself being gently turned as he spoke. She quickly pulled the veil across her face.

Lady Langton came a few steps closer. "Would it not be better if you put her in the barouche?"

Eleanor felt one strong arm go around her back and another slither under her knees. The next moment she was lifted into the air. She turned her head so it rested against Lord Allerdale's broad shoulder and gave a dramatic moan that would not have been at all out of place in a Shakespearian Tragedy. She felt his arms tighten around her and smiled, feeling herself to be quite safe now.

"It is not necessary, ma'am. My mother's home is only a few steps away. Good day."

He turned and strode in the opposite direction. He soon crossed the road and they entered Bruton Mews.

"You may take your head out of my shoulder now, Miss Edgcott," he said calmly, "there is no one to see you."

She gave a surprised little laugh as she did so, and her veil slipped from her face. "How did you guess?"

"I did not guess," he said. "Your veil fluttered as you fell, and I caught sight of your chin and lips."

His enigmatic gaze rested upon them now and Eleanor felt her cheeks grow warm.

"Are they so memorable?" she asked.

"Apparently so," Lord Allerdale murmured.

"Er, you can put me down now," she said, her heart beating a little faster. "I am not at all injured."

His lips twitched into a grin. "I was aware of that, ma'am, from the moment you moaned. It was a nice touch, I will admit, if rather melodramatic."

He put her down gently as he spoke. She became busy brushing the dust from her cloak.

"Thank you for coming to my assistance, sir," she said, glancing up at him, an unusually shy smile in her eyes. "I knew all would be well once I realised it was *you* I had rushed into. And I must say, I am very glad it *was* you and not the wall."

He laughed. "If I had behaved more like a wall, you might have been better served. I did move to one side, which is something a wall would never have done, you must agree, but to no avail. You changed direction."

"I could not see where I was going," she admitted.

"That much is clear," he said dryly. "But little else is." He quirked a brow. "Care to enlighten me?"

"Yes, I will, of course. But I must return to South Audley Street before Frederick comes down to breakfast or I may have to also enlighten him, and I would rather not."

"I shall walk with you, Miss Edgcott. Have you a pin about you to attach your veil?"

Eleanor reached into the pocket of her cloak and

quickly pulled out her reticule. The string that tied it had become loose and some of its contents dropped onto the cobbles.

Both of them quickly bent and picked up one of the items. Lord Allerdale examined the small pistol closely for a moment, a twist of a smile playing about his lips.

"You are full of surprises, Miss Edgcott. Do you know how to use it?"

"You may be sure, I do. My father…" she paused, a stricken look upon her face.

She gazed down at the pocket watch in her palm. The glass casing had smashed.

"It was Papa's," she said, a catch in her voice.

He gently plucked it from her small hand and put the pistol in its place.

"It is only the front that is damaged. I shall have it mended for you."

"Thank you," she said softly.

Her large brown eyes were brimming with tears, and she dashed a hand across them.

"Forgive me, sir. I am being foolish."

She fished a pin from the reticule, dropped the pistol into it, and pulled the strings tight, before swiftly pinning her veil back in place.

"There, I am ready."

"On second thoughts, it will be better if I drive you, Miss Edgcott. It will be both quicker and occasion less remark. It would look a little odd if I were to be seen strolling about with a maid on my arm. Promise me you will wait. My curricle is being readied as we speak; I was on my way to fetch it when I heard the commotion in the street. I will not be many moments."

"I will wait," she said quietly.

He was as good as his word, and the curricle swept out into the lane before she had had time to gather her thoughts. Not wishing to waste any more time, she did not wait for assistance but hopped lightly up into it.

"Did you manage to stop the duel?"

"No, it had already begun by the time I arrived. Your letter was only delivered to Duke Street this morning."

"I assumed you lived in Berkeley Square," she said. "How foolish of me not to realise you might have your own rooms. Was Lord Sandford injured?"

"Again, no. I have much to thank you for, Miss Edgcott."

"I felt sure you would wish to know," she said simply. "But this morning my fears seemed ridiculous and I wondered if I had overreacted, but there was no time for procrastination."

She had looked up at him as she spoke and was suddenly very grateful for her veil, for his intense glance held such warmth and gratitude that she felt quite mesmerised. She only realised she had been holding her breath when he turned his attention back to the road.

"Your letter to Bow Street ensured that the duel was eventually halted. You are extremely thorough, Miss Edgcott; you left nothing to chance. Why did you think that Sandford may have been injured?"

They were already approaching South Audley Street and she quickly told him of Diana's letter and their visit to the park, and how Lord Sandford had not put in an appearance.

He frowned. "You should not have gone, ma'am."

"But it was you who suggested that she speak to him," she protested. "And as you said, I leave nothing to chance which is why I took my pistol."

Until this moment he had shown no great surprise or disapproval at finding her in such a strange predicament, but now he fixed her with an incredulous stare and his next words were uttered with biting scorn.

"Miss Edgcott, there are at least a dozen things that could have gone awry, especially if your pistol had come into play. Lady Haverham should have spoken to Sandford at a ball or some other society event. What is more, if such a clandestine meeting had come to Haverham's ears it would not have looked well. Your actions this morning have been both stupid and dangerous."

Eleanor gasped at his rudeness.

"Set me down here, if you please," she said icily.

As they were almost at her door, he obligingly came to a halt.

"You have not yet explained why you then went to Bruton Street alone."

Eleanor jumped down. "I am very grateful for your help, sir, but that is no one's business but my own. Good day."

She turned on the words, hurried down the street a little way, and mounted a shallow flight of steps, grateful when Stanley opened the door to her immediately. She slipped a coin into his hand, tore off her veil, and ran up the stairs.

Diana was waiting for her in her room.

"Eleanor! You have been an age!"

She waved the veil and forced herself to speak calmly. "I found it so hard to see that I could only move at a snail's pace. I am pleased you are feeling better."

Linny said nothing, but her mouth was set in a disapproving line as she took back her hat and helped Eleanor out of the cloak, leaving her in no doubt that she would have to listen to more recriminations presently. Having known her from her cradle, Eleanor acknowledged that her maid had that right and would listen to them without taking umbrage. Lord Allerdale had no such right, however, especially when his own escapades were taken into consideration.

"I am much better," Diana said. "A cup of tea and a biscuit were all that I required. I think it was all that exercise on an empty stomach which caused me to feel ill. Eleanor! You will not believe it, but Sandford sent us on a wild goose chase; he never had any intention of meeting me, he only wanted to teach me a lesson. He is a horrid toad! Read this."

She thrust a card at her. Sandford's card. He had scrawled a few words on the back of it.

Lady Haverham,

How long did you wait, I wonder? It is so very tedious to have one's time wasted, isn't it?

Sandford

"Quite abominable," Eleanor agreed. "But at least you need no longer worry about him, Diana."

CHAPTER 13

Miles waited until Miss Edgcott had disappeared inside the house before driving on. He had not meant to cut at her; he did not have that right, nor did he wish to have it. He could think of nothing worse than to be saddled with a headstrong chit who always thought she knew best! He would admit that her quick actions concerning the duel were to be admired; they had shown she had a cool head and a quick wit in a crisis. He was very grateful to her, and when he had realised that the heavily veiled woman who had cannoned into him was not a maid but Miss Edgcott, he had not paused to consider why she should be masquerading in such a fashion, he had only been aware of a desire to shield her from harm.

Any fear that she had been injured by the fall had been swiftly put to flight. As soon as she had snuggled into his shoulder like a trusting kitten, and given that ridiculously exaggerated moan, he had not only realised that she was unhurt, but had suspected that she was positively enjoying herself. He did not think he had ever met a young lady with less sensibility. She had shown no discomposure when her imposture was discovered but had laughed with sublime unconcern, apparently convinced that he could be trusted to keep her secret, almost as if they had known each other for years rather than days. And he had been so sucked in by her smiling eyes that he had also made light of the whole episode, even talking some nonsense about not being a wall!

His expression softened. No, it was not true that she was devoid of *all* sensibility; when she had realised that she had damaged the watch her papa had left her, she had been powerfully affected. Her large eyes had swum with tears and her determination to overcome this momentary weakness had touched him. But when she had explained the reason for her disguise and the pistol in her reticule, amusement and sympathy alike had been supplanted by incredulity and anger that she seemed so oblivious to the dangers that could have upset her foolish plan. He did not believe for a moment that she would have pulled the trigger – and neither would Sandford have if he had kept the rendezvous – but he might well have discovered her identity, and he already had reason to resent her. He would not have hesitated to spread the story and would have rejoiced in her fall from grace.

Miles shook his head. Why he should have been moved to anger was beyond him; Miss Edgcott was no concern of his. Why she should trust him so blindly was a mystery; she knew full well that he had not lived a blameless existence. Perhaps that was it. It had probably never occurred to her that he would have been shocked by her escapade, and he did, after all, owe her a debt of gratitude. He gave a low laugh. What a sermonising fellow he was turning into. It was not yet ten o'clock, but he had already read two people a lecture this morning. Charles had taken his in much better part, however. Now that the issue of the duel had been resolved, he was his usual self and had taken his trimming down with cheerful unconcern.

Miles had been a little surprised that such a seasoned soldier had been so troubled over the whole affair, but Charles had explained it to him.

"It is not the same thing at all, old fellow. I am trained to kill an unknown enemy; it is my duty, but it is not personal. And once enjoined in the heat of battle, I have no choice; it is a case of kill or be killed. I do not particularly like Sandford, but I have known him for years. The thought that I might take the life of someone I have known since we were at school did not feel right. I would not have drawn his cork if I had been sober, of course, and I never expected him to call me out; he had deserved it after all." Charles had shaken his head. "He has always possessed a malicious tongue and lived life at a furious rate, but I do not remember him being quite so full of spite as he is now."

Miles thought that he might understand this change in their acquaintance. Sandford was a little older than them, and whilst he had been surrounded by cronies who lived life as hard and fast as he did himself, he had seemed nothing at all out of the ordinary. But as the years had passed, more and more of his fellow revellers had fallen by the wayside, either marrying or adopting a more sober way of life as they inherited their estates and the obligations that went with them.

It was perhaps not surprising that Sandford had seemed so scornful when he had discovered that Miles seemed to have joined their ranks. With each passing year he was becoming a more solitary figure, but he refused to let go of the lifestyle he had become accustomed to – a lifestyle Miles had gradually come to realise was hollow. He had known it even before he had returned to Brigham last summer to lay his latest folly before his father. But whereas Miles had a family whom he respected to temper his actions, Sandford had no one but himself to please, and he doubted very much that he respected anybody overmuch.

He drove through the gates of Lord's ground and nodded at one of the boys who hung about in the hope of looking after a gentleman's horses.

"My groom will be here presently, walk them until he arrives, will you?"

The match was to be played on the morrow, and most of the team were meeting later that day, but as he wished to spend it with Charles, Cranbourne and Somerton had arranged to meet him for a final practice this morning. He was surprised to see Carteret had also joined them.

"What is this?" he cried, peeling off his coat and striding onto the pitch. "Fraternising with the enemy?"

"Come, come," Lord Carteret said, "it is only a friendly match, after all."

Miles grinned. "There is no such thing as a friendly match!"

At the end of an hour, he had had the satisfaction of sending several of Carteret's quickly delivered balls sailing through the air – only Somerton had sent any further – and he was in high good humour.

"Well done, Allerdale," Lord Somerton said, "you shall not put us to shame, that is certain. We shall see you this afternoon."

Miles raised a surprised brow. "I thought I had explained that I was already engaged."

"We are all engaged, Allerdale," Cranbourne said, smiling. "Lady Bassington has sent us all invitations to join your party at Richmond Park. We are to bring a basket of something, she did not specify what, but I assume she meant food as we are to enjoy an al fresco luncheon."

"I was unaware of the expedition," Miles admitted.

"I only received my invitation this morning," Lord Carteret said.

"You too?" Miles said, surprised. "What is she up to, I wonder?"

"Why should she be up to anything?" Lord Somerton said. "She seems to take no common delight in the company of both Georgianna and Marianne and the day is fine, surely that is enough reason?"

"She has good taste," grinned Lord Cranbourne.

"Undoubtedly," agreed Lord Somerton.

"Do you know," Miles said, "I am suddenly grateful that I have not yet had time to break my fast, for to hear you two waxing lyrical about your wives after so many months of wedded bliss, fair turns my stomach."

As his words were not laced with malice, and an amused glint brightened his eyes, neither gentleman took the least offence at these cynical words.

"Why haven't you had time to eat your breakfast?" Lord Carteret asked, looking at him closely. "Had a late night of it, did you?"

"The chance would be a fine thing," Miles said dryly. "It seems that since I came to Town, I have had very little time to consult my own wishes on anything!"

As he drove to Berkeley Square, Tibbs cleared his throat and said, "His lordship wishes to see you the moment we get back, sir."

His gloomy tone put Miles on his guard.

"Thank you, Tibbs. I don't suppose he gave you any indication as to why the matter might be so urgent?"

"No, that he did not," Tibbs said. "But he did ask me as to your whereabouts this morning."

"Did he?" Miles said softly. "And what did you tell him?"

"Only that you had asked me to bring your horse to you early, sir. I knew nothing else, after all. But he spoke to me in precisely the same way as you are now. I swear you are becoming more like him every day. It gives me the shivers, so it does."

Miles chose to ignore the comparison.

"You did not mention the footman or the letter he brought me?"

"No, sir. But he looked at me as if he didn't believe a word I said, anyways."

A reluctant smile curved Miles' lips.

"Do not concern yourself, Tibbs. My father would not rate a groom who did not keep his master's secrets."

He entered his father's study with an unconcerned

smile on his face. "Good morning, sir. How can I serve you?"

"I cannot imagine," Lord Brigham said, laying down his pen and regarding him with the satirical gleam that he knew of old. "But you will tell me, if you please, why you allowed your cousin to embroil himself in a duel."

For a moment Miles was in complete sympathy with his groom, for his father's words, whilst softly uttered, left their recipient under no illusion that prevarication was an option.

"I did not *allow* him to do anything, sir," he said. "I had no notion that he intended to meet Sandford until this morning."

"And yet you asked Tibbs to bring your horse to you at five thirty."

"I did," he said, just as gently. "I have become used to rising with the sun, sir, and if one wishes to ride hell for leather down Rotten Row, it must be done at an early hour." He smiled wryly. "It is one of the inconveniences of residing in Town."

"May I ask why you wished to ride, er, hell for leather, as you put it?"

Miles shrugged. "I have a great deal of energy, sir, and for some reason I cannot quite fathom, I no longer find the amusements offered in Town quite use it up."

Lord Brigham sat back in his chair, a small smile playing about his lips. "You have never been a liar, Allerdale, I will give you that."

"I am unmanned by your praise, sir," he said, his tone quite as dry as his father's.

Lord Brigham's smile grew wider, but he said nothing.

"How did you come to hear of the duel, sir?"

"I know the magistrate they were brought before."

"I should have guessed. It seems there is no one in Town you do not know."

"It is something you should cultivate, Allerdale. I mean persons who might be of some use to you, of course, rather than those who might help you out of a brawl."

"But I *am* doing so, sir," Miles said. "I have just come from playing cricket with Cranbourne, Somerton, and Carteret. Cranbourne appears completely reformed, and as for the other two, well, I think even you must agree that you are not likely to meet two more respectable gentlemen."

Lord Brigham sat up, planted his elbows on his desk, and steepled his fingers. "I do agree with you. I have always thought Carteret the best of your friends, and Somerton is certainly a good ally for you to have in your camp. But if you think to distract me from my purpose, Allerdale, you will not do it. You will give me a plain tale with no roundaboutation of this morning's unfortunate encounter."

"I do not know why you did not just ask Charles," Miles said, a little resentfully.

"*He* is not my responsibility, thank God! *You* are. It is your actions in the affair that I am interested in rather than his."

"Very well, sir. You shall have them."

He told him the whole, from his ejecting Sandford from the ball and the reasons for it, to that morning's events, and how he had come to hear of them.

Lord Brigham again sat back in his chair, his eyes narrowed as he considered all that he had heard. After a few moments, he said, "I have the highest opinion of Miss Edgcott, and on the whole, you did very well, Miles."

Although his words held no hint of emotion, the use of his name as opposed to his title, left Miles in no doubt as to the depth of his father's approval.

"Thank you, sir."

Miles was not left long to bask in his father's rare praise, however. Lord Brigham's expression suddenly hardened.

"And now we come to the matter of the lady in the lane. I do hope, Allerdale, that you would not encourage any of your lightskirts to come within shouting distance of your mother's residence."

Miles' eyes flashed. He rose to his feet, saying from between gritted teeth, "I have no idea how you come to know of that, but if you think such a thing of me, I have nothing more to say to you, sir."

"That might be so, but I still have something to say to you. Sit down, Allerdale."

It was not his father's words, but the softening of his expression that made Miles obey him.

"My bed chamber gives me a tolerably good view of the far end of the lane. I saw you carry someone there, and a few minutes later, I observed you drive off with her. Judging by the way she was curled into your shoulder, and the smile on your face as you spoke to her, I assumed your acquaintance to be intimate. I must admit, I did not think you would do such a thing; you did, after all, tell me that you would not embarrass me whilst you were in Town, and I have never known you to break your word on the rare occasions you have given it. Your understanding has never been lacking, Miles, so I am sure you will see why I might have jumped to such a conclusion. Your reaction to my assumption tells me that I was wrong, however, and I am happy to offer you an apology."

"I accept it," Miles said, a little stiffly.

"Thank you. Now, perhaps you will unbend enough to give me an explanation."

He did not like to lie to his father, and he did not do so, but he left out the details of the maid's true identity, merely stating the bare facts of the case.

Lord Brigham looked fascinated. "I shall certainly allow you to live at Murton when you choose a bride," he finally said. "It seems to have done you more good than I had dared to hope, my boy. It appears you are turning into a regular Galahad!"

Miles put up his hands. "Do not tar me with that brush, sir, it is not a mantle I have any wish to wear!"

"Sometimes, Miles," Lord Brigham said gently, "our wishes have very little to do with it."

As at that moment, Lady Brigham poked her head around the door, he had no chance to reflect on this comment.

"Miles!" she beamed, "I had not expected you so early. We are not due to set out for another half an hour!"

He rose, went to her, and kissed her cheek. "I had no idea that we were going anywhere, Mama, until Cranbourne enlightened me not so very many minutes ago."

"Miles, do you not read your post? Frances wrote all the invitations last evening and they were sent out first thing this morning. Apparently, she was inspired by the sylvan scenes in the play; she said they reminded her of the glades to be found in Richmond Park. I must say, I think it will be a perfectly lovely way to spend Charles' last day with us, don't you?"

"Undoubtedly," her dutiful son agreed, allowing her to lead him from the room.

Lord Brigham waited until their footsteps became indiscernible, before saying, "You may stop listening at keyholes now, Frances."

A deep chuckle sounded, and the door behind Lord Brigham that had been very slightly ajar was pushed wide open.

"You've always had eyes in the back of your head!" Lady Bassington said, unabashed.

"And you have always had a prying disposition. I had thought that aspect of your nature had lessened the stouter and lazier you became."

"Then you were mistaken," she said, not in the least offended. "It is just that there is so rarely anything worth discovering these days, at least not at home."

She came around the desk and sat down. "How *did* you know?"

"The draught," Lord Brigham said dryly, standing and closing the door. "I had thought that dark, little parlour was never used, and that door always kept locked."

Lady Bassington held up a key in front of her.

"So it is," she said. "Papa always insisted upon it too, but I knew even then which key unlocked it."

"I suppose I should not be surprised," Lord Brigham said, taking it from her and locking it again.

"You always did seem remarkably well informed. Would you be so good as to explain to me why you thought there might be something worth discovering this morning?"

"A mother's instinct," she said promptly.

Lord Brigham raised a sceptical brow and regarded her steadily. His sister merely laughed.

"That look might put Julia or Miles in a quake, Brigham, but it doesn't worry me in the least. If you must have it, I heard that butler of yours ringing a peal over poor Michael."

"The footman?"

"Yes. I was awake ridiculously early this morning, and try as I might, I could not fall back to sleep. I came down to the drawing room to find a book I thought I might have left there. That is when I heard the poor boy being told that if he ever failed to check if a letter was marked urgent again, he would be given his marching orders and that he was very fortunate Lord Allerdale had not boxed his ears."

"And what did you deduce from this information?"

"That the letter must have been delivered late last night, for it was not on the table when we returned from the theatre, and that it was of some importance. I could only think that perhaps a friend of his might be in need of his help, or perhaps it was from a lady."

"Well, now you know you that you were right on both counts, that should please you, although I do not think Miss Edgcott is the kind of lady you had in mind."

"I can hardly be blamed for that assumption, Brigham. In the normal course of events no respectable lady would be writing to him, certainly not at that hour of the night."

"I hope, Frances, that you have not mentioned any of this to Julia?"

"Don't be such a gudgeon, Brigham. Apart from anything else, she would have fagged me to death with dozens of wildly improbable explanations."

"Such as a duel?"

Lady Bassington laughed. "Yes, such as a duel. I must admit it never crossed my mind. How silly of Charles."

"Silly? It was downright foolhardy. I might have expected even you to be a little more shocked by the news."

"Why?" she said. "I saw him safe and well only half an hour ago so what was there for me to be alarmed about? I am only surprised he has never found himself in such a position before, or perhaps he has, I don't suppose I would know if he had. I liked Miss Edgcott on sight, you know, and am in her debt."

"Yes, we all are, I am sure."

Lady Bassington smoothed a crease in her dress. "I find this business about the maid, quite intriguing."

Lord Brigham was not deceived by her casual tone. "Why?"

"You have always been extremely acute, Brigham," Lady Bassington said with a small smile. "And your eyesight is excellent. If you thought it looked like this person knew Miles, then she probably did. And then one must wonder why a maid would wear so heavy a veil that she could hardly see where she was going."

"Perhaps she was in mourning," Lord Brigham

suggested.

"Again, I say, why wear one so thick? It seems far more likely to me that this person did not wish to be recognised. And if she had been so injured that Miles felt the need to carry her, why leave her alone in the alley whilst he fetched his curricle?"

"Because she was not injured, and he was protecting her identity," Lord Brigham said slowly. "Perhaps because she was not a maid."

"Very good. And as we have established that this mysterious person was not a woman of questionable morals and reputation, she must be a lady. I must say, it was very chivalrous of Miles to come to her rescue in such a fashion."

"Out with it, Frances!" Lord Brigham said. "What notion have you got in that head of yours."

"I hope you don't mind me saying so, but I have never found Miles to be innately chivalrous," she said gently. "And I can think of only one lady towards whom he might be feeling *particularly* generous on this *particular* day."

She had the satisfaction of seeing her brother look surprised.

"Miss Edgcott? But why on earth would she be traipsing about alone, dressed as a maid of all things."

"Apparently, Brigham, she was shopping." Lady Bassington sounded a little disappointed. "I must admit, it was not a very exciting reason to go about incognito."

"But I would hazard a guess that it became far more exciting than Miss Edgcott would have liked," her brother said dryly. "Let us hope she has learned her lesson!"

CHAPTER 14

When Eleanor accompanied Diana down to breakfast, she was relieved to discover that Frederick had not yet put in an appearance, feeling that she needed a little time to regain her usual equilibrium.

She picked up the letter that had been placed beside her plate and opened it.

"Would you like coffee or chocolate, ma'am?"

"Chocolate, please," she said absently.

"Coffee for me, Stanley," Diana said. "Well, Eleanor? Is it an invitation?"

"Yes," she said. "It is from Lady Bassington. She has invited us to go with her party to Richmond Park. She has also invited Georgianna and Marianne."

Eleanor had already accepted an invitation to go there with Lord Allerdale, but now the prospect of spending so long alone in his company did not seem quite so attractive. It was not so much his words that had upset her but the horribly cutting tone in which he had uttered them. How dared he speak to her in such a way? This was a much better scheme, and although she thought it highly likely that he would be one of the party, it should be easy enough to ensure that he had no opportunity to cut at her again.

"When does she intend to go?" Diana asked.

"Today. She says she will call for us at twelve o'clock unless she hears otherwise."

"Who will call for you?" Lord Haverham said, coming into the room.

"Lady Bassington," Diana said. "She has invited us to go to Richmond Park with her. Would you like to accompany us?"

"Why not?" Lord Haverham said. "I can think of nothing I would rather do than stroll with my wife through the park. We might even catch sight of the deer; you would like that, Diana. But I shall take you myself, in the barouche, you are looking a little pale, my dear, and the fresh air will do you good."

"Thank you," she said softly, reaching for her coffee.

Eleanor pushed her chair back. "I had better go and write a note to Lady Bassington informing her that we have no need of her escort, and I will need to have a word with Mrs Finley as she has asked us to bring a basket of something. Apparently, we are to enjoy an al fresco luncheon."

"There is time enough, Eleanor," Lord Haverham said. "Eat your breakfast first; there is little enough of you as it is."

Eleanor had half risen, but she sat again and obediently nibbled at a piece of bread and butter. Diana put down her cup and suddenly slumped forwards, resting her elbows on the table and dropping her head into her hands.

"Diana?" Lord Haverham said, looking a little alarmed. "You do not look well."

She did not answer him, but sat drawing in long, slow breaths, apparently unable to speak.

"Are you feeling sick again?" Eleanor asked.

"Yes," Diana whispered. "I think it was the coffee."

This pronouncement seemed to act powerfully upon Lord Haverham. He rose so swiftly to his feet that his chair went toppling backwards, but he no longer looked alarmed, on the contrary, his eyes gleamed with a mixture of hope and excitement.

"My dear," he said, "my love, dare I to hope… could it be… what I mean to say is that the only time I have ever known coffee to make you feel ill is when you are in a delicate condition."

Diana roused herself enough to raise her head.

"You are right, Freddy," she murmured, her eyes widening. "Do you mind?"

"Mind?" he said, "Mind? My darling, my angel, I could not be more pleased."

He went to her and scooped her up. "I shall take you to your maid immediately. She will know what is best for you."

Diana wilted against him. "Yes, but hurry, dearest, I am afraid I am about to be dreadfully ill."

"Out of the way, Stanley," he snapped.

The footman sprang back from the chair he had just picked up and flattened himself against the wall. Eleanor offered him a sympathetic smile as Lord Haverham strode hastily from the room, and then considered the half-eaten slice of bread and butter upon her plate. After a moment she pushed it away. *My love, my angel, Freddy!* If that was what falling in love reduced one to, she hoped very much that she would not become a victim to its clutches. Whilst she was pleased that Frederick and Diana seemed to be enjoying a second honeymoon, she found these exchanges rather cloying.

She did not write to Lady Bassington, assuming that neither Diana nor Frederick would be accompanying her anywhere but instead penned a few lines to Miss Crabtree, sure that she would be on tenterhooks until she knew the results her letter had produced. She then went to the kitchen and desired Mrs Finley to pack whatever she thought would be appropriate for an al fresco luncheon.

It was not Lady Bassington who came to collect her, however, but Georgianna and Marianne, their carriage flanked by Lord Somerton and Lord Cranbourne on horseback.

"Lady Bassington asked us to bring you, after all," Georgianna said, once the door was closed behind her. "She had also invited Lady Selena Sheringham but seems not to have considered that five people would be rather too many in one carriage. Is Lady Haverham not coming?"

"She is not well," Eleanor said. "It appears that Diana is also expecting a happy event, but she is not as fortunate as you, Georgianna; she is suffering from all those horrid symptoms you described to me."

"Poor Diana!" Marianne said. "But perhaps it is all for the best, Eleanor, for I am afraid that both Georgianna and I are leaving Town the day after tomorrow, and so we will not be able to help keep Lord Sandford away from Lady Haverham. We will have much to do tomorrow as we will be leaving early the following morning."

"This is a little sudden," Eleanor said.

"I know, and I do apologise. My very good friend and neighbour, Lady Charlotte Bamber, has given birth to a little boy, and whilst he is perfectly healthy, her mama-in-law hinted in the letter she sent me that Charlotte is not quite herself. I feel I must go to her, for I am always able to lift her spirits and bolster her confidence, which is what I suspect she needs most."

"Yes, of course. And are you also to go, Georgianna?"

"No, although I shall certainly pay her a visit when I can; we all shared a room at Miss Wolfraston's Seminary. Besides, I wish to discover exactly what to expect when my time comes."

"I hope that it is not bad news that has called you away?" Eleanor said.

"No, although Somerton has received a letter from his father." An amused smile lit her eyes. "The duke is sadly out of curl. He said that he hoped we were enjoying gadding about Town and that we were not to spare him a thought for he was quite used to rattling around Rushwick Park on his own, after all."

"Oh dear," Eleanor said. "He is feeling sorry for himself."

"Precisely. Somerton said I should not be taken in by his humdudgeon, that he was a manipulative, overbearing old scoundrel who would manage very well without us for a few more weeks." Georgianna smiled. "He is all of those things, as I have often told him, but he is a dear underneath his gruffness, at least to me, and I am aware how selfish I am being in keeping my condition from him when I know he will be cast into transports by the news."

"I shall be sorry to see you both go," Eleanor admitted. "But only because I shall miss your friendship. I suspect that Haverham will send Diana back to Standon at any moment, and even if he doesn't, Lord Sandford is no longer a problem."

"Why not?"

Marianne and Georgianna had spoken as one, and Eleanor laughed. She did not hesitate to tell them of her morning's adventures. Marianne found no fault with her plan and fully entered into her indignation at the way Lord Allerdale had spoken to her.

"But I must admit, that apart from that, he behaved very handsomely," she said.

"Yes, he did," Georgianna said. "He behaved impeccably, and I am sorry if you do not like it, Eleanor, but I will go further. I can find no fault with his words to you, although I do, of course, understand that you did not like the manner of their delivery. But he was quite correct you know, there were many things that could have gone wrong, and in fact, something did go wrong when you decided, for some reason not yet entirely clear to me, to go to Madame Lafayette's."

"Yes," Eleanor agreed. "But I could hardly have foreseen that Eliza Langton would come to the shop and then accuse me of being a thief!"

"That is my point," Georgianna said. "You only accounted for the things you could foresee, but even the best laid plans may be ruined by chance."

"So it appears," Eleanor said, with a reluctant

smile. "But chance also sometimes works in our favour."

"True, but you cannot rely on it. I will admit, however, that it worked in my favour the day Somerton rode up the drive to my aunt's cottage."

"And it worked for me," Marianne said softly, "when Cranbourne came to Cheltenham after a chance encounter with his friend, Sir Horace Bamber."

"And I suppose it also worked for me when I ran into Lord Allerdale instead of another who might not have helped protect my identity."

Eleanor saw her friends exchange a smile.

She laughed but said firmly, "If either of you thinks that our encounter shall prove to be fateful and lead to a love match as it did for you both, rid yourselves of the idea. I have no wish for a husband who would rip up at me whenever I displeased him. And as I will admit that I like to have my own way quite as much as I am sure he does, we would be forever at each other's throats! Besides, I have other plans."

"Are you still set on having your own establishment in Town?" Georgianna asked.

"I would like to have my own house," she admitted. "But it seems that it would not be *quite the thing* for me to do so. It is yet another of those rules that make no sense to me; if I had a spinster aunt it would be entirely acceptable, but a hired companion will not do, at least not for a few years yet." She sighed ruefully. "And I had not considered that if I showed to the world that I preferred to live with a stranger, it would reflect badly on Haverham. When I go back to Standon, I shall search the family Bible and see if I can discover some obscure relative who might do. Although I do not need to reside in Town, there are reasons why it might be useful to have somewhere I can visit regularly."

"Such as?" Marianne asked.

Eleanor had not shared with anyone her intention to invest in Mrs Willis and put her in Madame Lafayette's premises.

"I know it would be considered going into trade," she said, a little defiantly. "And I am aware that Haverham will not like it, but my involvement does not need to be generally known, after all."

"I think it a splendid idea," Marianne said. "When next I am in Town, I will certainly buy one of your hats and tell all of my acquaintances where I purchased it."

"As will I," Georgianna said. "And I dare say that if your business becomes a success – and I cannot see why it should not – society will forgive you, should they discover your involvement."

"Thank you," Eleanor said. "But nothing is as yet certain. I shall go and see my solicitor tomorrow for he has not yet replied to my enquiries."

They joined Lady Bassington's party at the gate and the cavalcade moved into the park. Eleanor caught glimpses of rolling hills, wide grassy slopes, and groves of ancient trees and when they descended from the carriage at a spot chosen by Lady Bassington, she was presented with a delightfully picturesque view. The parkland spread out for miles in front of her, a ribbon of river glinted in the sunlight in the valley below, and in the hazy distance she could just make out the spire of St Paul's Cathedral.

Eleanor wondered just how many people Lady Bassington had invited, for although Lord Brigham, Lord Allerdale, Captain Bassington and Lord Carteret had all chosen to ride, there were two carriages drawn up in front of theirs. The doors of one suddenly burst open and two footmen sprang out, followed by three grooms, and another descended from the roof. All was bustle for a few moments as Lady Brigham took charge, ordering the footmen to carry blankets, cushions, and baskets to a shady spot under a stand of towering oak trees, whilst the grooms took charge of the horses.

Lady Bassington came over to them, chuckling.

"What a to-do," she said. "I can't think it necessary. Julia has treated the expedition like a military campaign, but perhaps it is just as well; I always leave the details of my schemes to take care of themselves."

Lady Brigham came up to them in time to hear these words. She smiled. "And it is a fortunate circumstance that I am well aware of that, Frances, but at least you remembered to ask everyone to bring a dish. You must have stayed up very late organising the menu."

"You're out there, Julia," she said, looking surprised. "It's only a luncheon after all. I simply asked everyone to bring a basket of something."

Lady Brigham's pretty eyes suddenly sparkled with laughter. "Frances! You ninny! We will in all likelihood find we have enough to feed a small army, and I shall not be at all surprised if we discover that everyone has brought the same dish! It will serve you right if you have nothing to eat but slices of beef!"

"It wouldn't worry me in the slightest, my dear,"

Lady Bassington said, quite unperturbed. "I am very partial to slices of beef."

Lady Brigham ordered everyone to go for a walk whilst she and her sister-in-law delved into the various baskets.

They fell into two loose groups and Eleanor found herself walking next to Lord Brigham.

"Allow me to thank you, Miss Edgcott, on behalf of both my sister and myself. Your actions may well have saved my nephew's life."

She looked up quickly.

"You look surprised," he said softly. "You should not be you know; my acquaintance in London is wide. Once the tale was carried to Bow Street, I was bound to hear of it."

"Oh, I see," she said, her brow wrinkling. "I had not considered that. I do hope that my informing on Captain Bassington will not lead to the event becoming more publicly known."

"I have taken steps to ensure it does not," he said, with a small smile. "It is always so difficult to envisage every outcome our actions might have, isn't it?"

Eleanor held her breath. Lord Brigham's eyes were very penetrating, and she felt for a moment that he knew everything about her recent activities.

"Have you seen any interesting sights since we last spoke, Miss Edgcott?"

She cast about in a mind that had suddenly gone blank for something to say. "I was very pleased with the examples of Mary Linwood's needlework," she finally said, "but I hardly think that they would interest you."

"I don't know why you should make such an

assumption," he said. "I think some of her work very good. I purchased one of her pieces as a gift for my wife. It hangs in her private sitting room at Brigham."

"What a lovely present," Eleanor said.

"I like to think that Lady Brigham thought so," he said. "What else have you discovered?"

"Oh, nothing really; we have been so busy. Although I did catch a glimpse of the Foundling Hospital whilst out driving. I had meant to learn more about it and perhaps visit it but have not yet had time."

"My family have always supported the school," he said. "What is it you would like to know?"

"A little more about the children. Are they orphaned?"

"Some are, but many are the illegitimate offspring of some poor soul who cannot look after them. The school takes the babes in their first year of life and sends them to a nurse until they are old enough to begin their education. It keeps them until they are old enough to be apprenticed to a respectable trade."

Eleanor looked thoughtful. "And what are considered respectable trades for the girls?"

"They often go into domestic service."

"I see. Would millinery be seen as a respectable trade, do you think?"

"That would depend on the milliner. If someone of standing vouched for her, then I cannot see why not. It might also depend on the cost, however. Have you someone in mind, Miss Edgcott?"

Eleanor smiled. "Perhaps. I am not yet sure. You have given me much food for thought, thank you."

Lord Brigham glanced down at her, his expression

enigmatic. "If, when you are sure, you would like me to put your scheme forwards to the board, feel free to come to me and discuss it."

"You are very kind, sir," she said, her wide smile lighting her face.

She had purposefully positioned herself as far from Lord Allerdale as she could but had become so engrossed in her conversation that she had not seen him drop back from the group ahead to join them. Her smile faded as Lord Brigham gave up his place beside her to his son.

"Am I still in your black books?" he said, with a disarming grin. "I do wish you had not stopped smiling; it was like watching the sun going behind a cloud."

She threw him a darkling look, determined not to respond to his flattery.

"I see that I am quite sunk beneath reproach and will hang my head out for washing. Go ahead, Miss Edgcott, rid yourself of your spleen and throw my past actions in my face. Tell me what a hypocritical fellow I was to drag you over the coals, and do not fear to call me impertinent, not to mention ungentlemanly to talk to you in such a way when it was none of my business after all."

"Odious, odious, man!" she said, a reluctant smile edging her lips. "You have even rid me of that pleasure; how can I now do so, when you have already owned it?"

"Despicable of me to steal your thunder, wasn't it? However, I do own it, and I apologise. I do not say that my views on the matter have changed but will admit that the manner of their delivery left much to be desired."

"How can I fail to accept such a handsome apology?" Eleanor said, eyeing him resentfully.

"My only excuse is that I had had a very trying morning, and my nerves were quite shot to pieces."

She laughed. "You, sir, are shameless! What a bouncer!"

"I am shocked to hear such an expression on your lips, ma'am," he said, shaking his head.

She gasped. "You… you… Oh, I don't know what you are! But I refuse to listen to any more of your faradiddles!"

They had walked a circuitous route and were now approaching the point at which they had started. Two large blankets had been laid end to end, and upon them sat a variety of dishes, which contrary to Lady Brigham's expectations, did not wholly comprise of beef. A tempting selection of cold meat, cheeses, pies, cakes, and fruit awaited them.

Lady Bassington had been reclining against a pile of cushions but sat up as they approached, smiled at Eleanor, and patted the place beside her.

"You see, my dear, it all worked out wonderfully in the end. I could not have planned a better spread! I don't hold with over organising every little thing. I have always placed great faith in serendipity, and it has never let me down yet."

"You do not fool me, ma'am," Eleanor said, a mischievous twinkle in her eyes. "You certainly plan ahead when it suits you. I have not forgotten the opera glasses in your reticule or the extraordinary uses to which you put your walking stick."

"You are as sharp as a tack, Miss Edgcott," she said, smiling. "I will admit that I will sometimes bestir myself to plan ahead if by doing so, I will add to my comfort or amusement."

A tinkle of laughter made Eleanor look up and she was surprised to see Lady Selena smiling up at Captain Bassington.

"I am pleased to see Lady Selena at such ease; she is usually so painfully shy with gentlemen."

"The Sheringham lands march by ours. She has known him all her life, although she can only have seen Charles a handful of times in the last few years. I was great friends with her mama and am really quite fond of Selena. I invited her today as she always shows to better advantage when not with her stepmother."

"Matchmaking?" Eleanor said. "I thought you preferred to trust in serendipity?"

"I do. I shall make no effort to push her in the way of any of the gentlemen here. Unfortunately, Lady Sheringham does not fail to do so. I do not believe she has any great understanding of those with less robust natures than herself. She has hopes of Lady Selena contracting a great match this season, but her tendency to shrink from anyone who is unknown to her has been a trial for them both."

"Has she always been so shy?" Eleanor asked.

"No. She only became so when she left childhood behind and turned into a young woman. But once she knows someone well, she is a different girl. She came to me often after her mama died." She sighed. "Poor Amelia. She understood how difficult it would be for her and so did not bring her out the moment she left the schoolroom. We discussed it and agreed that no good could come of it until she had grown up a little. Unfortunately, she died not long afterwards."

"Lady Selena must have been very thankful to have you nearby," Eleanor said gently. "It cannot have been easy for her when her father remarried so soon."

"He waited a bare nine months," Lady Bassington said. "I believe he did so largely for his daughter's sake, but why he picked such a Roman-nosed dragon, I do not know. Amelia was very pretty; Selena is the image of her."

They both glanced in her direction. Charles was leaning back on his elbows, his mouth wide open, trying to catch the grapes a giggling Lady Selena was throwing at him. Her cheeks had a soft pink bloom in them, and her eyes sparkled. Eleanor thought that she looked quite beautiful.

"Perhaps they will make a match of it," she said. "I have never seen her look so animated or behave in such a playful way."

"I have no such hopes," Lady Bassington said regretfully. "He has always treated her as a little sister, just as he is treating her now. He could always persuade her to join in with the games he played with her brothers, not that they always thanked him for it. And then, Charles has no great expectations and who knows when he will be home again? Lady Sheringham has her own daughter to bring out next season and Selena is approaching twenty, so I am sure she will make every effort to find her a husband before then." She frowned. "I only hope she will not be forced into marriage whether she likes it or not."

"Would Lord Sheringham allow such a thing?"

"I hope he would not," she said, "but Lady Sheringham is very determined, and I have known more than one gentleman capitulate to his wife's wishes if it will ensure she will stop cutting up his peace."

A gurgle of laughter escaped Eleanor. "Do you speak from personal experience, ma'am?"

"That's it," she said cheerfully. "I see you have guessed it; poor Bassington is dreadfully henpecked!"

"Boys! Behave! You are making yourselves look ridiculous!" Lady Brigham protested, her smiling countenance robbing her words of any power to make them obey her.

Lord Cranbourne and Lord Somerton had also leant back on their elbows and were exhorting their wives to join in with the game.

"Whoever catches the most grapes in one minute is the winner," Charles said.

"And what will be the prize?" Eleanor asked, amused.

Various ideas were batted back and forth, and when Lord Brigham forbade them to wager money on such a ridiculous game, it was finally agreed that the victor could beg the lady of his choice one favour.

Lord Allerdale had been quietly chatting to Lord Carteret, but he suddenly said, "In that case, I shall join in." He quirked an eyebrow at Eleanor. "Will you partner me, Miss Edgcott?"

As all eyes turned towards her, she smiled sweetly and said, "But that would leave Lord Carteret without a partner. Would you like to take part, my lord?"

"I thank you, Miss Edgcott, but I have no desire to make such an exhibition of myself."

"Then you shall join me in adjudicating this childish competition," Lord Brigham said. "Julia and

Frances, we will need you also. We shall each observe one couple, and if there is any cheating, we will impose penalties."

Eleanor felt Miles' triumphant eyes upon her.

"Then I shall, of course, partner you, Lord Allerdale," she said, suddenly all compliance.

Fortunately, nearly everyone had brought some grapes, and once the ladies had all collected a handful, and moved a similar distance away from their partner, the game began.

Eleanor was determined that she would not give Lord Allerdale the right to ask anything of her, and so deliberately aimed wide, making it very difficult for him to catch any of them. Her smile widened in direct proportion to his eyes narrowing. At the end of the minute, the judges compared notes and Charles was declared the clear winner.

"And what favour will you ask?" Eleanor asked.

An almost embarrassed smile crossed Charles' face. He turned to Lady Selena and said gently. "Would you write to me, Selena? I would like to know how you go on, and a little news from home goes a long way when you find yourself in dashed uncomfortable barracks."

She nodded, her cheeks reddening as she became aware that everyone was waiting for her reply. "Of course, I will, Charlie," she said. "I only hope my letters don't bore you to death."

Miles glanced at his father.

"Did you not say, sir, that anyone cheating would be issued with a penalty?"

Eleanor felt a trickle of unease run down her spine.

"So, I did, Allerdale," he said softly. "As Miss Edgcott clearly did not intend you to catch any of her grapes, you were undoubtedly handicapped. I think you may also ask her a favour of your choice."

She found herself being regarded by a pair of eyes that gleamed with malicious amusement.

"I would ask you to grant me the favour of taking you for a drive the day after tomorrow," he said.

CHAPTER 15

M iles grinned as he saw the relief in Miss Edgcott's expressive eyes.

"As I had already agreed to go for a drive with you, sir, that is an easy favour for me to grant you."

"For some strange reason," he murmured, "I thought you might have changed your mind."

The rueful smile she offered him, confirmed his suspicion. Having decided only that morning that she was not at all the sort of girl he would wish to have for a wife, he should not perhaps have pressed the point, but he had taken uncommon delight in sparring with her, and the temptation to tease her a little more had been too great.

"Why would Miss Edgcott change her mind?" Lady Brigham said.

She smiled reassuringly at Eleanor. "If it is because you are afraid he will overturn you, you need have no fear. Miles is a first-rate whip."

Miles thought the smile that curved Miss Edgcott's generous lips, a little mischievous. He was sure of it when her eyes turned to him with an innocent expression that did not suit her. It immediately put him on his guard.

"Is that so? That puts a completely different complexion on the matter. I have always wished to learn to drive a curricle and pair." She smiled sweetly at him. "Would you be so very obliging as to give me my first lesson?"

Charles gave a bark of laughter. "Allerdale never allows anyone but his groom to handle his horses, I am afraid, Miss Edgcott. You are aiming for the moon!"

"Something I am quite sure, Miss Edgcott is aware of," Miles said wryly.

"No! How could I be?" she said, disappointment writ clear in her widening eyes. "Of course, if you doubt your ability to teach me, I quite understand; excelling at something yourself and being able to pass your skill on to another, are two very different things."

Miles' lips twitched. He was fully aware that the little minx was trying to goad him.

"I am afraid you are quite right, Miss Edgcott," he said, shaking his head. "I don't like to admit it, of course, but I fear I'd make a hash of it."

He struggled to preserve his hangdog expression as he saw the flash of annoyance in Miss Edgcott's eyes.

"You allowed me to drive your horses," Georgianna said, a dimple peeping in her cheek.

"Yes, and if I remember correctly, it was a disaster! Tibbs said that if I ever allowed a female to handle the reins again, he would be forced to leave my service!"

"Nonsense!" Lady Brigham said. "He is quite devoted to you. Do not be so disobliging, Miles. Your father taught me, after all."

"Yes, but at Brigham, Mama," he said. "And it was there that I tried and abjectly failed to teach Georgianna."

"The failing was mine and not yours," Georgianna said ruefully. "Somerton says I am a hopeless case."

Lord Somerton raised her hand to his lips. "Completely cow-handed," he agreed, smiling fondly at her.

"That does not change the fact that it would not be safe to teach Miss Edgcott in any of the London parks."

"I have always found the avenues in Hyde Park to be remarkably quiet first thing in the morning," Eleanor said, the mischievous smile again playing about her lips. "I suggest you pick me up at eight o'clock."

This reference to her early visit to the park that morning both surprised and pleased Miles. It suggested that he was completely forgiven and for some reason that he could not quite fathom, he did not wish her to think badly of him.

"Very well," he said, unable to withstand the amused intimacy of her expression, which spoke of their shared secret.

"Come to breakfast in Berkeley Square after your drive, Miss Edgcott," Lady Brigham said, smiling. "I shall be very interested to hear how your lesson went."

It was at this moment that Miles realised he had lost sight of his reason for being in Town, but his mother clearly had not. Although he was fairly certain that Miss Edgcott would not read anything into his invitation, he felt sure his mama would if he paid his attentions only to one lady. He looked across at Lady Selena. She had appeared like a tongue-tied, pretty ninnyhammer at the ball, but seemed a different girl in his cousin's company.

"If I survive my expedition to the park with Miss Edgcott, perhaps you will consent to drive out with me on the following day, Lady Selena?"

Her gentle hazel eyes widened in alarm.

"Do not be such a goose, Selena," Charles said gently. "You will be quite safe in Allerdale's company. He is almost like a brother to me, just as you are almost like a sister to me."

She smiled tremulously. "Thank you, Lord Allerdale. That would be very pleasant, I am sure."

As they rode back to Town, Lord Carteret said, "I am not sure it was the best of good manners to ask Lady Selena to drive out with you in the presence of the lady you had just proffered a similar invitation to."

Miles laughed. "Miss Edgcott will not care a jot."

"And how do you know that?" his friend asked.

"I just do," he said. "She is not throwing out any lures at me. I do not believe she has any great interest in me at all."

"It did not seem that way to me. I intercepted a look between you that suggested otherwise. It was just after she had mentioned that Hyde Park was always quiet in the morning. It occurred to me that it is not usual in my experience for ladies of fashion to frequent the park at such an early hour, yet only this morning I discovered Lady Haverham there."

"How fascinating," Miles said.

A sly grin crossed Lord Carteret's face. "I begin to think it is. She was accompanied by a maid."

"I should hope so."

"I did not pay her much thought, at the time, for Diana had been taken ill and my only concern was to take her home. It was only later that I considered the maid's strange appearance. She was very heavily veiled. This circumstance muffled her voice somewhat, but when I heard Miss Edgcott speak today, the tone of her voice if not the manner of her speech, struck a chord. And then, Miss Edgcott is unusually petite, and so as it chances, was the maid."

"Coincidence," Miles suggested.

"I think not. Of course, if you do not wish to explain it to me, I will respect your wishes. I shall simply ask Diana when next I see her."

Miles frowned. "Damn you, Carteret. It is not my secret to tell."

"And yet you are clearly aware of it, old fellow. I cannot help but also wonder how you came to be in possession of the facts."

"Why are you so interested, Carteret? Do not tell me you are still carrying a torch for Diana. I thought you had realised that you would never have suited."

"I have," he said quietly. "I don't know if you will understand this, Allerdale, but when a woman confides in you in such a trusting and innocent way as Diana did to me at the ball, one somehow feels a little responsible for her."

Miss Edgcott's laughing countenance when he had revealed that he knew it was she behind the veil sprang to mind.

"I do understand," Miles said, with a wry smile. "I see I shall have to explain, after all."

Lord Carteret listened in silence, his brows gradually gathering in a frown.

"Whilst Miss Edgcott's actions were well-meant, and her intrepidity cannot be questioned, it was a foolish plan."

"I told her as much."

"And how did she take that?"

"Not well," Miles admitted.

Lord Carteret smiled. "She is rather spirited. Are you really going to let her drive your horses?"

"Yes." Miles grinned. "But I shall be a very bad teacher and make her so uncomfortable she will soon be glad to relinquish the reins to me."

His friend laughed, but after a moment he sobered.

"What are we going to do about Sandford? I cannot like him hounding Diana in such a way."

"I do not think we need do anything," Miles said slowly. "I wondered why he did not keep his rendezvous, but I think we may safely assume that he has found easier game to pursue."

He nodded towards an approaching curricle. The beauty they had seen in the park sat beside Lord Sandford, her eyes were modestly downcast, and her hands clasped demurely in her lap.

"Do you still wish to rescue her from his clutches?" Lord Carteret said.

Miles shrugged. "No. Why should I? Sandford said she was still playing the pretty innocent. If she is what she appears, he will get nowhere with her, and if she is not, then she will learn a hard lesson."

Lord Sandford kept his eyes fixed firmly ahead as he passed the party.

"Did you see that fine-looking girl Sandford had with him?" Charles said, coming up to them. "If she doesn't put him in a better mood, nothing will!"

"Just as Lady Selena put you in a good mood today?" Miles said, raising a brow.

"I am almost always in a good mood, old fellow. I was pleased to see Selena, however, for she looked so unhappy at the ball that I was determined to make her laugh today."

"You certainly did that," Miles said. "You reduced us all to schoolroom status with your idiotic game. But if you are not sweet on her, why did you ask her to write to you?"

Charles laughed. "Sweet on her? Don't be such a numbskull, Allerdale. I just felt sorry for her. Lady Sheringham makes her miserable, anyone can see that. You don't fall in love with a girl you've known since she was in her cradle. Why, I've fished her out of the river, helped her down when she got stuck in a tree, and teased her about her freckles."

"I didn't notice any freckles," Lord Carteret said.

"No, they've gone," Charles said, a little regretfully. "It's a pity; I rather liked them."

"And she doesn't seem the sort of girl to fall in the river or climb trees," Miles said.

Charles grinned. "She wasn't always the little mouse she is now. She didn't have any sisters, so she used to trail around after me and her brothers. She fell in the river when we were fishing, and she climbed the tree because Gregory, her eldest brother, told her she might as well go back to her governess as she would never be able to do it."

"What made her turn into a little mouse?" Miles asked.

Charles frowned. "I have no idea. It happened when she was about fifteen; I came home one year and discovered she had developed a painful shyness with strangers. Keep an eye on her whilst you are in Town will you, Allerdale? Don't let her stepmother push her into marrying someone she doesn't like."

"Now wait a minute, Charles," Miles said. "What could I do about it?"

"Oh, I'm sure you'd think of something," he said.

"Your faith in me, Charles, whilst touching, is quite misplaced," he said dryly.

After a family dinner, Miles bid his cousin goodbye and good fortune and returned to his rooms. He picked up a handful of letters from his desk, settled himself in front of the fire, and smiled his thanks at his man as he placed a brandy by his elbow.

He quickly discarded the invitations, telling himself that he would dutifully look through them later and applied his attention to the letter Janes had written him about a few matters of interest at Murton.

He carried a branch of candles to his desk and penned a reply before turning his attention to his last missive.

Miles smiled. It was from Rebecca, an old friend. The vicar at Brigham was the proud father to six children, of whom Rebecca was the youngest. Having no siblings of his own, Miles had roamed the countryside with them as a child, and when Rebecca came to London to make her way in the world, he had promised the vicar that he would look in on her now and then. He felt a twinge of guilt as he realised that he had not visited her for some time. He shrugged. She would have written to him if she had wished to see him, as she had now.

CHAPTER 16

Eleanor wished her friends a fond goodbye as they pulled up in South Audley Street, promising to write to them with her news.

"You are very welcome to visit me at Rushwick Park," Georgianna said. "Indeed, I hope you will, for if the duke lets me out of his sight before I produce his first grandchild, I will be surprised."

"And you may also come to Cranbourne any time you feel the need to escape," Marianne said, smiling.

"Thank you," Eleanor said, touched. "I would like that very much." She suddenly laughed. "Now all I need do is develop several other close friendships, and I can spend my time house hopping with very little expense to myself!"

Georgianna smiled but said, "I do not think you are suited to such a lifestyle, Eleanor. You grew up in many different places, but your father made every place you lived in feel like home. I know you wish to be independent, and I admire you for it, but it is not the bricks and mortar that make a home, but the people you share it with. I grew up in one house only, but Avondale never felt like my home. Rushwick Park does because Somerton is there."

Eleanor blinked as sudden tears started to her eyes. Georgianna had touched a wound that was mending but not yet completely healed.

Marianne took her hand. "She is right, Eleanor. I know you wish for a house of your own, but you already have one, in Scotland, yet you were not happy there. You were lonely."

"You may be right," Eleanor admitted. "But the house you speak of was far from anywhere; one cannot be lonely in London and that is where I mean chiefly to live."

She had barely time to change before it was the dinner hour. When she entered the drawing room, she found Diana and Frederick in an earnest discussion.

"Eleanor," Frederick said, "tell me please if you think Diana looks perfectly well."

"She is a little pale," Eleanor said, but when Diana sent her a pleading look, she added, "I am sure that is only to be expected when she was so ill this morning."

"But Diana is regularly ill in the morning when she is expecting," Frederick said. "I have been telling her that there is no point in her staying in Town. She will only tire herself out."

"But I do not wish to go back to Standon without you, Freddy," Diana said, pouting.

His rather belligerent expression softened. "And I am sure I do not wish to be parted from you, my dear. But neither do I wish you to put your health, or that of our unborn child at risk. I am firmly of the opinion that you should go back to Standon immediately. The journey is a long one I will admit, but Eleanor will take very good care of you."

"But it does not suit me to go back to Standon immediately," Eleanor said. "Amongst other things, I have promised to go driving with Lord Allerdale the day after tomorrow."

Frederick frowned, his concern for his wife warring for a moment with his desire for his cousin to find herself a husband.

"You have, eh?" he said. "I hear he is much improved this season. I was talking to his father only the other evening. He was very impressed with how well Allerdale has run his estate in Yorkshire over the last several months."

"Then might I suggest, Frederick, that we wait a few days and see how Diana fares before we make any plans?"

"Thank you, Eleanor," Diana said. "It is what I have been saying myself. And I do not need to go out every evening, you know. Didn't I send a note to Mrs Wrangton earlier, excusing us from her musical evening?" She looked quickly at Eleanor. "I hope you do not mind."

"Not at all, Diana. My day has been quite busy enough."

"Very well," Frederick said. "But if Diana is still suffering three days hence, she shall go back to Standon if I have to take her myself."

This pronouncement ensured that Eleanor visited her solicitor in the morning with a sense of urgency. If she was immured at Standon and reliant on the post for all her communications, the whole business might come to nought.

Mr Layton, a very thin, tall man with a slight stoop, received his diminutive guest with a condescending smile.

"Miss Edgcott. You need not have troubled yourself to come in person. Please, sit down."

He rummaged amongst a pile of correspondence on his desk, plucked a letter from it, and held it up. "This would have been delivered later today."

"I believe, sir," she said quietly. "That I marked my missive to you as of some urgency, yet it has been some days since I asked you to make a few simple enquiries on my behalf."

His smile faded a little, and a wariness entered his eyes.

"Yes, yes, I am fully aware of that, Miss Edgcott. But as you see," he said, gesturing at his desk, "I am extremely busy just at this moment."

"I am pleased to know it, Mr Layton," she said, rising to her feet. "I need then, have no qualms about taking my business elsewhere."

The solicitor regarded his client with dawning respect.

"Miss Edgcott, please, do not be so hasty. I served your father faithfully for years and he never found any fault with my service."

"Perhaps you were more prompt in dealing with his affairs," she said gently, holding out her hand. "That letter, please. Perhaps I will find something in it that will make me change my mind."

Mr Layton suddenly looked at the missive he still clutched in his hand as if it were a burning coal. He ripped it up and dropped it in the bin by his desk.

"Perhaps it is best, Miss Edgcott, that you have

visited me in person, after all. There is much room for misunderstanding in the written word."

Eleanor raised a brow but sat down again. Mr Layton retreated behind his desk, opened a drawer, and withdrew a sheaf of papers. He perused them for a few moments, nodded, and looked up.

"Miss Edgcott, as you know, your father was a younger son and forced to make his own way in the world. He was very proud, I am sure, to be awarded a baronetcy for his sterling work for his country." Mr Layton looked thoughtful as if he was choosing his next words very carefully. "I know that he would expect me to look after his daughter's affairs with great care. He made his own fortune through choosing his investments very wisely. I know that it was his wish that you would be well provided for, and I am certain that his aim was to ensure you would never have to trouble your head over monetary matters. I cannot think that he would wish you to sully your own fair hands by investing your money in the way you propose."

Eleanor had known within moments of entering his office that Mr Layton, like so many of his sex, thought that a woman's place was in the home and that he had not taken her enquiries seriously. He had taken one look at the slight young woman before him and had thought that he would easily be able to deal with her. She had no intention of changing her solicitor; he was very well versed in her affairs and her father had assured her he was a good man who was to be trusted. But neither would she have her ideas or herself dismissed out of hand.

"Mr Layton," she said, "I know that my father

trusted you, and I am aware that you believe what you say to be true, but my father also trusted me to make my own decisions. What reasons, other than the daughter of a baronet sullying her hands in trade, have you for thinking that my scheme is not a good one?"

Mr Layton sat back in his chair, clasped his hands together in an attitude of prayer, and brought his long fingers to his lips as he marshalled his arguments.

"Your fortune is substantial," he finally said. "And if invested wisely will keep you in comfort, but it is not so large that you can afford to lose any great portion of it in a speculative scheme that might fail."

"I am happy to have my affairs in the hands of such a cautious man as you, sir, but nobody would ever achieve anything if they allowed fear of failure to stop them. Whenever Papa was about to enter into a particularly difficult negotiation, he used to wink at me and say, "*Oh well, nothing ventured, nothing gained.*" Eleanor suddenly unleashed her mischievous smile. "Besides, I cannot think my venture is as risky as you suppose; the fairer sex, you know, have an insatiable appetite for bonnets. Do you like mine?"

Mr Layton was a serious-minded man, but he found his lips stretching into a genuine smile in response to his client's sudden playfulness. He regarded her bonnet of straw-coloured satin that she had edged and trimmed with green satin ribbons and ornamented with a cluster of spring flowers.

"I am no expert, but it certainly appears to be very modish, and if you don't mind me saying so, suits you admirably."

"Thank you. I designed it myself. I enjoy creating

my own designs. Ladies of fashion often comment on my bonnets."

He again stared at her bonnet for a few moments, his large, sloping forehead wrinkled in thought.

"It is still a risky business, Miss Edgcott," he said. "Consider Madame Lafayette's predicament."

"Ah, but her bonnets are quite ordinary and her prices too high."

"I will take your word for it, Miss Edgcott, as I cannot comment on that aspect of the case. But I do know that she has also suffered from some of her clients either paying their bills after a lengthy period of time or not at all."

"I have no intention of allowing such a thing to happen to me or Mrs Willis. If our clients do not pay for their first bonnet when the bill is sent to them, they will not have another from us."

"That is an admirable scheme in theory, but you may swiftly lose your clients if you put it into practice."

"I do not think we will, for I intend for our bonnets to become all the rage. I have been fortunate enough to make some influential friends. Two of them are extremely pretty and they have already promised to recommend my bonnets to their acquaintances. One is married to Lord Somerton, who is heir to the Duke of Rushwick, the other is the Countess of Cranbourne."

Mr Layton nodded thoughtfully. "That would certainly be helpful."

Eleanor could feel him weakening. She did not need his approval of course, but things would be much easier if she could get him on side.

"And I will of course, only be a silent partner. Mrs Willis will run things and the shop will bear her name; my only contribution will be to fund her and to offer some of my own designs. Hers, you know, are excellent, and she is quite wasted tucked away in Cranbourn Alley."

"You seem to have thought of everything," he said with a faint smile.

"So, will you arrange the lease on the shop for me as soon as it may be arranged?"

"I will," he said. "I can see you are not a lady to be dissuaded and have not just dreamed up the idea one rainy afternoon without thinking it through carefully."

A gurgle of laughter escaped Eleanor. "I knew you harboured some such idea."

Mr Layton's answering smile was a little rueful. "Forgive me for my assumptions. You have surprised me, Miss Edgcott."

"You are forgiven." Her countenance took on a serious aspect. "I am not without sympathy for Madame Lafayette and if she will sell her stock at a reasonable price, I think we should purchase it from her. Oh, and once I am sure that the enterprise will succeed, I have some thought of Mrs Willis offering apprenticeships at a very low premium to girls from the Foundling Hospital. Lord Brigham has offered me his assistance in this matter."

Mr Layton's rather spare eyebrows rose at this. "You are well connected, ma'am," he said. "I begin to think you will succeed."

"And will you arrange for the sale of my house in Scotland?"

"Are you quite sure you do not wish to keep it?" Mr Layton said.

"Quite," Eleanor said firmly. "I was born there, but until recently I had not been there since I was a small child. After my mother died my father would not go there, you see."

"My agent in Scotland, who keeps an eye on the property, informs me that it is a substantial house. It was the only property of your grandfather's that was not entailed, and I believe he gifted it to your father on his marriage. It is, of course, yours to dispose of as you please, but it occurs to me that Lord Haverham may not wish it to go quite out of the family."

"I shouldn't think he will care a groat," she said. "He has never been there after all. But if he does not like it, he can always purchase it himself."

"Would you like me to broach the matter with him before I cast my net a little wider?"

"No!" Eleanor said quickly. "I have not found the right moment to discuss it all with him, but I see now that I must, of course."

She gave an instruction to the coachman and smiled at Stanley as he helped her into the carriage. Frederick had insisted she take him with her when he had discovered her about to leave the house and she had told him that she was going shopping; he appeared to think females quite incapable of carrying the smallest of parcels. The footman closed the door behind her and climbed up onto the roof.

"Well, Miss Eleanor? Are you finally going to tell me what plot you have been hatching?" her maid said in tones of deep foreboding.

"I shall tell you, Linny, for I am more confident that it shall happen now."

Eleanor was quite prepared for her maid to scoff, but when she explained the full sum of her plan, it was a small smile and not a frown that appeared on Linny's face.

"Linny!" Eleanor said, grasping the maid's hands. "Are you not going to try and stop me?"

"I've rarely been able to do that," she said dryly. "As far as your plans go, I'd say this one was the most sensible I have ever heard you come up with."

As Eleanor smiled fondly at her, the maid added, "But that's not saying much when most of them are completely outrageous! As you don't seem of a mind to wed, it will at least keep you out of mischief. You will be so busy designing bonnets and organising Mrs Willis, you shall have very little time to concern yourself with helping other people out of their difficulties, and that is what usually leads you into trouble." Linny's stern expression softened. "I will say this for you, Miss Eleanor, you have one of the kindest hearts I have ever known."

"Thank you, Linny," Eleanor said meekly.

"That show of humility is wasted on me, missy," Linny said, swiftly recovering from her momentary display of weakness. "You've also got a stubborn nature, no respect for the notions pertaining to the behaviour of young ladies of quality, and no idea of caution at all! In short, Eleanor Edgcott, when you think no one will know any better, you are a regular hoyden!"

A gurgle of laughter escaped Eleanor. "That is

why I'm not of a mind to wed, Linny. Who in their right mind would have me?"

The carriage had reached Leicester Square.

"I must inform Mrs Willis that she must not renew the lease on her shop," Eleanor said. "But there is no need for you to come with me."

Linny ignored her and followed her out of the carriage. "If you think I'm going to let you face those trollops – for nothing will convince me that is not what they are – alone, you've windmills in your head!"

She need not have worried, for the ladies she referred to did not step into the alley.

"You see, you need not have troubled—"

Both Eleanor's speech and her person came to a halt outside Mrs Willis' shop window. She saw the tall, handsome figure of Lord Allerdale inside. He was talking with Mrs Willis. Perhaps he had come to buy his mother a present. She watched him pass Mrs Willis a handful of notes, and then gasped as that lady, who had seemed so respectable, suddenly smiled, put her hands on his shoulders, leaned towards him, and kissed his cheek.

"I think we've seen enough," Linny said. "Come along, Miss Eleanor."

But Eleanor was frozen to the spot, a painful mix of disillusionment and anger running through her veins. She was not sure who she was most disappointed in; Lord Allerdale for proving himself a rake, or Mrs Willis for ruining her hopes. One thing she was sure of, however, was that she was not going to go meekly away. They should both know the discomfort of being discovered.

She marched through the door, a look of disdain

on her face. As the little bell that hung above it tinkled in an inappropriately cheerful manner, they both turned towards her.

"Miss Edgcott!" Lord Allerdale said, bowing. "What an unexpected surprise."

"Don't you mean an unwelcome surprise?" she said coldly.

Her gaze swivelled to Mrs Willis. That lady bowed her head in a modest manner and said in her well-modulated voice, "Good day, Miss Edgcott."

"It would have been a very good day, Mrs Willis, if I had not happened to witness the exchange that has just occurred between you and Lord Allerdale. It is rare that my instincts about people let me down, but I apprehend that in this instance, they have failed me completely. I should not, I suppose, be so shocked as to Lord Allerdale's actions, his reputation is hardly unknown, but you had me completely fooled! You would not be out of place on the stage, ma'am."

"How dare you speak to Rebecca in that way?" Miles' voice was soft, but his tone ice. "She is a vicar's daughter and one of the most respectable women I know."

Mrs Willis looked down at the notes she held in her hand and coloured. "Miles, hush. I am sure it was an easy enough mistake to make when the other shops have become so disreputable."

Rebecca? Miles? A vicar's daughter? Something told Eleanor she had made a dreadful mistake.

"I don't understand…" she began.

"That is patently obvious," Miles said, scathingly. "I had no idea you had such a commonplace mind, Miss Edgcott."

Although Linny spoke freely with her mistress, she was not in the habit of speaking to those above her unless they first addressed her, and so Eleanor, who had been momentarily silenced by these harsh words, was considerably startled when she suddenly burst into speech.

"Now wait a minute, sir," she said. "I am sure Miss Edgcott cannot be blamed for thinking such a thing, for it is what I thought myself." She raised her chin at his haughty look. "And if you dare tell me *I* have a commonplace mind; I might just forget my station and give you the sharp edge of my tongue!"

Eleanor looked in his direction, a little alarmed, but saw that it was no longer anger, but amusement that glinted in his eyes.

"Mrs Willis," she said quickly, feeling shame wash through her. "Please accept my sincere apology. I would never have believed such a thing of you if I had not seen you kiss Lord Allerdale immediately after he passed you some money. I would not have jumped to such a horrid conclusion even then if it were not for those, those… er…"

"Harlots," Lord Allerdale supplied for her helpfully.

"Those forward girls who haunt the alley," she said, ignoring him. "Can you forgive me for insulting you so?"

Mrs Willis smiled gently at her. "Do not give it another thought."

"Thank you," she said. "I do not deserve such easy forgiveness."

Her conscience would not allow her to ignore Lord Allerdale any longer. She raised troubled eyes to his, hot colour flooding her cheeks. "I also beg your forgiveness. I was too quick to judge… I do not understand what has just happened here, but I do know it was not anything disreputable." She dampened her suddenly dry lips with the tip of her tongue. "It was such a shock, you see, because I never thought that you… that you…"

She had got herself into a muddle, but Lord Allerdale's lips twisted into a queer smile and he said gently, "You are forgiven, you foolish girl. I was only angry on Rebecca's behalf. Her father is the vicar at Brigham, and when she finally persuaded him to allow her to become apprenticed to a milliner in London, I promised him I would keep some sort of watch over her. We grew up together, you see."

"Oh!" Eleanor groaned. "What a complete idiot I have been."

"The money you saw exchanging hands," Mrs Willis said, "was a repayment of a loan Miles made to me. You see, the lady I was first apprenticed to, Mrs Loosely, ran a shop along similar lines to the others in this alley. Miles not only extracted me from her clutches but paid the sum required to apprentice me to a more respectable lady." She smiled fondly at him. "He also managed to come up with a story to satisfy my father, for if he knew the truth it would have reinforced all his prejudices and I would have been forced to return to Brigham. As if this wasn't enough, he helped me acquire the lease on this shop when I first came here. I asked him here today to repay the loan, but he gave it back to me when I explained that I hoped soon to move to a more salubrious part of Town."

"I told you at the time, Rebecca, that it was not a loan but an investment, and I do not choose to withdraw my investment at this moment."

Eleanor suddenly wished the earth would open up and swallow her. She could not bring herself to look at him but closed her eyes.

"And this, Miles, is the lady I was telling you about. Miss Edgcott designs all her own hats; isn't the one she is wearing ravishing?"

"Quite ravishing," he agreed.

Eleanor's eyes snapped open and she saw that he was regarding her with an enigmatic look that reminded her forcibly of his father.

"And it is she who has proposed we go into partnership. Do you have any news on the premises in Bruton Street, Miss Edgcott?"

Eleanor saw comprehension lighten Lord Allerdale's eyes and dragged her own away.

"I do indeed," she said. "I came to tell you not to renew the lease on this shop, for I have just come from my solicitor, and he is confident that there will be no difficulty regarding the Bruton Street property. We should have it by the end of the summer." She smiled ruefully. "If, that is, I have not persuaded you that I am the last person in the world you would wish to be your silent partner."

Eleanor saw a sudden twinkle in the demure Mrs Willis' eyes. "Well, Miles?" she said. "Do you think I should go into business with Miss Edgcott?"

Eleanor's eyes flew back to his, a challenge in them.

He suddenly laughed. "Why not? Your business

acumen and Miss Edgcott's connections could well be the perfect recipe for success."

As Eleanor bestowed her wide smile on him, he added dryly, "I shouldn't think she will remain very silent, however, but I am sure your common sense will be the perfect foil to any of her wilder ideas."

Eleanor opened her mouth to protest, but Mrs Willis said calmly, "Do not gratify him with a response, Miss Edgcott. All of the ideas you have thus far lain before me have been both practical and sensible."

"I stand corrected," Miles said, grinning. "Miss Edgcott, allow me to take you home. I wish to further my acquaintance with the practical and sensible you. As I am on my way to Lord's ground, it will not be at all out of my way."

"Thank you," she said. "But my carriage is waiting in the square."

"You relieve my mind. It can take your estimable maid home."

"You go with the gentleman," Linny suddenly said.

Eleanor looked at her in some surprise. "Linny!"

"I speak as I find," she said. "And I've always held that actions speak louder than words. Lord Allerdale has behaved very gentlemanly to both you and Mrs Willis, so the least you can do is gratify his wish to drive you home."

Miles offered the maid his most charming smile.

"Don't think you can turn me up sweet with that smile of yours, Lord Allerdale, for you won't do it. Just take good care of Miss Eleanor, and I'll be satisfied."

"Very well," Eleanor said. "I will just have a quick word with Mrs Willis—"

"I am not married, you know," Mrs Willis said. "But it sounds more respectable. If we are to be partners, would it be unbecoming of me if I asked you to call me Rebecca?"

"Not at all. And you must call me Eleanor. Now, could you perhaps give me Miss Finchley's precise direction?"

Once she had been furnished with this information, she smiled at Miles and followed him from the shop.

CHAPTER 17

"I get the feeling," Miles said as he handed her up into his curricle, "that your maid has been with you a long time."

"She has always been with me. My mother died when I was four, and apart from my father, Linny has been the one constant thing in my life."

"He never married again?"

"No. He said he could never set another in Mama's place."

"That must have been difficult for you," Miles said gently.

"Not at all. I don't really remember my mama, and no matter how busy Papa was, he always made time for me." She grinned. "There were a few ladies who tried to make him fall in love with them. They would talk to me in caressing accents and make a great fuss of me once they realised how important I was to him."

Miles glanced down at her dancing eyes. "Did you scare them away?"

Eleanor laughed. "Not quite that, although I admit that when I was still a child, I would sometimes devise little tests to see if they were as kind as they appeared. Nothing too horrid, I assure you. I once knocked against a lady so that her wine spilled on her dress."

"You little imp."

"She went into hysterics," Eleanor said dryly. "Any lady worth her salt would have laughed it off, or said it was of no matter. Are you thinking that I wished to keep him all to myself? I am not so selfish. If it would have made him happy, I would have been glad for him to marry. But sooner or later the latest lady to try and catch his interest would do or say something, and Papa would give me a look and a small smile. I always knew what that meant; *Your mama would never have done that.* I knew then that I would probably never see them again."

"Did you never wish to settle in one place?"

Eleanor shook her head. "Every time we moved, I viewed it as a great adventure. I have never been shy you see."

"No, you are unusually open."

Eleanor smiled up at him. "Only with my friends."

Miles was surprised to feel a little twinge, somewhere in the region of his heart. He had eaten his breakfast rather quickly that morning, perhaps it was indigestion.

"You are fortunate, Miss Edgcott, to have the knack of making friends easily. I hope you choose them carefully."

"I almost always know immediately if I can trust someone," she said. "Speaking of friends; it is a little unusual, is it not, for the son of a marquess to be good friends with a vicar's daughter?"

"My parents have never been particularly high in the instep, and the vicar's lineage is perfectly respectable. Besides if we restricted ourselves to only mixing with the highest born families in Cumberland, we would be a very restricted circle."

"I, too, have had many friends who did not move in the first circles," Eleanor said. "I have always thought it contemptible to disregard someone only because they were born into less fortunate circumstances than you were."

When her confiding chatter suddenly ceased, he looked down and saw her brow wrinkled in thought, as if she were trying to remember something. Her eyes looked far away, but they suddenly brightened.

"Cumberland is very close to Westmoreland, isn't it?"

"Yes. Do you know someone there?"

"No, but do you perhaps know of a Sir Roger Crouch?"

Miles burst out laughing. "I should think I do! Do not tell me the tabbies are still gossiping about that? He was always a rum old stick and never came to Town and so the news of his marriage was a seven-day wonder. But it all happened years ago; why would anyone be talking of it now?"

"I believe his widow is in Town, although she has not been received anywhere."

"I should think not. It is one thing to have a friend who is not from your own class, but to marry a commoner, and one that has for years been your mistress, is quite another!"

Eleanor's eyes grew round.

Miles suddenly frowned. "Forgive me, Miss Edgcott. Perhaps I was a little too frank. I can see that I have shocked you."

"Oh no!" Eleanor said. "I hope you will always be frank with me. I am four and twenty after all."

A smile twisted his lips. "You are a very unusual combination, Miss Edgcott. You look upon the world with an innocent optimism that makes you seem little more than a child, yet you carry a pistol in your reticule, take the most shocking episodes in your stride, and it seems, have quite a head for business."

"But then I have had an unusual upbringing," she said. "We sometimes visited dangerous places, and my father took pains to teach me how to protect myself."

Miles looked down at her, a stern expression in his eyes.

"At those times, he should have sent you to school."

"I would not go," Eleanor said simply. "And when I told him that if he forced me to, I would find my way back to him, he believed me."

Miles shook his head. "You must have worried him greatly."

"Not at all. Besides, nothing bad ever did happen to us. I did once give him a fright though."

"Only once? You surprise me."

She threw him an arch look.

He grinned. "Do not pucker up. What did you do to give him a fright?"

"I got lost in the streets of Naples when I was about ten years old and was gone for some hours. When I became very tired, I went up to a group of men who were sitting outside a coffee house, told them I was tired, hungry, and thirsty, and asked if one of them would show me the way home."

"And did they?" Miles asked.

"Yes. But first, they ordered me something to eat and drink. Then one of them took me by the hand and led me home. I discovered later that the man had been the head of some criminal organisation. I found it very difficult to believe for he was very kind, but Papa would not have lied to me, so it must have been true."

Miles said nothing for a moment, a rather grim expression on his face.

"Miss Edgcott," he said finally. "How you have come through life thus far unscathed is beyond me."

"Linny says I have always had a guardian angel. I like to think it is my mama."

They had arrived at South Audley Street. Miles handed her down and stood for a moment holding her little hand in his.

"Try not to need your guardian angel before I collect you at eight o'clock tomorrow morning."

Eleanor laughed. "I shouldn't think I will; Frederick refuses to allow Diana out past eleven o'clock at the moment. She is in a delicate condition. We are to go back to Standon soon." She sighed. "I hope it will not be too soon, for I will need to sign the lease for Bruton Street and discuss several things with Mrs Willis. Enjoy your cricket match."

Miles watched her enter the house, a frown between his eyes. He would be sorry to see her go, he realised. Town would be dull without her.

Eleanor found her cousin at breakfast.

"Is Diana unwell again this morning?"

"Yes, and she is likely to be for weeks yet to come. Doctor Lampton took very good care of her the last time she was with child which is why I think she should return to Standon."

"Of course," Eleanor said.

"I hear you bumped into Allerdale whilst you were out, and he drove you home. It seems he likes you."

Eleanor considered this. "Perhaps, sometimes."

Lord Haverham looked pleased. "Very good. Very good. I noticed that Stanley returned without any parcels. Didn't you find anything you liked, my dear?"

Eleanor smiled as the footman poured her usual cup of chocolate.

"Thank you, Stanley. Would you mind leaving us for a few moments?"

As her cousin eyed her a little warily, Eleanor drew in a deep breath.

"I am afraid that I told you a little fib, Frederick."

"Oh?" he said, his expression of unease deepening. "And why did you feel the need to do that?"

"Because I was afraid that you would not approve of my errand."

Lord Haverham lay down his fork, wiped his mouth with his napkin, and sent her a stern look.

"I suppose it would be useless for me to point out that if you knew I would not approve of whatever it is you have been about, then you should not have done it?"

Eleanor looked a little shamefaced. "I did not wish

to make you unhappy," she said. "I have a great dislike of making the people about me unhappy."

"And *am* I about to be made unhappy?"

Eleanor looked across at him. "I do not know that for sure, but you are not at all like Papa, so it is difficult for me to tell. I certainly did not wish to upset you before I knew if my idea would come to anything."

"Eleanor," Lord Haverham said sharply. "Where have you been?"

"I went to see my solicitor."

"If you are about to tell me that you have gone directly against my advice and taken a house—"

"No, I have not," Eleanor said quickly. "I realised that if I did so, people might say that I was not happy with you. I would not wish to embarrass you in such a way. I have decided that I shall search the family Bible when we return to Standon for some relative who might be glad of a home with me."

"That is something, I suppose," he said begrudgingly. "Not that I think you will find anyone suitable. Now, enough of this prevarication. Out with it, cousin. Why did you visit your solicitor?"

Eleanor took what she felt sure to be the easiest option first. "Would you mind very much, Frederick, if I sold my house in Scotland?"

His brows rose in surprise. "No. Why should I? It has nothing to do with me, and you have no need of it as I am perfectly willing to offer you a home for as long as you wish. I daresay the money you will raise will be just as attractive to a husband as a house in such a far-flung place. But you had better run any offers you receive past me; I daresay you wouldn't know a good offer from a bad one."

"Yes, of course, Frederick," she said meekly.

He looked at her suspiciously. "Was that the whole of your business with your solicitor?"

She suddenly smiled. "I'll say this for you, Frederick, you are not at all stupid."

She surprised a reluctant grin from him. "I am glad you realise it. Dash it, Eleanor, just let me have it. The more you beat around the bush, the more worried I become."

"Oh, very well, I will tell you, but only if you promise not to breathe a word until I have finished."

Eleanor soon discovered that she had underestimated her cousin, for although he looked a little alarmed when she first rushed into her tale, by the time she had explained Mrs Willis' origins, her connection with the Brighams, and both Georgianna's and Marianne's assertion that they would spread the word, his heightened colour had receded. When she followed this by showing him her sketchbook of designs and mentioning Diana's assertion that if ever Eleanor lost her fortune, she could certainly make her living as a milliner, his eyes held something approaching respect.

"She was only joking, of course," Eleanor admitted, "But Diana does genuinely admire my designs."

Frederick blew out his cheeks and said, "You will definitely be a silent partner?"

"Absolutely."

"Diana has very good taste, and if she likes your bonnets, so will everyone else. Do you not think that you will be tempted to claim some of the glory if your business becomes a roaring success?"

"No," she said, smiling. "Knowing I have accomplished something will be enough. I like to accomplish things, you see. And you will know of it, Frederick, and so will Diana and my closest friends. That will be quite enough for me."

"I am pleased that my opinion is of some importance to you, cousin, even if you did not trust me enough to seek my advice before you went headlong into action."

"I thought that might rankle, but be honest, Frederick, would you have approved of my plan if I had laid it before you without having all the facts I have put before you at my fingertips?"

"No, I would not. You are a clever girl, Eleanor, I will give you that. God help anyone who gets leg-shackled to you."

Eleanor laughed.

"Yet Allerdale knows of this scheme and approves of it?"

"Oh, yes, but remember Mrs Willis is his friend therefore that is not so very surprising."

Frederick gave her a quizzical look. "I know you think you are awake upon every suit, Eleanor, but you may take it from me that you are not!"

Eleanor was far too pleased to have come out of this interview unscathed to begrudge her cousin the pleasure of having the last word in their encounter.

She paid a brief visit to Diana, whom she found propped up in bed, a resigned look on her face and a biscuit in her hands.

"I had forgotten quite how tedious this is," she said softly.

Eleanor perched on the edge of the bed. "Poor, Diana. Frederick says it will go on for weeks."

"Yes, but it will pass, and then I will feel wonderful."

"Do you think you will feel well enough to attend Lady Bessinborough's rout party, this evening?"

Diana looked dismayed. "Oh, dear. There is never anywhere to sit at a rout, and they are always so crowded that one cannot move. I don't think I can face it."

"No," Eleanor agreed. "I think some fresh air will serve you much better. I shall take you for an airing later."

"Y-yes," Diana said hesitantly, "but not in Hyde Park."

Eleanor interpreted this to mean that Diana did not wish to run the risk of seeing Lord Sandford.

"Then we shall take a stroll through Green Park."

Just then a maid bustled in carrying a pretty posy of flowers.

Diana suddenly sat up, a delighted smile on her face.

"Who are they from?"

Eleanor took them from the maid and read the card that accompanied them.

"They are from Lord Carteret," she said. "He sends you his best wishes and hopes that you are restored to your usual good health."

"He is such a gentleman," Diana said. "It is a shame you don't seem to care for him, Eleanor. He would make a very good husband, I think."

"He has shown as little interest in me as I have in him," Eleanor said. A small smile tugged at her lips. "Besides, he is *too* gentlemanly for me; I don't think I would deal well with an extremely correct husband."

Diana giggled. "Perhaps not; he would be shocked by your antics, I should think."

"Undoubtedly," Eleanor said. "Especially as I am about to follow your advice, my dear, and set up as a milliner."

"Oh, Eleanor, no!" Diana cried, bolting upright.

Eleanor had only meant to tease Diana but regretted her impulse when she saw tears start to her eyes.

"Frederick will never forgive you."

"He does not mind at all," Eleanor said, "or at least, not as much as I thought he would."

By the time Eleanor had explained more fully her role in the business, Diana was enraptured by the idea, and very happy to think she had planted the seed for it.

"I will, of course, get all my hats from you. When will Mrs Willis open the shop?"

"In September, in time for the little season," Eleanor said.

She left Diana in a much happier frame of mind and went to pay a call on Miss Finchley.

The house in Castle Street, whilst of genteel proportions, was rather dark. A severe-looking housekeeper showed Eleanor to a shabbily furnished drawing room. She took in at a glance the threadbare carpets and the faded damask-covered chairs and sofas and reflected how fortunate she was to be in a much more comfortable position. She turned as the door opened and Lady Crouch, dressed in a low-cut gown of deep purple, came into the room.

"Miss Edgcott," she said in accents of delight. "I heard how you had taken a turn about the square with my little Emily. It was very kind of you to approach her, for she is such a shy little thing that she will never put herself forward. You must forgive our shabby-genteel surroundings, rented properties are to be despised, aren't they? I declare Sir Roger would turn in his grave if he could see what I have been reduced to."

The idea that Sir Roger might have found it within his power to ensure that Lady Crouch was not so unfortunately circumstanced did flit across Eleanor's mind, but she firmly dismissed the uncharitable thought.

She took the plump hand offered to her, resisting the urge to sneeze as a strong floral scent assailed her nostrils.

"I was happy to renew my acquaintance with Miss Finchley," she said.

"Of course, you were," Lady Crouch said. "I am sure there is not a sweeter girl to be found anywhere in London."

She reached an arm behind her and grasped Miss Finchley's hand, pulling her forwards.

"Do not hang back, child, but welcome our guest."

When Miss Finchley, who had been quite obscured by her aunt's formidable bulk, had regained her balance after being propelled so hastily forwards, she curtsied, her cheeks a fiery red, and said in her soft voice, "I am very happy to see you again, Miss Edgcott."

"Please, sit down," Lady Crouch said.

Eleanor had hoped to have a private word with Miss Finchley, but it soon became clear that Lady Crouch had no intention of leaving them alone.

"I hear you reside in South Audley Street. Such a respectable address. Is it your own house, ma'am?"

"No. I live at present with my cousin and his wife, Lord and Lady Haverham." She was suddenly struck by inspiration. "I had hoped that Miss Finchley would call on me there; Lady Haverham has expressed a wish to meet her."

"There, Emily," Lady Crouch said with some satisfaction. "Did I not tell you that you need not think we would be imposing on Miss Edgcott if we visited her."

"Yes, Aunt," Miss Finchley said, squirming a little in her chair.

Eleanor did not care to imagine Frederick's reaction if he were to discover Lady Crouch in his drawing room. Even if he had not heard of her infamous marriage, he did not at all approve of vulgar persons.

"You certainly would not have been an imposition. But unfortunately, we are no longer receiving visitors just at the moment. Lady Haverham is in a delicate condition and feels dreadfully ill every morning and is then quite worn out."

"Oh, that is a shame," Lady Crouch said, her disappointment clear.

"But I am taking Lady Haverham for a drive later this afternoon. We could easily pass this way and take Miss Finchley up with us."

Lady Crouch's eyes narrowed. "How very kind of you. As it happens Emily is free this afternoon, but I could not let her go alone. Would there perhaps be room in your carriage for both of us?"

Eleanor said regretfully, "I am afraid not. I would, of course, have invited you also, Lady Crouch, if there had been. Lady Haverham will not go anywhere without her maid just at present, and there will not be room for five of us in the barouche." She stood to take her leave. "I quite understand your reservations, Lady Crouch. It is a pity, for I am not sure how much longer we will be in Town. Thank you for your kind hospitality. It has been very pleasant to see you again, Miss Finchley. Goodbye."

As she turned towards the door, Lady Crouch said, "Wait a moment, Miss Edgcott."

Eleanor turned and raised an enquiring brow.

"I have reconsidered," Lady Crouch said. "I feel sure I can trust my dear niece to you and Lady Haverham."

"We will take very good care of her." She offered Miss Finchley a friendly smile. "We shall pick you up at half past four, if that suits you, Miss Finchley?"

"I shall be ready," Miss Finchley said, coming forwards and taking the hand Eleanor was holding out to her.

She said no more but she did not need to; Eleanor could see both relief and gratitude in her eyes.

CHAPTER 18

When Eleanor returned to South Audley Street, she discovered Mr Pavlov had called and left his card. She stood for a moment in the hall looking down at it, chewing her bottom lip as she sometimes did when she was thinking. She had only meant to see if she could discover Miss Finchley's feeling towards him today, but it suddenly occurred to her that if the young lady did return his regard, it would be the perfect opportunity for them to speak with each other.

She took the card upstairs with her and dashed off a note to Mr Pavlov before going to see Diana. She found her idly tinkling the keys of the pianoforte in the drawing room.

"I have not heard you play since we came to Town," Eleanor said.

"No, there have always been so many other things to do." Diana gave her a small smile. "I thought that there was nothing that I enjoyed more than racketing about Town, but I think I am beginning to look forward to going back to Standon."

Eleanor sat on the stool beside her. "Nothing is as much fun when you are not in the best of health."

"It is not just that," Diana said quietly. "I have been thinking about all that you have done for me and all that you are going to do for yourself." She sighed. "I wish that I was more like you, Eleanor."

"That would not do at all," Eleanor said, laughing. "Frederick would not like it if you turned into a managing female!"

"No," Diana said. "I will never be that. But I think I could manage better than I do. Mrs Finley brought me a glass of hot milk after you had gone – dear Freddy asked her to – and when I suggested we discuss the menu for dinner, she said there was no need for me to bother my head as you had already done so."

"I always do so."

"Yes, I have imposed upon you dreadfully whilst I have thought of nothing but my own pleasure."

"You have not imposed on me," Eleanor said, taking her hand. "Or if you did, it was only because I let you. I wanted to be busy; it stopped me thinking about Papa and made me feel useful."

Diana squeezed her hand. "Is it still so terribly painful?"

"Only sometimes," Eleanor said.

"Then, would you mind very much if I take back the reins of my household?"

"I would be delighted," Eleanor said firmly.

"Thank you." Tears misted Diana's eyes. "It was only when I thought I might lose my lord's good opinion forever that I realised how much I could not bear for that to happen. He has given me so much, and I have given him so little." She wiped at her eyes and sat a little straighter. "I intend to make him very comfortable and take more of an interest at Standon. Do you know, Eleanor, I do not even know what his favourite dishes are?"

Eleanor smiled. "Talk to your housekeeper and ask her advice. You are a little starched up with the servants, and you will find they will respond much better if you unbend a little."

"I have always felt a little out of my depth," Diana admitted, "but I had a very nice talk with Mrs Finley today, and I discovered I enjoyed it."

"I am glad," Eleanor said. "Diana, do you trust my judgement?"

"Of course."

"Then will you trust me when I tell you that I am sure the lady you saw in Lord Sandford's carriage is not his mistress and that she is a dear little thing who might need our help?"

"In what way does she need our help?" Diana asked, cautiously.

"I think her aunt, Lady Crouch——"

Diana gasped. "Eleanor! We can have nothing to do with them."

"We are not going to have anything to do with Lady Crouch," Eleanor reassured her. "Only Miss Finchley."

When she had explained Mr Pavlov's situation, Diana looked thoughtful.

"I can think of only one reason Lady Crouch would spurn the advances of such a respectable gentleman," she said slowly, "and that is if she had someone else in her eye."

"And I think we can both guess who that might be," Eleanor said gently. "And you of all people know how persistent he can be."

Diana's eyes hardened. "Very well, Eleanor. I shall withhold any judgement on Miss Finchley until I have seen her myself."

They took Linny rather than Diana's maid, and both she and Diana stiffened as Lady Crouch, quite unable to resist the opportunity to speak with Lady Haverham, brought Miss Finchley out of the house.

"I am very pleased to make your acquaintance, Lady Haverham," she said, inclining her head. "What a pretty picture you all make. I am not at all sure I should let Emily go with you, for if you don't have every park saunterer ogling you, I will own myself amazed."

When Diana did not reply and gave only the frostiest of nods, Eleanor said quickly, "You may be sure, ma'am, that we would not pay them any heed, and Mrs Linwood here, would certainly know how to deal with any gentleman who dared to approach us."

Lady Crouch eyed the rigid, stern-faced maid and said dryly, "I can well believe it."

As they began to drive away, Eleanor said, "Miss Finchley, let me introduce my cousin, Lady Haverham."

Diana's expression thawed a little as Miss Finchley raised her bowed head to reveal two spots of flaming colour in her cheeks and eyes brimming with mortification.

"I am very pleased to make your acquaintance,

Lady Haverham," she said, her voice barely more than a whisper.

"And I yours," Diana said gently. "Please do not look so alarmed, Miss Finchley."

These words did not have the intended effect, for Miss Finchley suddenly gave a strangled sob, slid off her seat, and sat in a huddle at Diana's feet.

"Miss Finchley! Please, compose yourself," Eleanor said.

They were now driving along Piccadilly towards the park, which at that hour of the day was always crowded with carriages. Eleanor looked over her shoulder to see what might have caused Miss Finchley to behave in such an odd manner. She saw Lord Sandford's curricle coming in the other direction. She hastily pulled off her shawl and dropped it over Miss Finchley's cowering form.

"Do not look," she said as Diana began to twist in her seat.

Diana's eyes widened as the curricle swept past them.

"You may take your seat again," Eleanor said gently. "He has gone."

As Miss Finchley dutifully began to rise, Diana pushed her gently back down again.

"No. Wait a moment more, if you please."

The next carriage to pass them held Lady Langton and her sister. They exchanged nods, but fortunately, the road was far too busy to allow them to pull up and exchange any speech.

"You may get up now," Diana said when they had moved some distance away.

Linny put out her hand and helped Miss Finchley to arise from her cramped position.

"I am sorry," she said in trembling accents, "you must think me quite mad."

They had by now reached Green Park. The carriage pulled up and the ladies alighted.

"Come back in an hour," Eleanor said to the coachman.

They had gone no more than a few steps into the park, when Diana said, "Miss Finchley, has that man, for I will not call him a gentleman, done something to cause you to almost lose your senses?"

Miss Finchley's eyes darted uncertainly to Eleanor.

"You may speak freely. Nothing you say to us will go any further and we will help you if we can," she assured her. "We know that Lord Sandford took you up in his curricle the day I first met you."

"Yes," Miss Finchley said. "I had twisted my ankle, you see. I thought it very kind of him at first, but then he looked at me in such a way, oh, I cannot explain it."

"You need not," Diana said, "I quite understand."

Miss Finchley threw her a grateful look. "And then my aunt encouraged him to call on me and take me out driving. She was delighted that I had caught the attention of a marquess."

"But you do not seem to share her delight," Diana said.

"No, I do not," she said, her usually soft voice, surprisingly vehement.

"And yet you have entertained him at your house and allowed him to escort you about town," Diana said gently.

"I did not wish to," Miss Finchley said, tearfully. "But my aunt became very angry when I said I would not. She said I should be grateful to her for putting such an opportunity in my way, but I have never liked him." She gulped and tried to overcome the feelings that threatened to overwhelm her. "I had thought my aunt only had my best interests at heart, but… but..." Her voice wobbled. "I have discovered I have been quite mistaken in her. Last night we went to Vauxhall and he… he…"

"Kissed you?" Diana said helpfully.

Miss Finchley nodded and searched in her reticule. She pulled a handkerchief from it and mopped at her streaming eyes and blew her nose.

"I n-nearly swooned, and h-he just laughed and said he would wait, b-but not for much longer. H-he said he had a nice little c-cottage not far from London where I would be v-very comfortable."

"And what did your aunt say to this?" Eleanor asked.

"I thought she would be shocked, but she boxed my ears and said that I was n-not in a position to be so choosy and that there was more than one way to catch a g-gentleman if only I learned how to p-please him." Her cheeks flooded with colour. "She t-told me that she was Sir Roger's mistress before he wed her. Now I understand why Papa and Mama would have nothing to do with her. But I did not know, and she was so kind to me at first that when Mr Nutley, who was my father's solicitor, asked me if I wanted to go with my aunt, I said yes."

"It is very bad," Eleanor said. "But perhaps your aunt, although misguided, is fond of you in her own way. She has spent a great deal in bringing you to Town and fitting you out in the latest style."

"She has not!" Miss Finchley cried. "She has used the money my papa left me, and it is now nearly all gone!"

Linny had been walking a few steps behind, but she suddenly burst out, "It's downright unchristian, that's what it is."

Eleanor had not failed to note that Miss Finchley had not once mentioned Mr Pavlov's name, and as they were now approaching the fountain near the Queen's Walk, where she had asked him to wait, she said, "And is there no other gentleman who has taken your fancy, Miss Finchley?"

Miss Finchley gave a great sob and came to a standstill as if paralysed by her emotions. "Yes! Oh yes!" she spluttered. "There was a gentleman who was so gentle, so handsome, and I thought… I thought that he admired me, but he suddenly stopped calling."

"No, Miss Finchley, he did not," Eleanor said. "Your aunt refused him admission when he came calling."

Eleanor felt sorry for Miss Finchley, but she privately thought her a milky sort of girl, and so she was surprised when the drenched eyes before her suddenly hardened and flashed with unmistakable anger.

"How dare she? How dare she?"

"I think your aunt would dare almost anything," Eleanor said, quietly. "But look ahead, Miss Finchley."

She did so and saw a tall, slim, blond figure. "Mr Pavlov!"

For a moment they stood like statues, each

devouring the other with their eyes, and then both burst into sudden motion. Mr Pavlov caught her to him, and Miss Finchley melted into his embrace.

Eleanor was surprised to hear Linny give a sniff.

"You know I don't normally hold with you interfering in other people's business, Miss Eleanor, but if that gentleman is going to marry Miss Finchley, you have done a very good thing this day." She looked at Diana. "Both of you have."

"Perhaps the best thing I have ever done for anyone else," Diana said, her eyes misty. "I must admit to feeling a rather happy glow inside."

Eleanor was aware only of a feeling of satisfaction at a plan well executed. She could not help but wonder if she was lacking in some way. Although she had loved her father, their relationship had not been one of cloying embraces, even when she was a child. There had been an almost uncanny channel of communication between them that had been beyond words, a look, smile, or grimace, had been enough to convey their feelings. They had talked, of course, on any number of things, nothing had been taboo, and their conversations had always been frank and frequently laced with humour.

He had not raised her as if she had been a boy, precisely, but neither had he attributed to her a feminine delicacy that she did not possess. He had encouraged her to have an enquiring mind and fostered the independent spirit that had been hers from an early age. It had been very hard for her when he had lain dying and she had not been able to go near him, for his presence had always felt like an extension of herself, and she had felt as if a limb had been torn from her when he died, but even then, she had not been overcome by an excess of sensibility. Her heart had been frozen within her, but she had calmly discussed with his secretary the arrangements for her journey home.

He had always told her to follow her instincts, insisting that they were her greatest gift, and so she had gone to the house in Scotland and licked her wounds in private. She was not unfeeling, but neither did she seem to possess the finer feelings that were expected in a young lady of quality. Hysterics and swooning alike were quite unknown to her.

For several minutes they had walked at some distance behind the couple, who were oblivious of everyone else about them, their heads bent closely towards each other as they spoke earnestly in hushed tones, but Eleanor judged it was time to return to their carriage. She quickened her steps until she came up to them. Mr Pavlov turned to her and grasped her hands.

"How can I ever thank you, Miss Edgcott?"

She smiled at him. "What are you going to do, Mr Pavlov?"

"I am going to take her to Aunt Jemima, and then I am going to marry her."

Diana, clearly swept away by the romance of the occasion, said in awed but not disapproving tones, "An elopement!"

"No," he said, frowning, "I will not behave in such an underhand way, but neither will I allow Miss Finchley," he smiled down at her, "Emily, to remain under her roof another night."

"Then what are you going to do?" Eleanor said.

"I shall take Emily home and wait whilst she

collects her things. I shall explain to her aunt exactly what I think of her and what I intend to do."

"But do you think she will let her go?" Diana said.

"As I have told Emily, she will not be able to stop me. I do not believe for one instant that Lady Crouch is Emily's guardian in any formal way; Emily was nearly twenty when her parents died, and even if she is, I shall threaten her with exposure for immoral behaviour if she tries to take any sort of action."

"Then you are nearly of age," Eleanor said, surprised. She seemed younger.

"I will turn one and twenty next week," she said.

"Miss Edgcott, Lady Haverham," Mr Pavlov said, "I know I should not ask any more of you, but I will have to set my affairs in order and will not be able to leave town until tomorrow. I do not wish to leave Emily alone at a hotel. Could I bring her to you for tonight?"

Eleanor baulked a little at this, but strangely, Diana did not.

"Certainly, you may," she said. "But I would rather you did not mention her whereabouts to Lady Crouch."

"No, I shall give her the impression we are leaving this very day," he promised.

"Diana," Eleanor said as they returned to the carriage. "What about Frederick?"

"I think you underestimate, Frederick, and me for that matter. You are not the only one who can think of a plan, you know."

"Go on," Eleanor said, intrigued.

"Has it not occurred to you, Eleanor, that Miss Finchley looks rather like me. Our colouring is almost identical, although her hair is more golden than mine."

"Yes, I suppose that is true."

"And she has such a modest manner and shy demeanour that Frederick will only have to spend a very little time in her company before he realises what a sweet girl she is."

"Of course," Eleanor said. "And we will only tell him of her circumstances after he has already taken a liking to her. All his chivalrous instincts will be aroused."

"Exactly," Diana said. "But it is I who shall tell him of her circumstances, Eleanor, not you."

"You are right! When he sees you are not shocked, he will not be overruled by an overwhelming desire to shield you from one who is so closely connected to Lady Crouch." Eleanor laughed. "You sly thing, Diana. He is bound to also admire you for the kindness and consideration that you have shown Miss Finchley!"

Diana raised a brow. "And will I not have deserved his approbation?"

"Undoubtedly," Eleanor agreed.

"If ever I knew such a scheming pair," Linny said in severe tones. "Poor Lord Haverham doesn't stand a chance against the two of you."

"And do you disapprove of our scheme, Linny?" Eleanor said.

"Now, I didn't say that," the maid said. "Needs must when the devil drives."

CHAPTER 19

Miles awoke with a thumping head. He had returned to his rooms very late after the cricket match. His team had been the victors, and he had enjoyed the privilege of hitting the winning ball. He was carried from the field on the shoulders of Somerton and Cranbourne, a grin on his face. He had been surprised to discover as he raised his hand to the cheering crowd, a wish that Miss Edgcott had been amongst them, which was quite ridiculous, for what did women know of cricket?

They had put him down in front of his father, who had shaken him by the hand and said coolly, "Thank you, Allerdale, you have just won me a considerable amount of money."

"I had no idea of it," he had said grinning, "and I am pleased that I did not. If I had known, hitting that last ball might have seemed like a Herculean feat."

"That is why I did not tell you, but I have rarely known you to fail at anything you have set your mind to, whether it be an honourable goal or a disreputable one. Now, go and celebrate with your friends."

He had not hesitated to do so and had been borne off to several taverns to celebrate. He had abandoned himself to male company and a great quantity of wine, although he did seem to remember saying to his friends at some point during the evening, "Aren't you meant to be leaving early in the morning?"

"We are," Lord Cranbourne had confirmed.

"And aren't you supposed to be taking Miss Edgcott for her driving lesson at eight o'clock?" Lord Somerton had said.

"I am," he had agreed.

But they had, by that time, reached the stage where the morning might as well have been next year.

Lord Carteret, rarely a heavy drinker, had been the most cast away of them all. He had hiccupped and said, "I'm dashed glad I've got no female waiting for me to make an early appearance, for there's no doubt about it, I couldn't do it!"

Miles rolled over and groaned. He was not at all sure he could do it either. He had not imbibed such a great quantity of alcohol for nigh on a year! He was on the point of sending his man around to South Audley Street with a message when he suddenly remembered that Miss Edgcott had said something about leaving Town soon. He swore softly under his breath, threw off his covers, and staggered to his feet.

After he had thrown a quantity of cold water over his head and partaken of a substantial breakfast, he felt much more the thing. But even so, when Tibbs arrived promptly ten minutes before the hour, he took one look at his master and said, "Are you sure you want to be teaching a *female* to drive these greys today, sir?"

"I'm not sure of anything," he admitted dryly, "but I have always been a man of my word, and I'm damned if I'll break it just because I made a night of it."

"No, sir," Tibbs said in mild accents that in no way deceived Miles. "And if she breaks your neck, I'm sure that'll give you some comfort."

Miles laughed. "If she breaks my neck, Tibbs, I don't suppose I'll need any comfort."

Miss Edgcott had clearly been watching out for him, for she tripped down the steps looking as fresh as a daisy in a green pelisse, and a hat of chip straw, embellished with a plume of cream and brown feathers, the moment he came to a stop.

"Good morning, Lord Allerdale," she said, her smile almost blinding him.

Before he could move, she hurried around the vehicle, sprang lightly up, and gave him a very clear look. Miles had the uncomfortable feeling that she could see past his smiling countenance to the mess that lay beneath. His fears were confirmed when she said, "You have the look of a man who has had one bottle too many and is now regretting it."

"I cannot deny it," he admitted, his smile souring. "But it is not at all the thing for a lady to comment on it."

Her eyes lit with laughter even though her lips only curved up at the corners by the smallest degree. "I could confine myself only to the subjects ladies are supposed to talk about if you think it would amuse you."

The only thing he thought might amuse him at that moment was to press a kiss to each smiling corner of her mouth, before nibbling at her luscious lower lip. His hands loosened on the reins as this thought crossed his mind and the horses jolted forwards.

"It would not," he said, encouraging them into a smoother gait, "but I cannot help but wonder how an unwed lady with no brothers should recognise so precisely the state I find myself in this morning."

"I have always had more men about me than women," she explained. "I have often witnessed one of my father's employees come to the table looking the worse for wear. In my experience, it was usually because they had been cast down by something, or quite the reverse, and they had been thrown into transports of delight by something and celebrated in fine style." She raised a brow. "Tell me, did you win or lose the cricket match?"

"You, Miss Edgcott, are too clever for your own good," he said in the soft tone that Tibbs would have known to be wary of.

"I am sure you are right," she said mildly. "Mind your horses, sir, you very nearly scraped the pillar as we entered the gates."

Miles gritted his teeth as he heard a swiftly strangled chuckle issue from Tibbs. He brought his pair to a halt and handed the reins to Miss Edgcott, a satirical gleam in his eyes.

"Perhaps you would like to show me how it is done?"

"If you insist," she said, expertly flicking the whip.

The horses moved into a swift trot. Miss Edgcott threw him a glance quite as satirical as his own, before encouraging them into a canter and then a gallop.

It was not often that Miles was speechless, but this was one of those rare occasions. As he glanced down at Miss Edgcott's face, he realised that it was not triumph that had caused the wide smile to cross it, but happiness. He was certain that her joy had been enhanced by the knowledge that she had surprised him, but he somehow knew that its main cause was the experience, the freedom, of being in charge of a first-rate pair of horses and bowling along at a spanking pace on a fine spring morning.

"I wouldn't have believed it if I hadn't seen it," Tibbs said.

"Is this another thing your father taught you, Miss Edgcott?" Miles said, his smile now quite as wide as Eleanor's.

"Yes," she said. "He was always prepared to teach me anything I wished to learn."

"Anything?"

"Almost anything," Miss Edgcott amended. "He drew the line at teaching me to fence. I do not know why, for he taught me to shoot and drive."

Miles briefly closed his eyes. Thank God he had not let her free with a sword, the thought did not bear thinking about.

"You would be disadvantaged in any sword fight with a man, Miss Edgcott, you are not tall, and any man's reach would put you at a severe disadvantage."

"I suppose so," she conceded, slowing the horses to a sedate trot.

"Walk with me, Miss Edgcott," Miles said. "I need

to clear my head. And by the way, I was celebrating; we won."

"Congratulations." She suddenly laughed. "Did Lord Cranbourne and Lord Somerton celebrate with you?"

"They did. Why do you ask?"

"Oh dear," she said. "If, as I suspect, they are in just such a case as you this morning, I fear they will receive a severe scold. Georgianna and Marianne cancelled their plans last evening so they would be ready for an early start."

Miles grinned. He rather thought that they would both be in a worse case than he, for he had been the first to leave to the party, although he was not about to admit this to Miss Edgcott.

"I am sure they will rise to the occasion."

Eleanor handed the reins to Tibbs. "I am pleased to think I did not terrify you."

"No, ma'am," he said respectfully. "Far from it. It was a privilege to witness your skill. I wouldn't ever have expected to see such a fine performance from a female, except perhaps at the circus."

"Thank you," she said, laughing. "If ever I need to find employment, I will now know where to look."

They left the path and wandered over the grass. Eleanor came to a halt under a stand of trees, her eyes resting on the Serpentine glimmering in the distance.

"I think this quite the best time to visit the park," she said softly. "I used to wander for miles around the loch by my house in Scotland before I came to live with Frederick and Diana."

"You sound fond of the place," Miles said.

Eleanor shook her head. "No, I am selling the property. I will admit that the scenery is beautiful, but the house had not been lived in for years. Most of it was shut up, I lived in just a few rooms with a skeleton staff. I had thought that it was the damp, cold climate that I did not like, but I have come to realise that it was living alone, and without Papa in particular."

There was no self-pity in her voice, just resignation and a hint of pain. Miles discovered that he wished very much to banish that pain. He reached for the silver chain that he had draped about his neck and pulled it over his head. His eyes never left Eleanor's and he felt a spurt of pleasure as hers widened when the pocket watch that it was attached to was revealed. She held out her hand and he dangled the chain so that the watch rested in her palm. She ran one slender finger across the repaired glass face and then closed her hand about it, glancing up at him with such fierce gratitude that he lost his head.

He suddenly pulled her to him and did what he had wished to from the moment he had set eyes on her. His kiss was not gentle but greedy, and Eleanor responded without hesitation, matching his passion but in an innocent, untutored way that recalled him to his senses. He lifted his head but did not release her.

Her eyes were huge in her face, filled with passion and wonder. His heart turned over. Words that he had no idea he was about to utter tumbled from his lips.

"Eleanor, my clever, outrageous, fascinating, brave, madcap, darling. Will you marry me?"

He watched the flame in her eyes dwindle until it was just an ember and felt his gut twist in uncertainty when she did not immediately answer but straightened her bonnet.

"Ask me again, tomorrow," she finally murmured.

"Why?" he demanded. "What difference can a day make?"

She raised her hand to his face. "Miles, my impetuous, passionate, reckless, honourable, restless love. A day can make the difference in any negotiation. Ideally, you should leave three days, but I don't think I can wait that long."

"Why three days?" he said, interested despite his impatience.

"Because on day one you feel sure of your position. On day two you have had time to reconsider and might discover that you are not quite as keen as you supposed. And by day three, you have had time to view all aspects of your proposition in an objective way and are therefore fit to make a decision."

"Then it is not your own position that you question?"

"No," she said. "I am almost certain of my position."

His eyes glistened with intent, but even as he moved to pull her to him again, determined to rid her of any lingering doubts, she pushed him away and he immediately released her.

"No. I cannot think when you touch me, and I must. I had drawn up in my head a list of the things I desired in a husband, and although I had not thought you the man to fulfil them, my heart tells me otherwise. Ask me again tomorrow, Miles, after you have taken Lady Selena for a drive, or don't. I wish you to be as certain as I, and I will not hold a man whose head is thick from a night's carousing accountable for his actions today."

He reached for her hand and raised it his lips. "You, Eleanor Edgcott, are an extraordinary woman."

"An unusual one, perhaps," she conceded. "Before you ask me again, Miles, *if* you ask me again, you should consider that I am unlikely to be a comfortable wife; I am as stubborn as you and I like to have my own way unless I am provided with a very good reason why I should not."

Miles raised his brows. They had, it seemed, entered into negotiations. He made an effort to concentrate.

"That sounds reasonable," he said. "My only stipulation would be that you should discuss what it is you wish to have your own way about with me *before* you do it."

Eleanor nodded. "That also sounds reasonable. And you should know that I like to take an interest in everything about me. I like to be busy."

He smiled. "We will live at Murton, one of my father's estates near York when we are not in Town. It is a large estate and there will be much to keep you occupied."

"I would expect you to discuss with me your business also and consult my wishes before you make any decisions that would affect me or our children."

Miles took a deep breath. *Our children.* Those two little words struck him forcibly; he already felt a fierce protectiveness towards their unborn children.

"Certainly, and I would expect the same courtesy."

"Of course. I also like to travel, and I would expect you to grant me that freedom," she said a little doggedly.

Miles realised that Eleanor expected this to be the stumbling block in their negotiations. He hoped it would not be, but if she thought he would allow her to leave the country without him by her side, she was chasing at rainbows.

"Once it is safe to do so, *we* shall certainly travel abroad but you will not go without me. If you wish to come to London on a matter of business and I cannot accompany you, then my mother will. I will be surprised if she does not take an active interest in your project." He smiled. "She will adore you when she knows you a little better."

He watched as she caught her lower lip in her teeth and did not realise he had been holding his breath until she nodded.

"Very well," she said. "There must always be some compromise in any negotiations. Now, we have set out our terms and you have until tomorrow to consider them carefully. I will not hold it against you if you change your mind."

"I will not, I assure you," he said, offering her his arm. "We had better return; my mother will be waiting with some impatience for us to join her for breakfast."

~

As they drove the short distance to Berkeley Square, Eleanor felt the bubble of happiness inside her grow.

When Lord Allerdale had kissed her, the last frozen part of her heart had melted. There had been no gentleness in his embrace, and she had not wished there to be. His energy had flowed into her, mingling with her own and it had felt perfect, she had felt complete, and she had known that she had finally come home. She had suddenly understood why her father could not replace her mother, for surely such depth of feeling was rare. It was beyond rational thought; it was as elemental as thunder and lightning.

She smiled. For a moment Lord Allerdale had looked thunderstruck, and she had known that he had been taken as much by surprise as she, and so had allowed him a cooling-off period. But even as they drove through Mayfair, seated a respectable distance apart in the curricle, she could feel that they were still connected, that their energies were still reaching out and mingling. They had always had this connection she realised, from the moment she had looked into his eyes at Lady Brigham's ball, she had somehow known that she had found a friend, but she had not allowed herself to think that she might have found more. She had been sure that they would not suit, and she finally admitted to herself, she had been afraid to love someone again.

"Wait for me to help you down."

Eleanor blinked at this growled command and realised they had arrived. As she stood up, Miles ignored the hand she held out, but grasped her about the waist and lifted her down.

"Miles," she said. "Someone might see us."

"Let them," he said, unrepentant.

She glanced up at the house and thought she saw a hand twitch a curtain. As they entered the breakfast parlour, Lady Brigham rose from the table and burst into rather breathless speech, "There, Brigham, I told you Miles would bring Miss Edgcott to us."

She hurried towards Eleanor, her hands outstretched. "I hope you don't mind that we started without you, my dear, but Brigham seemed to think that Miles would be indisposed this morning."

"Not at all," she said, taking the hands offered.

Lord Brigham had also risen. He bowed. "Good morning, Miss Edgcott. I am pleased to discover that I was mistaken." He glanced at his son. "My compliments, Allerdale. Forgive me for doubting your resilience."

"I doubted it myself, sir," he said with a grin.

"You won't mind if I don't get up, I know," Lady Bassington said, nodding at Miss Edgcott. Her eyes twinkled. "Do you know, now I see you and Julia standing side by side, I cannot help but notice how alike you are. I wonder I had not noticed it before; you could almost be her daughter. Don't you agree, Brigham?"

"There is a passing similarity, I grant you," he said.

"In more than looks," Miles murmured.

Lord Brigham's lips twitched.

"Thank you, Lady Bassington," Eleanor said, smiling at Miles as he held out a chair for her. "I shall take that as a compliment, but I fear it is not as complimentary a comparison for Lady Brigham; she is far prettier than I will ever be."

"Sweet girl," Lady Brigham said. "Now, tell me, did you enjoy your lesson?"

"Yes, it was very…" Her eyes sought out Miles'. "Very exhilarating."

He laughed. "Miss Edgcott, Mama, is an excellent whip. I dare say she could even take the shine out of you!"

Lady Brigham gave a gurgle of laughter. "So, you were just teasing my poor boy when you asked him to teach you?"

"The temptation was irresistible," Eleanor said.

"Well, I should like to test my skill against yours, Miss Edgcott—"

"Not in Town," her lord said firmly.

"No, of course not," Lady Brigham said, the tiniest bit of disappointment lacing her words. "It would give the horrid gossips something to dine out on for weeks. Not that I would care a button."

"Miss Edgcott might, however," Lord Brigham said gently, "and I certainly would."

"Then it is, of course, out of the question," Lady Brigham conceded, "but I do not think you would object if we were to race at Brigham?"

"Not at all," he allowed.

"Do say you will visit us at Brigham this summer, Miss Edgcott," Lady Brigham said, her eyes sparkling. "It would be such fun."

"Mama!" Miles said, frowning. "Racing is dangerous, you should not—"

"I would very much like to see Brigham," Eleanor interrupted, "and I also think a race would be fun."

Lord Brigham sent an amused look in his son's direction. "Then that is settled. I think I should just mention that there will be certain conditions attached to this race."

"Oh?" Lady Brigham said.

"Each lady must have a gentleman seated beside her so that in the unlikely event that the excitement of the occasion should lead either of you to be overcome by a dangerous recklessness generally unknown to the gentler sex, your safety will be ensured."

"In that case," Miles said, grinning, "I withdraw my objection."

"But Brigham—"

"That is my final word," he said softly.

"Oh, very well," Lady Brigham said, "but I cannot think it necessary."

Neither could Eleanor, but she smiled anyway. She rather thought she would enjoy being part of this family.

When Miles returned her to South Audley Street, he bowed over her hand and said, "Until tomorrow, then."

Eleanor nodded, not daring to speak lest she begged him to ask her again immediately.

"Ah, Eleanor," Frederick said as she entered the house. "You've just missed Miss Finchley. Mr Pavlov took her off ten minutes ago, but not before I questioned him closely about his intentions. He seemed a very sensible young man. I also sent one of our maids with her for propriety's sake. I told her to go back to Standon afterwards." He shook his head. "I shudder to think what would have become of that sweet young lady if you and Diana had not befriended her. But all's well that ends well, eh?"

"It is a happy outcome indeed," Eleanor said.

He had been glancing up at her intermittently as he rifled through the post on the hall table, but he suddenly sent her a rather penetrating glance.

"Have you changed your style in some way, Eleanor? I can't quite put my finger on it, but you look different somehow."

"Do I? I can't imagine why," she said casually.

"Did you enjoy yourself this morning?" he said. "You should have invited Lord Allerdale into the house."

"I thought it might be a little awkward to explain Miss Finchley."

Lord Haverham's brows shot up. "By gad, it would."

"But I am expecting a visit from him tomorrow."

Something in the tone of her voice made her cousin look at her closely.

"Eleanor!" he said. "Now I know what is different, there is a softness about you, a glow almost. Has he proposed?"

A squeak came from the top of the stairs. "Eleanor! Is it true?"

"Yes," she said, "It is true."

Lord Haverham came quickly to her, put his hands on her shoulders, and beamed down at her.

"Congratulations!"

Diana ran down the stairs and threw her arms about Eleanor from behind.

"I shall miss you terribly, but I hope you will be very happy."

Eleanor suffered herself to be wedged between them for a moment before disengaging herself.

"I should perhaps mention that I have not as yet given him my answer."

Lord Haverham's smile wavered. Diana's mouth opened. They spoke at the same time.

"But you haven't refused him?"

"Don't you like him?"

Eleanor smiled. "I have not refused him, Frederick, and I do like him, Diana."

Lord Haverham looked relieved and gave her an understanding smile.

"Of course, your acquaintance with him is not long—"

"It is not that," Eleanor said. "I feel quite sure of my affections. I have asked him to ask me again tomorrow if he still wishes to when he has had time to consider my terms."

"Your terms?" Frederick said, looking a little uneasy.

"Yes, my terms. The things that I would expect from a husband."

Lord Haverham groaned. "You mean all that nonsense about listening to his wife's counsel and considering her feelings—"

"You listened to my counsel, Frederick," she said gently, glancing at Diana.

"Yes, well, I will allow that there are some things—"

"And you consider my feelings, Freddy," Diana said.

"Of course I do, my love, but—"

"And I am sure that if Lord Allerdale is worthy of Eleanor, he will not be put off by her terms."

"We shall discover *that* tomorrow," he said, retreating to his study.

Eleanor and Diana turned as the knocker on the front door sounded. Linton glided past them and opened it.

"Miss Crabtree," Eleanor said, coming forwards to greet her.

"I cannot stay," she said, smiling at them both. "I have just come to say goodbye. We are on our way home. Papa is waiting in the carriage."

"You must be very happy," Eleanor said, taking her hands.

"I am," Miss Crabtree said, her eyes crinkling in amusement. "Papa has told me that I am a very tiresome girl but that if I want Mr Shaddon, I shall have him."

"I hope you will be very happy," Diana said.

"Oh, I will be," Miss Crabtree said with certainty. "I only hope Lord Allerdale will find someone he can like as much."

"I think he already has," Diana murmured.

Eleanor sent her a reproving look.

"I thought there was something between you that night at the theatre," Miss Crabtree said. "It was nothing either of you said, but there was something in the way you looked at each other, as if a deeper communication existed between you. Or was I being fanciful?"

"No," Eleanor said softly, "You were not, only I had not quite realised it then."

An exasperated voice came from the carriage. "Come along, Anne!"

"I must go. Goodbye and good luck."

As the carriage pulled away, another took its place and Georgianna and Marianne descended from it.

"Take them up to the drawing room, will you, Diana, whilst I take off my bonnet and pelisse?"

Diana raised a brow. "Yes, Eleanor, it is my house after all."

Eleanor laughed. "You'd better hope Miles does not change his mind, for a house, it seems, cannot have two mistresses."

When she entered the drawing room some ten minutes later, it was clear that Diana had not been able to resist sharing her news.

"We knew it!" Marianne said, rushing across the room and hugging Eleanor.

"We suspected it," Georgianna corrected her.

Marianne laughed. "It is the same thing. It was something about the way—"

"We looked at each other," Eleanor finished for her. "It seems that everyone knew it but me."

"I did not," Diana said, a little peevishly.

"You would have if you had come to Richmond," Marianne said.

"I begin to wish I had."

"Nothing is settled yet," Eleanor reminded them.

"It will be," Georgianna said. "Once Allerdale makes up his mind about something he rarely changes it. I think you were very wise to give him a list of conditions, however. But it seems to me that your list wasn't very comprehensive. I think you missed a trick."

"Oh?" Eleanor said.

"Did you stipulate, for example, that he must never lose his temper with you?"

Eleanor smiled. "But then I would have denied myself the pleasure of provoking it."

"Very true," Georgianna acknowledged. "But you might have at least asked him to promise never to allow his dogs into the house."

Eleanor raised a brow. "Does he have dogs?"

"All gentlemen have dogs," Marianne said. "Georgianna used to be quite terrified of them."

"I am no longer," Georgianna said. "But I do not like them to roam the house at will. The duke's do."

"Well, I can't see any problem with that," Marianne said. "I think you should rather have asked him to bring you breakfast in bed each morning."

"Does Cranbourne do that?" Eleanor asked, laughing.

"Yes, and it is very pleasant."

"But I do not like to eat breakfast in bed," she pointed out.

Marianne gave her a knowing grin. "I did not think I did, either."

"I wonder if I should ask Freddy to do that?" Diana mused.

"Not at the moment," Eleanor said dryly.

Diana giggled. "No, you are quite right. He almost ran from the room when I was ill the other morning."

"But he did carry you there, knowing you were about to be," Eleanor said gently.

"Yes, he did, didn't he?" Diana said, on a sigh.

"I think," Georgianna said, her eyes kindling, "that the most pertinent thing you should have demanded of him, is *never* to go on a drinking spree the night before a journey."

"Definitely," agreed Marianne, looking unusually stern.

"Oh dear," Eleanor said. "I assume that is why you are still here. Miles was not on top form when he called for me this morning, but he was not incapacitated."

"Then I can only assume he did not imbibe as much as Somerton or Cranbourne," Georgianna said. "Neither of them have as yet, managed to emerge from their bed chambers."

CHAPTER 20

Lord Brigham had asked Miles to return to Berkeley Square. He found him awaiting him in his study.

"Sit down, Allerdale," he said, pouring them both a glass of claret.

Miles accepted the glass offered to him but looked at it dubiously.

"Drink it," Lord Brigham said gently. "I know you do not think it, but it will make you feel better."

When he had done so, he said, "Congratulations, Miles. I think Miss Edgcott will lead you a merry dance, but you will, at least, avoid the biggest causes of unhappy marriages; boredom and incompatibility."

Miles grinned. "You are premature, sir. Miss Edgcott has asked me to ask her again tomorrow when I have considered our negotiation."

As Miles explained, Lord Brigham's eyes glinted with amusement.

"I think you got off lightly," he said.

"So do I, sir."

"I hope you will not change your mind."

"There is not the remotest chance of it. I adore her."

The door behind Lord Brigham was flung open. Lady Brigham and Lady Bassington tried to come through it at the same time and became wedged in the doorway, and after a brief moment's undignified struggle, Lady Brigham shot forwards like a cork from a bottle.

Lord Brigham caught her and pulled her onto his knee.

She laughed and kissed his cheek. "Thank you, my dear."

Lord Brigham eyed his sister with disfavour. "I thought I had hidden the key to that door?"

Lady Bassington smiled. "You need to be a little more imaginative, brother."

"Oh, never mind that," Lady Brigham said, jumping off her lord's lap and rushing around the table to envelop her son in a scented embrace. "Miles! Oh, Miles! You have made me so happy."

"Stop strangling the boy, Julia," Lady Bassington said, dryly. "Although I must say, I am very pleased with him myself. Never knew he had so much sense."

"You have never valued him as you should," Lady Brigham said.

"On the contrary, I have always valued him exactly as I should, and I still loved him, warts and all."

"None of you seems very surprised," Miles said, ignoring this interplay. "And yet I had no idea I was going to propose until the words came out of my mouth."

"There was a certain charged atmosphere between you and Miss Edgcott when we were at Richmond," Lord Brigham said.

"And an even stronger one this morning," Lady Bassington said, chuckling.

"And the way you looked up at her before you lifted her down from the carriage, Miles," Lady Brigham said, softly sighing, "reminded me of the way Brigham used to look at me."

"Used to?" Miles said, laughing. "Everyone who has ever witnessed you and Father waltz has seen that look. Which reminds me, I have not yet had the pleasure of waltzing with Miss Edgcott. That must be remedied."

"Moving onto other, more mundane topics," Lord Brigham said. "I have received a letter from Mr Willis this morning, it was nothing of import, but it has reminded me that you have always taken upon yourself the task of keeping an eye on his daughter. Is she still prospering?"

"She is doing very well, sir, but two new milliners have set up shop in Cranbourn Alley, ones who, I am afraid to say, employ young women of questionable morals."

"Mr Willis will be most displeased at this news," Lord Brigham said, frowning.

"There is no need for you to inform him of it," Miles said. "Rebecca would not wish you to."

"But it is my duty to do so."

"Rebecca will be moving into premises on Bruton Street soon," he said.

"But, Miles," Lady Brigham said. "That will be very expensive, surely? And it seems only two minutes since she completed her apprenticeship. Is she ready, do you think, to compete with the established shops in Mayfair?"

"She completed her apprenticeship two years ago, Mama, and I have it on the best authority that her hats are something above the ordinary."

"Whose authority?" Lady Brigham said sceptically.

"Miss Edgcott's."

"Ah, I begin to see the light," Lord Brigham said.

"I will admit Miss Edgcott's hats are always very stylish," conceded Lady Brigham.

"She designs them herself," Miles said proudly. "She stumbled upon Rebecca's shop and intends to go into business with her, as a silent partner. It is Miss Edgcott who discovered that the lease on Madame Lafayette's shop would soon be available. She has already asked her solicitor to acquire it for her."

"I always knew that girl was something out of the ordinary," Lady Bassington said, "the moment I set my eyes on her."

"And you are happy with this arrangement?" Lady Brigham said, a little doubtfully.

"Why not?" Miles said. "Rebecca deserves this opportunity, and I will support my wife in her endeavours, as I hope you will, Mama."

"Of course, I will, dearest," Lady Brigham said, her eyes suddenly brightening. "I wonder if I will get a discount?"

Although Eleanor had assured Miles that she was almost certain of her feelings, that word *almost* ensured that he did not sleep quite as soundly as he would have liked. He did not feel much inclined to take Lady Selena for a turn about the park, but Charles had asked him to keep an eye on her, and so he did not fail to call.

He grimaced as Lady Sheringham pushed her out of the house saying, "Come, come, Selena, do not keep his lordship waiting."

Lady Selena flushed with colour and murmured something incoherent.

He handed her up into his curricle and offered her a reassuring smile.

"That's the way," Lady Sheringham said. "I can see you'll know how to handle a shy young lady, Lord Allerdale."

"I shall take very good care of her, ma'am," he said coolly.

"Yes, yes, I am sure you will," she said. "Take your time, we have no other engagements this afternoon."

Lady Selena's colour deepened even further.

"Do not be embarrassed by that old dragon," Miles said.

"Oh, no," she murmured, "I am not—"

"Yes, you are," he said smiling. "And I don't blame you. Subtlety is unknown to her."

"Well, perhaps," she said hesitantly.

"And you needn't be shy with me," Miles said, "As Charles regards me as a brother and you as a sister, we are practically related."

This drew a small smile from her.

"That's better. I know all about you, Lady Selena. You are a girl who falls in rivers and climbs trees, what other scrapes did Charles get you into?"

She smiled. "It would be more correct to say I used to be a girl who fell in rivers and climbed trees."

"Very well, I stand corrected. But I will share a secret with you; I have always admired girls who do such things."

He felt her withdraw a little way back into her shell.

"Do not fear that I am flirting with you," he said. "I am about to propose to quite another lady."

"Miss Edgcott?"

He laughed. "Is there anyone who doesn't know?" He glanced over his shoulder. "Tibbs, did you know?"

His groom grinned. "I had a feeling the way the wind was blowing when you let her drive your greys, and I was sure of it when you came back to the carriage smelling of April and May."

"Charlie said that you liked her," Lady Selena said.

"Well, I do," he admitted. "And although my heart is set on another, I hope you will consider me your friend, Lady Selena, in Charles' stead."

"I would like that," she said.

"Good. And you needn't be on your best behaviour when you are with me; as well as knowing what a hoyden you were as a child, I have seen you throwing grapes at Charles, so there is no point."

"Very well."

"That's better," he approved.

He set the seal on their friendship by regaling her

with tales of the least disreputable scrapes he and Charles had rescued each other from.

As they came near the place where he had walked with Eleanor the day before, something caught his eye. He pulled up his horses, jumped down from the curricle, and walked quickly over to the clump of trees they had stood beneath. He bent and with a slightly unsteady hand picked up a hat. The crown was crushed, as if someone had trod upon it. He smoothed out the bent brown and cream feathers, his heart beating uncomfortably fast. It was the hat Eleanor had worn only yesterday. He suddenly turned and sprinted back to the curricle. He was sure there would be a simple explanation; there had to be a simple explanation. Perhaps she had come for a walk, sat under the trees, and then removed her bonnet, forgetting all about it when she returned home. But he knew that Eleanor would never forget her bonnet.

"Lord Allerdale," Lady Selena said, picking up the hat he had thrown on the seat, "what is wrong?"

He turned his horses, flicked his whip, and drove towards the gate at a recklessly fast pace, "I pray to God nothing is wrong," he said, "but that is Miss Edgcott's hat and I wish to know why it was left lying crushed in the park."

He reached Audley Street in a matter of moments and took the steps two at a time. He rapped the knocker against the plate with such force that he dented it. As the door opened, he brushed passed Linton and said curtly, "Is Miss Edgcott in?"

"No, sir," he said, his countenance rigid, "she went out some time ago."

"What the devil is all this noise?" Lord Haverham

said, coming into the hall. "Ah, it's you Allerdale, well I can understand your impatience to see Eleanor, but she stepped out some time ago and is not yet back. She is expecting you, so I am sure she will not be much longer."

He held up the battered hat, "Was she wearing this when she went out?"

"I don't know," he said. "I never take much notice—"

"Yes, she was," Diana said, leaning over the banister. "What on earth has happened to it? And where is Eleanor?"

"That, Lady Haverham, is what I intend to find out. Where did she go?"

"I am not sure, but she took Stanley with her, so I assumed she had gone to do some shopping."

The band around Miles' heart loosened its grip by a fraction. "He is your footman, I presume."

"Yes," she said.

"And did she also take her maid?"

"No, I don't think so."

"Fetch Linny to me, would you?"

Linny, having heard the commotion in the hall, was already descending the stairs.

"Lord Allerdale," she said. "I don't know where she went; she's always disappearing off somewhere when my back is turned, but I didn't expect her to do so today. She shed a few tears last night when she suddenly got the notion in her head that you might not come. Don't you worry none, she'll turn up, she always do—" She gasped. "That is her hat! Oh, my, and look at the state of it. What can it mean?"

"I wish I knew," he said, running his hand across

his head. "But I will not stand here and wait to discover it. I shall take Lady Selena home and then go to my parents to see if she is there. Haverham, send someone around to Somerton's house in Mount Street, and Cranbourne's house in Brook Street, they were still in Town this morning."

⁓

Eleanor had awoken from a restless night, wishing she had not given Miles time to change his mind. Although she was almost certain he would not, a nagging doubt still remained. She was unusually indecisive, changing her dress three times before she was satisfied, and then, after coming down to breakfast and discovering that she could barely eat a morsel, she returned to her room and changed again.

When she came down to the morning room, to discover if she could distract herself with her sketchbook, Stanley handed her a card.

"This was delivered about half an hour ago," he said.

Her stomach clenched as she saw it was Miles' card. She swiftly turned it over and read the brief message. The hand was untidy, as if it had been written in haste, and it took her a moment to decipher it. She sagged with relief when she understood that he was not informing her that he had changed his mind. She drew in a long, slow breath and read it again.

My dearest love,

I cannot wait. Meet me beneath the leafy bower where our lips first met, and my heart was forever lost.

Allerdale

A slow smile spread across her face. He too must be as little like himself as she was this morning, for somehow the words did not seem like his. She could well believe the first part; *I cannot wait*, but the second seemed too romantic, too sentimental. She gave a low laugh. Diana might enjoy such treatment, but if Miles thought she wished to hear such stuff, he would soon learn otherwise. She would enjoy provoking him out of such flowery nonsense.

She found that she too, could not wait. And when she ran up to her room and Linny was not there, she threw on a pelisse and grabbed the first reticule her eyes alighted on. Knowing that Miles would not be pleased if she came alone, she resolved to take Stanley. He, she knew, would keep his distance and turn his eyes the other way if it became necessary.

As they approached the place where Miles had kissed her, she motioned for Stanley to stay back. She was not unduly alarmed when she did not immediately see Miles but peeped behind the trees, half expecting him to grab her and laugh. Someone did grab her from behind, but she sensed immediately that it was not Miles.

"Stanley," she shouted.

A hard hand clamped over her mouth. "Stand very still and I will not hurt you," a voice whispered in her ear.

She heard a cry followed by a thud, and even though she knew it to be useless, began to struggle.

"If you wish your footman to live, desist."

She immediately stilled and found her head suddenly forced backwards. As she opened her mouth to protest, a hand holding a flask appeared and she felt a hot, fiery liquid course over her tongue and sting her throat. She began to cough.

The whisper came again. "Drink it."

The flask tilted again, and she found she had little choice but to swallow or choke. Then the world went black.

CHAPTER 21

When she awoke, she found herself laid out on a sofa. The room was dim, the only light coming from the fire and a branch of candles. Her head felt thick and her senses dulled. As she turned onto her side, she felt something hard press against her hip. She pushed herself into a sitting position and took a deep breath, willing the nausea that gripped her to subside. She brought her hands up to her face and choked back a sob. If only she had listened to her instincts. She had known that the words on the card did not sound like any Miles would have written.

Her reticule was still attached to her wrist, and as it gently bumped against her arm, she suddenly understood what had dug into her hip. Her pistol! She had been so annoyed with Miles when she had returned to the house after her near-disastrous visit to Madame Lafayette's, that she had impetuously thrown it aside without putting the gun back in her drawer.

She bit her bottom lip. Although its presence

offered her some protection, she would not use it lightly. Her skin suddenly felt clammy. Miles' words came back to her; *Miss Edgcott, there are at least a dozen things that could have gone awry, especially if your pistol had come into play.* She had dismissed them, in truth, she had never expected to have to use it. Her father had made her practise over and over again and when she had become proficient, had told her not to think, just choose her spot and fire. But she suspected that a live, moving target would be a very different thing. She stood and walked a little unsteadily to the closed shutters, but she soon saw that the bar that secured them was padlocked.

"There is no escape for you that way, Miss Edgcott."

She spun around, closed her eyes, and staggered as a wave of dizziness hit her. She felt a hand grasp her arm and lead her back to the sofa.

"Here."

She took the glass of water offered to her and drank greedily. Her vision cleared and she looked up at her captor. He smiled maliciously down at her, before seating himself on the chair set on the opposite side of the fire.

"Lord Sandford," she whispered.

He leaned forwards a little and bowed from his waist. "Did I not tell you, Miss Edgcott, that it was unwise to meddle in my affairs? Yet not only have you turned Diana against me, and I suspect informed the authorities of my duel, you mortify me in public, and to add insult to injury, you whip Miss Finchley from under my nose. I do not think you can have expected me to withstand such provocation."

Eleanor shook her head as if to clear it. "You turned Diana against you, sir, I only helped keep you at arm's length. I did not wield the cane that tripped you up, although I will admit I derived some enjoyment from the spectacle. And I did not take Miss Finchley away from you, I merely enabled one who loved her to do so."

Lord Sandford sneered. "Love! Love is nothing but an intense burst of lust that soon wears off."

"Mr Pavlov will at least marry Miss Finchley and provide a home for her."

"I would have provided a home for her," he said bitterly.

Eleanor remembered Miss Finchley mentioning that he had offered her a nice little cottage not far from London.

"Is that where you have brought me?" she said. "To the cottage you keep for your mistresses? If you think I will take her place, you are mistaken. I would rather throw myself from the roof."

Eleanor was surprised to see a glimmer of respect in his eyes.

"I believe you. But no, that is not my plan."

"Then what do you want? Is it money? I have heard you are very expensive. Do you think to hold me to ransom? Or ruin me so I will marry you?"

He gave a harsh laugh. "This is not about money, Miss Edgcott, this is about revenge. I do not wish to marry you, only to ruin you."

Eleanor felt a cold shiver run down her spine. "If you attempt to lay one finger upon my person, you will be sorry.".

"But I don't wish to lay a finger upon you," he

said. "I prefer my women to come willingly to my bed."

"Miss Finchley was not willing."

"That was not the impression her aunt gave me."

"What about the impression Miss Finchley gave you?"

He shrugged. "I thought she was playing with me. It is not unusual. Women always play games; they think it adds to their allure."

Eleanor realised he was in earnest and that there was no point in arguing with him. She changed tack.

"I assume that you saw what happened between Lord Allerdale and myself in the park yesterday."

"Not personally," he said. "I am not often abroad at that ungodly hour, you understand. But after Lady Crouch informed me of your interference in the matter of her niece, I put a man on to watch you, hoping he would discover something I could use against you."

"You do realise that Miles will kill you for this."

"He may try, Miss Edgcott, but he is unlikely to succeed. You need a cool head in a fight, and Allerdale is known for his hot-headedness."

Eleanor went cold with fear and then with anger. She would not let this man ruin her reputation, her chance of happiness, and above all, she would not allow him to kill Miles.

"Let me go," she said quietly. "If you do so, I will say nothing. This sordid episode will be forgotten, and no one will get hurt."

"Do you expect me to believe that, Miss Edgcott? I have never known a woman yet who could keep her tongue between her teeth. No, my hand is dealt, and I will play it out."

"Very well," Eleanor said softly, drawing her pistol from her reticule.

"I am about to leave, do not try and stop me."

Lord Sandford laughed and drew a key from his pocket.

"I locked the door before I spoke to you."

"Throw the key to me," she said, backing towards the door.

"No," he said baldly. "That is a very pretty piece you have there, Miss Edgcott, but I do not believe you will use it."

One moment he was lounging in his chair, and the next he was on his feet and striding towards her. "Give it to me."

Eleanor aimed and fired. Lord Sandford went reeling backwards, his hand clutched to his shoulder, a stunned expression in his eyes.

"I'll be damned," he said, sinking into his chair.

"Undoubtedly," Eleanor said.

She turned and tried to put the key in the lock, but her hand was shaking so much that she dropped it.

Lord Sandford gave a weak laugh.

"You do have some nerves then."

Eleanor ignored him, retrieved it, and this time managed to insert it into the keyhole. She twisted it, pulled the door open, and stepped into a small, dark passageway. Reaction set in and she stood there for a moment breathing in short, rapid gasps, her legs trembling beneath her. She became aware of a rumbling noise, and then the sound of horses' hooves. She found she could breathe again and rushed to the front door and wrenched it open. She blinked, blinded for a moment by the sunlight, and then a curricle drew up before her, and she found herself in Miles' arms.

He held her to him fiercely for a moment. She could feel relief and anger within him in equal measures.

"Are you hurt?" he said harshly, his arms gentling a little.

"No." She looked up and gave a small gasp. His jaw was clenched, his dark eyes almost black, and they burned into hers with an intensity that made her a little afraid.

"He never touched me," she said quickly. "He never intended to, he only meant to ruin my reputation by keeping me here."

Miles lifted her into his arms.

"I will kill him; I will throttle the life out of him inch by slow inch and enjoy every moment."

She said in a small voice. "I think I may have done so already."

Her words seemed to break through his fury. A humourless grin twisted his lips and he pressed them briefly to hers.

"Good girl!"

He deposited her in the curricle and strode into the house. She moved as if to follow him but felt Tibbs' hand on her shoulder. "You stay there, miss. Whatever he says, he won't lay a finger on him if he's injured. And besides, here comes the cavalry."

She realised that the thunder of horse hooves had not stopped and twisted around. Four horsemen emerged through a cloud of dust. Lord Somerton arrived first and dismounted with a swiftness that made her blink. He sprinted into the house with a speed she would not have thought possible for so large a man. Lord Cranbourne came next; he nodded at her and strode hastily towards the cottage. Lords Brigham and Carteret arrived together.

Lord Brigham paused by the curricle. "You are unharmed, Miss Edgcott?"

"Yes," she said. "It is Lord Sandford who is injured."

He raised a brow and said softly, "I am happy to hear it; now I know my son will not be accused of murder."

She swallowed. "If anyone is, it will be me. I shot him."

He took her hand and squeezed it gently. "My compliments, Miss Edgcott. But do not concern yourself. If you have killed him, he will have come by his just deserts. I shall see to it that you do not suffer any ill consequences."

"Thank you, sir."

As he and Lord Carteret began to walk towards the house, she suddenly cried, "I don't know where Stanley is."

Lord Brigham glanced over his shoulder. "He will be found, never fear."

Miss Edgcott began to fidget.

"I cannot just wait here, Tibbs," she said, for the first time taking in her surroundings.

The curricle took up most of a narrow lane, that judging from the grass that lined the middle of it, was rarely used. She thought the cottage might have at one time been a farmhouse, for a wide gateway a little way ahead gave onto a large courtyard and she could see a long barn at the far end of it.

"Where are we?"

"About eight miles from London, ma'am. As we appear to be blocking the lane, miss, I intend to drive into the yard. Do you think that you could lead the horses?"

∽

Miles stood over Lord Sandford's slumped body, his fists clenched. The marquess was unconscious, his face deathly pale, his breathing shallow, and dark blood still welled from the hole in his coat. Even though it galled him, he could not let Sandford bleed to death. He would not have his blood on Eleanor's hands.

"Miss Edgcott is full of pluck, it seems."

Miles whirled on his heels and saw Somerton bend and pick up Eleanor's small silver pistol. It looked like a child's toy in his hands.

Somerton turned his head as Cranbourne came into the room. "Go and discover if you can find some clean sheets, will you?"

Cranbourne nodded and went quickly out of the room.

"I know precisely what you are feeling," Lord Somerton said with a wry smile.

Miles gave a hollow laugh. "The circumstances are not the same."

"Not *quite* the same," Somerton amended. "But you did abduct Georgianna and would have ruined her if it had suited your purpose."

"That is very true," Lord Brigham said coming into the room. "And she had not provoked you in the way Miss Edgcott has Sandford. I am afraid it was I who did that."

"My God! I do not know how you prevented yourself from wringing my neck, Somerton," Miles burst out.

"Ah, but you had the merit of bringing her safely home. If I had found you before you had done so, it would have been another story, so I fully understand your wish to murder Sandford. However, we must make a push to save him, I think."

"I know it, damn you!" Miles said.

"We will think of a way to punish him," Lord Carteret said softly.

The marquess suddenly groaned and his eyes fluttered open.

"I am sorry I cannot offer you any refreshments, gentlemen," he murmured, a ghastly smile on his face. "I was not expecting company."

Somerton firmly pushed Miles to one side and picked him up.

"Save your breath, Sandford, whilst you still have some to save." He strode towards the door with his burden. "I shall take him upstairs. Cranbourne is finding sheets, Carteret, see if you can find me some water and some brandy."

As he left the room, they heard a carriage pull up outside.

"Who the devil—"

Even as Miles spoke, Lady Brigham came into the room, followed by Lady Bassington, Georgianna, and Marianne.

"I thought, my dear," Lord Brigham said without

an ounce of surprise in his voice, "that I asked you to wait for news."

Lady Brigham quickly embraced her son, before turning to him. "I do not like to go against your wishes, but it occurred to me…"

Lady Bassington cleared her throat.

"To us," she continued, "that there might be a few things you had forgotten. We have brought Doctor Carston and a change of clothes for Miss Edgcott should she need them."

"Eleanor!" Miles suddenly said. "I must go to her."

This did not prove to be necessary as she just then appeared in the doorway.

"I have found Stanley," she said. "He is tied up in the barn and has a huge lump on his head. Tibbs is seeing to him." She looked at the empty chair. "Is… is Lord Sandford dead?"

"No, Somerton has taken him upstairs. Come here, you little fool."

Miles opened his arms, and Eleanor ran into them.

Lord Brigham turned to the slender, bespectacled man who stood in the hall.

"Ah, Carston. I am pleased to see you. I believe your patient is above stairs."

"Very well, sir," he said.

Lord Brigham pulled out his snuffbox and deftly took a pinch.

"Carston is a good man, very discreet, you did well there, Julia. However, I cannot help but think that we are a little overcrowded." His cool grey eyes swept over the company and came to rest on his son. "Miles, you are to be congratulated on your friends. We did not need them *all* perhaps, but once they knew what was in the wind, I could see there would be no stopping them. Perhaps if Sandford also had such friends, we would not now find ourselves in this predicament."

"What will happen now, sir?" Eleanor asked, her voice subdued.

"That remains to be seen. I suggest you ladies wait for us at The Bull, on the Highgate road. I expect you are in need of some sustenance, Miss Edgcott. In fact, I consider that we will all need some sustenance presently for it is nearly seven o'clock."

He went to his wife and kissed her hand. "Julia, secure us a private parlour at the inn, large enough to hold us all, and bespeak us some dinner, will you? I expect we will be with you in about an hour."

Lady Brigham briefly laid her hand on her lord's cheek and nodded.

"Come, child," she said, wrapping her arm about Eleanor and leading her from the room.

CHAPTER 22

Eleanor found herself wedged between Marianne and Georgianna in the carriage, but she did not mind; she needed the comfort and when they each took one of her hands, she smiled gratefully at them.

"How did you find me?"

"Miles came to Berkeley Square to see if you had paid us a visit," Lady Brigham said. "When Brigham discovered that he had found your hat crushed in the park and you and your footman had been missing for some time, he sent for Lady Haverham and your maid, wishing to question them himself." She smiled gently. "Miles you see, was quite out of his mind with worry and Brigham felt that he would do a better job of it. Meanwhile, at Miles' request, Lord Haverham had sent out servants to see if you had visited either of your friends and so not only the Haverhams but also the Cranbournes and Somertons descended upon us."

"Closely followed by Lord Carteret," Lady Bassington chimed in. "He was on the hunt for Miles;

apparently, he had lost a bet with him over the cricket match and wished to pay his debt."

"Thank you, Frances," Lady Brigham said. "Now, where was I? Oh, yes, Brigham was about to question Lady Haverham. He wished to know if there was anyone who might bear you a grudge."

"She wasn't much use," Lady Bassington said dryly. "She kept throwing anxious glances at her husband, wringing her hands together, and saying she could not think."

"And so I mentioned that Lord Sandford had not been very pleasant to you on the night of Lady Brigham's ball because you had been keeping him away from Lady Haverham," Georgianna said.

"Yes, and she burst into tears and said it wasn't her fault," Lady Bassington said.

"I could have boxed her ears," Lady Brigham said, "because then precious time was wasted whilst he comforted her and told her of course it wasn't."

Lady Bassington snorted. "I've never known a man yet who didn't chase a woman if he hadn't had a little encouragement. I told him, of course, that I had also thwarted Sandford that night at the theatre. But I did point out that Lady Haverham had seemed frightened."

"Yes, and so we wasted yet more time while he demanded to know why he hadn't been told of it," Lady Brigham said.

"What did she say?" Eleanor asked.

"Nothing," Lady Bassington said. "She just snivelled into her handkerchief."

"I told him it was because she was afraid he would

call Sandford out and told him about our plan," Marianne said.

"That was very clever of you," Eleanor approved.

"And then Mrs Linwood spoke up," Lady Brigham said. "She, I am pleased to say, seems to have a great deal of sense. She saw it all immediately. She thought to mention what had happened between Sandford and Miss Finchley, and how you had discovered that Mr Pavlov was in love with her and arranged for them to meet."

"Oh," Eleanor said. "And how did Miles react?"

Lady Brigham smiled. "I think we had better draw a veil over that. But Lord Haverham was quite impressive in his defence of you, dear. Miles seemed to have the impression that she was not quite the thing, but Lord Haverham insisted that she was the sweetest girl and that both you and Lady Haverham were, er, ministering angels."

Eleanor said in a voice that was not quite steady, "And what did Miles say to *that*?"

Lady Bassington chuckled. "I fear we need another veil."

Eleanor seemed pleased by this, but after a moment said, "But how did he know where to find me?"

Lady Bassington and Lady Brigham exchanged a look.

"You have run out of veils," Eleanor said firmly.

"Mrs Linwood said that he had intended to bring Miss Finchley to a cottage somewhere near London," Lady Brigham said.

Eleanor frowned. "Well, that was not very much to go on, was it?"

Lady Brigham waved an airy hand. "He had been to a bachelor party there, apparently, years ago."

As Eleanor's eyes narrowed, Marianne squeezed her hand and said gently, "so had Cranbourne. You can't blame men for the disgusting way they behave before they marry, you know. They all do it."

"My Adolphus never did," Lady Bassington said in a tone of regret.

"In that case," Eleanor said decisively. "I think I would like to be married as soon as possible."

"Splendid," Lady Brigham said. "Ah, we have arrived."

Fortunately, The Bull did have one parlour large enough to comfortably accommodate nine people. Once Lady Brigham had discussed with the innkeeper what dinner he could provide for so many in an hour, she acquired a bedchamber for Eleanor and went up to it with her. When Eleanor had washed, she helped her into the dress she had brought for her. It was of a pale green silk, and if it was a little more daring in its cut than Eleanor was used to, at least it fitted perfectly.

"You look charming, my dear," Lady Brigham said. "It is fortunate we are the same height, build, and colouring, is it not? Now sit down and I will comb out your hair."

When she had finished, she laid her hands lightly on Eleanor's shoulders and met her eyes in the mirror.

"You have made me very happy, my dear, and you are the perfect girl for Miles. Welcome to our family."

"Thank you." Her thoughts turned to Frederick. "I am surprised my cousin did not also come. Is he very cross with me?"

"He was not best pleased that you had taken the

matter of Sandford's dealings with Diana into your own hands," she admitted. "But he was far more worried than angry. He did not come because he knew Brigham and Miles would do what was needed, and besides, Lady Haverham was quite overset by the whole thing and he could not leave her."

"Of course."

"May I give you a little advice?"

"Yes," Eleanor said quietly.

"You remind me very much of me in some ways. I used to find myself in scrapes. I was," she smiled, "I am quite strong willed, and I did not like to be chafed and constrained by the restrictions set upon ladies. But I have learned to be guided by Brigham. I do not like him to be made unhappy by my actions, and he, in turn, does not like me to be made unhappy by restricting me too much. So, he does not object to me racing a curricle, but he prefers that it is done at Brigham. He does not mind me gambling, but I must set a reasonable limit on my play, and so on." She suddenly laughed. "I make it sound so easy, but it is not. It has taken us years of negotiation, something I am sure you will understand. And yet it is not that hard either, if you love each other."

When they returned to the parlour, Eleanor paid little heed to the chatter of the other ladies, but sat by the fire, sipping the glass of wine Lady Brigham had insisted she take. She had been very kind, and the relationship she had described with her husband was, she realised, very similar to the one she had shared with her Papa. But she had not been able to bear the idea of anyone else taking over that role and had decided that she was quite old enough to make her own decisions without any counsel from anyone else.

It was her actions that had led to this horrible day. Linny had always said that one day she would come by weeping cross, and she had been proven right. She knew her motives in all her dealings had been good, but it had all gone horribly wrong somehow. She closed her eyes, but instead of a restful darkness, she saw her bullet tear into Lord Sandford's shoulder. Her fingers tightened on the wine glass. She hoped she had not killed him.

The sound of footsteps and voices in the hall brought her to her feet. The door opened and the gentlemen came into the room. Her anxious eyes fixed on Lord Brigham.

"Be easy, child. Lord Sandford has lost a great deal of blood, but the injury is not fatal and will cause no lasting damage. The doctor will stay with him tonight, and then a nurse will be found to watch over him whilst he recovers. When he is fit enough, he will go back to his estate and remain there until at least next season."

Lady Brigham gasped. "Is that all you mean to do?"

"Remember that he has already suffered a bullet through the shoulder, my dear."

"It will be torture to him," Lord Cranbourne assured her. "It is in Devon, and he cannot bear to be so far from civilisation. It was Carteret who suggested it."

"It will have the added benefit of hopefully restoring him to health in body and mind," Lord Brigham said gently.

"But how do you know he will stay there?" Eleanor asked.

Lord Brigham's lips curled. Eleanor had never realised that a smile could look quite so menacing and sinister.

"Oh, he will stay there," he said softly. "When he opened his eyes to discover us all standing around his bed, he understood the danger he was in."

His smile gentled. "Carteret has ridden back to Town to inform Lord and Lady Haverham that all is well. Now, Miss Edgcott, my son is waiting for you in the parlour across the hall."

Eleanor flew across the room, surprising Lord Brigham when she suddenly raised herself up on tiptoes and kissed his cheek. "Thank you, sir."

"For what it is worth, you have my blessing on both your marriage and your business venture. And when you are ready, there should be no difficulty in arranging for a girl from the Foundling Hospital to be apprenticed to Rebecca Willis." He took her hand. "Do not judge yourself too harshly, child. Your actions have not all been wise, but you meant well."

Eleanor felt her heart lighten. She was, she realised, very fortunate to have found a family who were prepared to love her despite her faults.

"Thank you, Lord Brigham."

She entered the much smaller parlour opposite and closed the door firmly behind her, leaning back against it for a moment. Miles stood, legs astride, in front of the fireplace. She felt his eyes roam over her for a moment and then a wicked smile curved his lips. He crooked his finger.

"Come here, Eleanor."

The words sounded like a caress, and Eleanor shivered in anticipation. She was no longer in the state of high anxiety she had been earlier, however, and did not fling herself in his arms, but walked slowly towards him, a shy smile on her lips.

He watched her appreciatively for a moment before reaching out one long arm and pulling her hard against him. She wound her arms around his waist, looked into his glittering eyes, and sighed as he cupped her face between his hands. They stood like that for some moments, speaking without words, apologies were offered and accepted and declarations of love made. Then he lowered his head until his lips whispered gently against hers.

"If you ever," he murmured, "scare me like that again, I shall lock you in a tower and throw away the key."

She smiled and nuzzled her lips against his neck. "But that would be against the terms of our agreement," she whispered. "Perhaps I should reconsider."

He growled and kissed her deeply. She felt heat rise both within herself and all around her, as if the very air shimmered, and when he finally pulled his head away, she sighed, pressing herself closer. He laughed, picked her up, and sat in the armchair set beside the fire. She curled up on his lap, her head resting against his chest, listening to the rhythmic beat of his heart.

"Eleanor," he said softly, "will you marry me?"

She tipped back her head and smiled up at him. "Yes, my love, but I have thought of a few amendments I would like to make to our agreement."

He raised a brow.

"Will you bring me breakfast in bed?"

"It will be my pleasure," he grinned.

"And will you promise never to go on a drinking spree before a long journey?"

"Yes, my darling."

He looked wary as mischief suddenly danced in her eyes.

"And will you teach me to fence?"

"Never!" he said, stopping her words with another kiss.

ALSO BY JENNY HAMBLY

Thank you for reading Allerdale!

Thank you for your support! I do hope you have enjoyed Miles' and Eleanor's story. If you would consider leaving a short review on Amazon, I would be very grateful. It really helps readers know what to expect and helps raise my profile, which as a relatively new author is so very helpful.

I love to hear from my readers and can be contacted at: jenny@jennyhambly.com

Other books by Jenny Hambly

Belle – Bachelor Brides 0

Rosalind – Bachelor Brides 1

Sophie – Bachelor Brides 2

Katherine – Bachelor Brides 3

Bachelor Brides Collection

Marianne - Miss Wolfraston's Ladies Book 1

Miss Hayes - Miss Wolfraston's Ladies Book2

Georgianna - Miss Wolfraston's Ladies Book 3

Miss Wolfraston's Ladies Collection

ABOUT THE AUTHOR

I love history and the Regency period in particular. I grew up on a diet of Jane Austen, Charlotte and Emily Bronte, and Georgette Heyer. Later, I put my love of reading to good use and gained a 1st class honours degree in literature.

I have been a teacher and tennis coach. I now write traditional Regency romance novels. I like to think my characters, though flawed, are likeable, strong, and true to the period. Writing has always been my dream and I am fortunate enough to have been able to realise that dream.

I live by the sea in Plymouth, England, with my partner, Dave. I like reading, sailing, wine, getting up early to watch the sunrise in summer, and long quiet evenings by the wood burner in our cabin on the cliffs in Cornwall in winter.

ACKNOWLEDGMENTS

Thank you Melanie Underwood for catching so many things that I missed!

Thank you Dave for patiently waiting for me to return from Regency England!

Printed in Great Britain
by Amazon